BITTEN AND BOUND

HELEN BRIGHT

VINCI
BOOKS

Vinci Books

vinci-books.com

Published by Vinci Books Ltd in 2026

1

Copyright © Helen Bright 2015

The author has asserted their moral right to be identified as the author of this work in accordance with the Copyright, Designs and Patents Act 1988.
This work is a work of fiction. Names, characters, places and incidents are the product of the author's imagination or are used fictitiously. Any resemblance to actual persons, living or dead, places and incidents is entirely coincidental.
All rights reserved. No part of this publication may be copied, reproduced, distributed, stored in any retrieval system, or transmitted in any form or by any means, including photocopying, recording, or other electronic or mechanical methods, nor used as a source for any form of machine learning including AI datasets, without the prior written permission of the publisher.
The publisher and the author have made every effort to obtain permissions for any third party material used in this book and to comply with copyright law. Any queries in this respect should be brought to the attention of the publisher and any omissions will be corrected in future editions.
A CIP catalogue record for this book is available from the British Library.
Paperback ISBN: 9781036707682
The EU GPSR authorised representative is Logos Europe, 9 rue Nicolas Poussion, 17000 La Rochelle, France
contact@logoseurope.eu

By Helen Bright

The Night Movers Vampire Series

Bitten and Bound
Blood & Secrets
Gregor's Reason
Sergei's Angel

Chapter One

Alex

I, Alexander Staithes, one of the most powerful Born Immortal vampires in Europe, was nervous.

I was trying to appear calm and collected; apparently, I wasn't pulling it off.

"Alex, what on earth is wrong with you this evening? You haven't stopped pacing since you walked in."

"Nothing's wrong, Maggie," I replied hastily. "I have a lot of work to do tonight, that's all."

"I could interview Julia on my own if you're busy. I mean, it's not as though we don't know her, or her background," Maggie said with a knowing smirk.

Maggie Saunders had been my employee and friend for over thirty years. The cunning yet adorable human could read me better than anyone, and it appeared she was trying to push me into admitting why I wanted to sit in on this interview so badly.

Julia Layton was the daughter of another employee, George Browne. I co-owned the import/export company, Night Movers International, along with my brother, Josh, and good friend Nik. Both George and Maggie had joined the company within two years of each other, having been school friends before that. In fact, many of our human employees were friends of mine. It's what I liked most about the company we'd worked so hard to build. It made it easier to trust who knew I was a vampire without the need for mind control to erase the knowledge.

Both George Browne and Maggie Saunders were among the few in this company who knew we were vampires, and which visitors were vampires too.

I first noticed Julia—who was then Julia Browne—when she accompanied her father to one of the company's Christmas parties. Night Movers always held parties for our employees because it encouraged the friendly, almost familial atmosphere that kept the company performing well. It also helped the humans and vampires to mingle and find common ground.

Julia held onto her father's arm as they chatted with other partygoers, and I was struck by her innocence and beauty. I hadn't seen her since she was an awkward fourteen-year-old with a permanent ponytail and braces, and though I spoke with George regularly about his family, I hadn't expected Julia to have blossomed into the beautiful young woman before me.

Julia stood as tall as her father in the high heels she wore, which put her around five-foot-seven barefoot. She was quite curvy, with a defined hourglass figure and long, chestnut brown hair that tumbled around her shoulders in waves.

I went over to talk to George and ask where his wife was that evening. He told me she was caring for a sick friend, so George had brought Julia, who was then only eighteen years old, instead. George explained she was going away to university that year, so he was glad to be spending time with her while he could. Armed with this information, I began a conversation with her about the university course she had chosen and her career options.

Julia was quite shy and seemed a little nervous, her blue-eyed gaze never holding mine for very long. So I bid her farewell for the time being and told her I'd come back over for a dance later.

I couldn't wait until later came. I felt like I'd do anything to hold her, even for a short while.

Nikolas and Joshua, both vampires and co-founders of my company, came over to quiz me about what had kept me occupied for the last half hour, but they quickly noticed Julia for themselves. Nik went in for a hug from Julia, which annoyed me to the point that I saw red. I mean literally saw red when my eyes changed, forming a red ring around the irises as my temper rose. I quickly looked away before Julia could see, but Josh noticed and placed a hand on my arm before enquiring if I was okay.

"Julia, my lovely, you have grown into a beautiful young lady. I think it's about time we ran away and got married so you can make an honest man out of me," Nik announced in a booming voice, which had infuriated me further, and I could feel my fangs about to descend.

Julia giggled and replied, "Mr Harding, no one could ever make an honest man out of you."

Nik smiled, looking over at a table across the room for a second before he gazed back at Julia. "Oh, you have me pegged, sweet Julia. So alas, it will never be." He bowed low in front of her, saying goodbye with dramatic flair.

I regained my composure when Nik left and went with Joshua to sit at a table nearby.

"What was that all about?" Josh asked. "Alex, you never normally react like that in front of people."

"I'm not sure," I replied. "Perhaps I'm just a little tired."

"Did you feed before the party, Alex? Maybe it would be best to nip out and grab a bag of blood before it happens again."

"No, I'll be fine, Josh, I promise. I just need a bit of peace and quiet for a while," I told him.

"So you wouldn't mind if I went and asked George's daughter for a dance, then?" Josh asked with a hint of humour in his voice.

I couldn't help the growl that seemed to come from my throat, and Joshua burst out laughing.

"Oh, Alex, don't you think she's a little young?"

I looked away, embarrassed at the situation I found myself in. I knew he was right, of course. She was young and needed to experience life before I could even think of her being in my world. Although it didn't mean I couldn't hold her for a short while, I thought, as I walked over to her and claimed my dance.

I knew when I held her in my arms that I wanted her there always. She looked up at me and shivered with what I believed was desire.

Did she feel the same things I was feeling?

As we slow danced to the Elvis Presley song, "Can't Help Falling in Love," I knew something powerful was happening. The way she felt as she moved with me to the music, how soft her hair felt against my cheek, the perfume she wore and her own natural scent that captured my senses. It was a potent combination that was almost too powerful to resist.

Before I did something I regretted, when the song ended, I walked her back to her father. I thanked her for the dance and wished her all the very best at university.

I thought I saw disappointment in her eyes when I said goodbye, but I had to leave the room. Josh followed, concerned about me and my premature departure.

"Alex, wait, what happened in there?"

"I'm not sure. I just have this feeling about Julia... A knowing," I explained. "I feel like she belongs to me, Josh. And I know I've only danced and spoken with her, but I already want more."

"How much more?" Josh asked warily.

"I want everything," I replied.

I decided it would be best to let Julia live her life a little before I sought her out again. I wanted her to complete her studies and return to Barrowfield a confident grown woman, ready to accept what I was.

A year later, Julia announced her engagement to Gavin Layton, and genuine pain pierced my heart.

I had lived nearly a thousand years and, at the time, thought that was long enough. With the help of my work friends and my sister, I kept myself plodding on through everyday life as much as I could without revealing the true depth of my anguish.

Nik and Josh knew what was wrong and tried to help in any way they could. Nik's Russian friend Sergei offered to kill Gavin Layton so that Julia was free again, but I declined hastily. Despite wishing he didn't exist, I wasn't about to start killing humans to achieve that.

I watched her many times without her knowledge over the last fourteen years. She seemed to be happy, and though I loved to see her beautiful smile, I always wished it was me who'd put it there.

Then, in a car accident earlier this year, Julia was seriously injured and lost her unborn baby. George contacted me immediately because of the healing properties of my blood, wanting me to help his daughter recover from her injuries.

I was there when they brought her around after the emergency surgery to fix her hip and deliver her stillborn daughter. I gave her only a small amount of my healing blood because I didn't want to arouse suspicion from the hospital staff.

Julia was desperate to see her daughter, even though she knew she was dead. It had been hours since they had delivered her, so none of the staff thought it was good for her to see the baby. As well as being cold, the infant would have the waxy pallor that death brings.

Using mind control, I got the staff to bring Julia her daughter, giving her better images than what she was seeing. During this most devastating time, her husband was asleep on another floor of the hospital, so he couldn't interfere with my actions. Although, to be honest, my only thoughts were of comforting Julia; I wouldn't have allowed him near, anyway.

I visited Julia several times over the past few months, offering her friendship and support in her hour of need. It was also a way to give her small amounts of my blood to speed up the healing process.

The strain of what happened was too much for her

marriage to bear, and they ended up separating. I was glad she was now free of the man who had kept us apart for so many years, but I knew this was just another kick to the already fragile shell she'd erected around herself.

I needed a way to keep her close and take care of her like I should have done all those years ago. The job I was about to offer her could do just that.

Chapter Two

Julia

"Don't be nervous, love. Maggie says this interview is just a formality, and the job is already yours if you want it."

My dad had been saying that for the last five days, ever since Maggie, our old family friend, had decided to go from full to part-time. She wanted to help her daughter out with childcare when she went back to work after her maternity leave.

Both my dad and Maggie had worked for the import/export company Night Movers International for over thirty years and were well-respected employees.

It was refreshing to see a company keeping its main hub here in Yorkshire. It was good for the area, providing a number of jobs and also funding for local charities and various community projects.

I found myself in the position of job seeker for the first time in almost fourteen years. Apart from the part-time sales advisor role I held in a clothing store during my time at university, I'd never needed to interview before.

I'd met Gavin, my soon-to-be ex-husband, in my first year at uni. We were both doing a degree in business management and had many of the same classes together. He was effortlessly gorgeous, with wavy dark-brown hair and striking hazel eyes. He took me out to a comedy club on our first date, and for the first time since I'd left home, I had fun without missing my parents. I fell in love with him instantly. It was hard not to, and we were engaged within a year.

We married as soon as we finished uni, and after our honeymoon, we went to work for his father's transport company just outside Birmingham.

Our life together seemed perfect for many years. We built up the business, holidayed all over the world, bought a beautiful home and had a busy social life.

We started trying for a baby six years ago. For the first year, we didn't worry too much when I didn't become pregnant. I was coming off the pill and understood it could take a while for its effects to leave my system. When it didn't happen after two years, we began to worry.

Our doctor referred us for fertility tests in our third year of being unsuccessful. Both of us were healthy, and after several tests, they could find no reason why either of us couldn't be parents. So their advice to us was, *"keep taking the prenatal vitamins, keep fit and healthy, and try not to get stressed."* Hello?! Not getting pregnant was the only thing stressing me out.

By this time, most of our circle of friends had children, and we found it hard to remain positive. We argued more and more, both of us finding faults with each other that were seemingly never there before. Then, sixteen months ago, when it seemed like I was never going to conceive, I became pregnant.

We were thrilled, and Mum, Dad and Gavin's parents were ecstatic. To be honest, the pregnancy helped repair the almost cavernous cracks that had appeared in our marriage from both sides, and once again, Gavin became an attentive, loving husband.

It was during a shopping trip two weeks before my due date that my life was ripped apart, and my heart was shattered.

A young man, not even two days out of prison, had stolen a car and was being chased by police when he lost control of the vehicle and drove into the front passenger side door of our car, straight into me.

Gavin and I spun off the road and ended up down an embankment.

We both lost consciousness immediately after the impact, but according to the police officers who were following the car, we were both only out for about five minutes. The driver of the stolen car wasn't wearing a seatbelt and was thrown from his vehicle. He died at the scene.

Gavin regained consciousness first, and to this day, I will never forget the screaming panic and utter devastation in his voice when I finally became aware of our situation.

At first, I didn't think of the baby because of the agonising pain in my hip. I knew it was broken, as was my arm. But Gavin was touching my very pregnant tummy, asking if we were both okay, and I knew then that my darling baby would never get to sleep in the new crib we'd just bought.

A fire crew was on the scene within five minutes, but it took them over an hour to free us both.

My labour pains started when I was placed on the

stretcher. The air ambulance arrived, and I was flown to our nearest hospital, so it didn't take long to get there. They quickly scanned my tummy in A&E, but as I already knew instinctively, there was no heartbeat to detect.

Due to all my other injuries, despite my strong contractions, they had to deliver our baby via C-section.

My beautiful daughter came into the world but never took a breath.

My hip had to have extensive surgery, and they set my arm in a cast. Due to the amount of blood I'd lost during surgery, I didn't wake up until the early hours of the morning. My parents were there and quickly explained that Gavin was okay, but because of his broken ribs and concussion, he was on another ward.

Also in the room was Alex Staithes, my dad's boss, although I didn't question his presence at the time.

Apart from being a bit groggy and having a slightly metallic taste in my mouth, physically, I didn't feel as bad as I thought I would. The pain from my hip seemed to lessen within seconds, and I marvelled at the effectiveness of the pain medication they must have given me.

When I found my voice, the first thing I asked for was to see my baby. That set my mum off crying, and my dad said he didn't think it was a good idea.

Mum told me that Gavin had held her after she was delivered, but that was over eight hours ago. I knew what she was saying, even without the words. My baby was cold, dead and too long passed to give me any peace.

Rage and unfathomable grief consumed me. I wanted to climb out of bed and throw people out of my way so I could get to her. I knew this was the maternal instinct to gather and protect kicking in, and although I would never get to take care of my child, I was still her mother, and I needed to feel the bond with her—if only for a short while.

Screams tore from my throat, and tears came seconds later. I remember Alex standing up and telling the nursing staff forcefully that my daughter needed to be brought to me. Not thirty minutes later, wrapped in a pink hospital blanket, she was placed in my arms.

It was hard to hold her at first because of the cast on one arm and the IV in the other, but I was so relieved to finally have her in my arms, and I was determined to cuddle my beautiful baby girl.

I named her Megan, after my late grandmother. She passed away two years ago, and it comforted me to know she was waiting in heaven to take care of my daughter until I could get there, which I hoped would be very soon.

I sobbed uncontrollably into the dark hair peeking out from her pink hat, and the nurse moved to take her away from me. I tried to turn away to stop her, and then I noticed Alex stand and walk over to us.

I thought he, too, was going to try to take her, but he didn't. I remember him lifting my chin, moving the hair out of my eyes, and wiping my tears away with his thumb. Alex stared into my despairing soul with his beautiful grey eyes and began talking to me. He said Megan was such a pretty baby, and she had my hair colour, which I noticed was true. He also remarked how smooth and pink her skin was and how she felt warm to the touch, which seemed strange as I hadn't thought that earlier. But I could see that I'd been wrong, and it appeared as though Megan was only sleeping.

He kept on speaking, telling me that although she wouldn't be here with me physically, I would always feel her presence. Alex said Megan knew that I loved her, and she loved me too, more than words could ever say. He said she wanted me to live a long and happy life and to remember always that I am her mother.

I looked down at my baby and began telling her about everything we'd planned for her. I spoke about her family, who loved her so very much, and with tears in my eyes, I told her she'd stay in our hearts forever.

About an hour after I first held her, my beautiful baby Megan was taken away, and at Alex's suggestion, I fell into a deep and restful sleep.

Gavin came to see me the following day, and we cried in each other's arms for the child that would never be part of our future. He'd been cleared to go home, but he'd broken two ribs, and his neck was hurting quite badly. Even sitting still in a chair at my bedside was awkward for him. After an hour, I sent him home to rest.

Over the next four days, with the help of our parents, we arranged Megan's funeral.

Six weeks later, I was still undergoing physiotherapy for my hip, neck, and shoulders. The crash had caused severe whiplash, which hadn't become apparent until three days after the accident.

The doctors said I wasn't improving as quickly as they would like, but they thought my emotional and mental state was a factor.

Gavin and I couldn't be in the same room without bickering, so I went to stay with my parents. They lived in a bungalow, which was a big help when moving around with my sore hip.

While I was there feeling sorry for myself one evening, Alex came by. It was the first time I remember seeing him since the accident. I was speechless when I opened the door and saw him standing there. Mum was out, and my first thought was of my dad, but Alex must have sensed this or noticed the panicked expression on my face. He quickly reassured me that my dad was fine and that he'd actually stopped by to see me. I invited him in and offered him tea or coffee, which he declined for water. He waited for me to take a seat on the sofa before he came to sit beside me.

Alex is an extremely handsome man with dark blond hair and stunning grey eyes that have always captivated me. I found it hard to look away from him. He also never seemed to age, like most men, which is utterly unfair to us women.

I remember dancing with him at a Christmas party years ago and totally crushing on him. But obviously, he hadn't been interested in me because he'd left the party early. Probably to meet up with some gorgeous, sophisticated woman—unlike the nervous eighteen-year-old I had been.

I left my memories in the past and thanked him for coming to see me at the hospital, apologising for all the upset he must have experienced. I told Alex I didn't think I could have managed without all the support he'd given me that night.

I didn't know why he'd been there at the hospital, but I told him I appreciated his thoughtfulness and assistance.

Alex explained that he'd been in a meeting in the area and met my dad at the hospital to offer his support to our family. He said he considered my father a good friend, which meant he saw all the family that way too.

I remember thinking, and not for the first time, how great this man was. He was running a multimillion-pound business yet made time to come and see me. Alex Staithes was a kind, genuine man who was a great boss to all his employees. He was just too good to be true.

We talked about his business, my slow recovery, and the problems I was having with my marriage. Honestly, it was a relief to talk about that with someone. Most of my friends were also Gavin's, and I didn't feel I could open up to them.

Alex agreed that time apart would probably do Gavin and me some good, and he offered to be there if I ever needed to talk. It was refreshing to have a man actually listen for a change, and I couldn't help but wonder what it would be like to be in a relationship with this sweet guy.

While thinking about how nice it would be to have his arms around me, I fell fast asleep on the sofa beside him.

For the first time in months, I didn't have a nightmare. Instead, I dreamed I was dancing again with Alex, not as an eighteen-year-old, but as the woman I had become.

It wasn't until I stepped over the bathtub into the shower the following day that I realised I no longer felt any pain in my hip, arm, or neck. Also, my very pronounced limp had completely disappeared. Even the scar had healed to a faint silvery line. I didn't question the reason why; I was just glad to move around without physical pain. And for the first time in weeks, I felt happy to be alive.

Despite how much better I felt, I decided to stay with my parents for another week. Alex came to see me again several times before I left for home, and his presence by my side felt right. Like we could be more than just friends. Although, I never presumed he'd want to be anything other than friends with me. I mean, let's face it, my husband didn't even want to be in the same room as me, never mind someone as wonderful as Alex.

When I eventually went home, I found the situation with Gavin was the same as before, and around five months after our daughter's funeral, we separated. Gavin and I are still friends, but our divorce is in progress.

Although we let our lawyers handle most of our divorce, my father-in-law bought my share of the house Gavin and I owned. He also gave me a pretty good bonus in my severance pay as a thank-you for putting so much time and effort into the Layton family business, which I'd helped grow into the successful company it was today.

It seems strange not to be as close to Gavin's family, and as I'm now back living with my parents again, I'm no longer near the friends Gavin and I shared.

So, after fifteen years of living away, I returned to South Yorkshire. Starting my life all over again means getting a new job and a place of my own, and that's why this evening, I'm all smartened up in a skirt-suit and blouse for an interview at Night Movers International.

Chapter Three

Alex

I could tell from the moment Maggie brought her into the room that Julia was anxious. Maggie immediately tried to get her to feel at ease, asking about a trip that Julia's mum was organising to a shopping centre in Manchester.

Why women would want to go to Manchester when we have the Meadowhall shopping centre in Sheffield is beyond me, but it got Julia chatting, and she relaxed a little as she spoke.

I waited for the brief conversation to end before I said, "So, Julia, you already know this interview is for Maggie's full-time position. It covers the day-to-day or, rather, the night-to-night running of the business. Our night office hours run from five in the evening until five in the morning. We have two daytime staff who look after local transportation requests. They only span a radius of up to 200 miles and are mostly from retailers. We also have two warehouses that store goods for a set length of time before they move on to their end journey. Our warehouse team handles all our goods in and out invoices, but we need to collate all files and records to keep track of storage space. We ship some of our stock abroad, so we also have to keep track of all HM Revenue and Customs documents."

Julia looked directly at me when she replied. She seemed more confident and focused now.

"At Layton's Transport, we mostly covered UK retail runs, along with several pickups in France, so I'm familiar with what's required to a certain extent. Because Night Movers venture further into Europe and beyond, I know that will be harder to set up and organise, but I'm looking forward to learning how to do that."

"We'll give you all the training you require before Maggie goes part-time," I replied, eager to ease Julia's mind regarding her suitability for the job. It was a way to get her near me most nights, and I had to make her see that she was more than qualified for the position.

Maggie lay Julia's C.V. on the table. Looking at it was pointless. She knew we'd find no better candidate.

"Julia, I have every confidence that the technicalities of this job will cause you no issue. However, I must let you know this has been more than just a job for me. Alex, Nikolas and Joshua have always been like family," Maggie said before turning to me and smiling. She grabbed my hand, then added, "Because of this, I find it easier to put up with their moods and the silly man stuff that goes on in this office."

"I don't get moody," I quickly interjected, glaring at her before pulling my hand away. "And what silly man stuff?"

"Making loud farting noises when I'm on the phone with important clients, for one."

"I didn't make the farting noises; it was Nikolas," I replied truthfully.

"But it was you who replaced my sugar with salt, Alex, and don't you deny it!"

No, I couldn't deny that one.

"But in my defence, Maggie, it was that horrible low-calorie sweetener stuff that makes you not want to drink the tea or coffee it's in, anyway. So I did you a favour, really."

"Do you see what I have to put up with, Julia? And Joshua is no better. He pretended I had a virus on my computer and I'd lost all my work. He kept it up for over an hour."

"I'm sorry about that, Maggie," I said, and I meant it... sort of.

"Well, you weren't sorry when you were doubled over on the floor laughing about it," Maggie stated.

Julia started giggling, and it was clear to see she was much happier to be in this room with us than when she'd first walked in.

I regained my composure and asked, "Do you have an up-to-date passport? You might have to accompany me occasionally, both here in the UK and out of the country?"

She nodded and said she had about five years left on her passport before it needed renewing. We went over a few more items that Maggie had listed for us to discuss, and before we knew it, the interview had come to a close.

"I hope you choose to accept the position, Julia. If you could let us know before the end of next week, we'd be really grateful," I said, knowing I'd do anything I could over the next few days to get her to say she'd work for us, whether in this role or another I had to invent.

"I would be happy to take the job. When would you like me to start?" she asked eagerly.

I was thrilled. Maggie stepped forward and hugged her tightly.

"I'm so glad you'll be joining us, Julia. I know you'll love it here, and we'll love you, too." She took Julia's hands in hers, then said, "Promise me you'll keep an open mind about everything else you see and hear tonight. We are all good people here, and we work well together. Please don't let prejudice prevent you from being happy."

Maggie turned to look at me and smiled. "I think you should take Julia on a tour of the premises while I get the paperwork ready. I can take over the rest of your workload for tonight."

I could tell Maggie's words had puzzled Julia, but before she had the chance to ask questions, I took her hand in mine and led her out of the room.

I tried to sound professional as I led her through the cafeteria and break rooms. We descended the stairs of the old stone building to our basement-level gym, then to the medical room, and all the while, her hand was still in mine. After we'd toured the lower levels, we walked back up towards the compound where all our lorries and vans were, and only when she spotted her father did she let go of my hand.

We chatted for a few minutes before he said he had to get back to work. They were busy getting ready for a large shipment tonight. I debated what to do next and ended up jumping into one of the small golf cart-type vehicles we used to get around. I drove her around the site, ending up down the lane at the row of small cottages that Nik, Josh, and I called home.

"Would you like to come in so we can discuss the job and what Maggie was talking about in more detail over a glass of wine?" I asked cautiously.

She spoke quickly while reaching out to take the hand I offered.

"Alex, I'm not sure what Maggie was referring to, but I have honestly held no prejudice that I can think of, and it's got me a little worried about the meaning behind her words."

We entered the kitchen, where I offered to take her jacket. Thankfully, I'd remembered to put the central heating on.

Autumn in Yorkshire can be mild or freezing, with various types of weather in between, but this evening, there was a definite chill in the air.

Despite what you read in fiction, vampires do feel the cold, although it bothers us very little.

I removed my jacket and placed it over the chair next to hers. I'd opted to wear a grey suit tonight, teaming it with a white shirt and grey tie that Maggie bought me. She said it matched my eyes.

I've never been fond of wearing a tie, so I removed mine and placed it in the pocket of my jacket before rolling up my shirt sleeves. When I looked up to ask what type of wine Julia preferred, I found her gazing at me. I didn't want to presume, but from the look in her eyes, she seemed to like what she was seeing. The sad thing was, I knew what I was about to tell her could change all that.

Chapter Four

Julia

I sat at Alex's small kitchen table and looked around the room. I thought his home would be quite masculine, with plenty of steel or chrome, but it was traditional in style, having cream-coloured walls and plush, deep-blue fabrics in the curtains and chairs.

He'd caught me looking at him earlier, and I was so embarrassed. But honestly, I couldn't look away from him while he removed his jacket and tie.

Alex was about six-foot-three with a lean muscular build, so good-looking and sexy in an understated way. When his pale-grey eyes gaze into mine, it hits me low in the belly and radiates south, if you know what I mean.

Alex asked which wine I preferred. I told him I usually drank Shiraz, so he selected one from his wine rack and poured us both a glass. We took our first few sips in silence, and then he spoke so quietly that I almost didn't hear him.

"Julia, I am a vampire, and so are Nik and Josh."

What the...?

"Alex, I'm sorry, I know you just said something, but I think I misheard you," I told him as calmly as I could.

"No, Julia, you heard me correctly. I'm a vampire and have been for nearly a thousand years. Nik and Josh have also been vampires for several centuries, though not as long as me, and we've been friends for a very long time. I consider Josh a brother, although we're not blood-related.

"Although revealing ourselves to humans and mixing as one with them in society has its drawbacks, it's become easier over the years, especially during the last century. Humans are no longer as controlled by religious beliefs as they used to be."

He paused to let me speak, but I couldn't find any words.

"Say something, Julia. Please."

"Okay," I said, looking around the room. "Where are the hidden cameras? This must be what Maggie warned me about with your silly man stuff."

"No," Alex replied while looking down into his wineglass. "It's not some silly joke, Julia. There are no hidden cameras in this room, and I assure you, every word I have spoken from entering my home is the truth."

He said that with utter sincerity, and I felt a little overwhelmed. "I'm sorry, Alex, I don't know what you want me to say. You've just told me you and two other men I've known for years are vampires. What am I supposed to say to that?"

He stared at me, those grey eyes of his never leaving mine, and eventually, I said, "Prove it."

What happened next will stay with me for the rest of my life.

Fangs descended from his slightly parted lips, and

when I looked into his eyes, they'd developed a deep-red ring around the now silvery grey of the iris. His nails had lengthened and looked more like claws. I jumped up out of my chair, and it fell to the wooden floor with a loud thud.

"What the hell, Alex? What kind of mind fuck are you trying to pull with me? Do you think I'm so gullible that I'd believe this shit you're telling me? And how the hell did you do that with your eyes, teeth, and nails?"

Before I could blink, Alex appeared beside me and held my arms so I couldn't escape.

"Please, Julia, just listen to me. I'm not making this up, but I promise I won't hurt you."

I struggled to get away from him, but my efforts were in vain. Alex had me in a vice-like grip, and although his eyes and teeth were normal again, I was still frightened.

I was alone with a madman who thought he was a vampire.

Alex inhaled sharply and quickly released me from his grip.

"Julia, I can smell the fear in you—I hear it in the acceleration of your heartbeat, and it kills me to know it's me that put it there."

"Then stop with all this vampire nonsense and just admit you're playing an idiotic, over-the-top prank," I cried.

"I only wish I could," he admitted sadly. Then he placed his arms around me and stared deep into my eyes. For a second, I forgot what he'd just told me, captivated by the insanely attractive man before me. His fangs descended again, his beautiful grey eyes changing to silver with deep-red rims. I knew then, without a doubt, that Alex wasn't human.

He held me like that for a few minutes more, and the

fear began to dissipate, like bubbles slowly popping until suddenly there were none.

Eventually, Alex asked, "Would you like to sit down again and finish your wine? I promise I'll answer any questions you have truthfully."

I nodded and looked down at my chair, which was still upended on the floor. Alex picked it up and placed it beside the table for me to sit on. I quickly sat and drank the rest of my wine in one go while he took his seat. He looked over and raised the bottle again, silently asking if I wanted another drink. I nodded, so Alex poured me another glass and then set the bottle down. Looking at me, he sighed, then spoke.

"I'm sure you have plenty of questions, Julia. But let me start by saying that you will never be in danger from me. Please believe me. I would lay down my life for you in a heartbeat."

"Do you have one? A heartbeat, I mean?"

"Yes, I have a heartbeat," he said with a smile. "But it's slower than yours, and I can decelerate it enough that it almost appears to have stopped."

"Do you bite people and drink their blood?" I hurriedly asked, thinking that should have been my first question, being as I was alone with a vampire.

"Yes, Julia, but only with their permission," he said seriously. This brought about thoughts of Alex holding me in his arms, kissing my neck, and asking in a sultry voice if he could taste my blood.

Those thoughts turned me on for some insane reason, and I felt my nipples harden against the lace of my bra. I looked up and found that Alex had a knowing smirk on his face.

"Can you read my thoughts?" I asked angrily.

"No," he replied. "But I can hear your heartbeat pick up speed and see the peaks of your nipples through your blouse. I can also scent your arousal."

"I am *not* aroused!" I stated crossly, reaching into my bag for the small perfume bottle I carried. After spraying a little on my wrists and throat, I finally allowed myself to look at him. Alex was trying not to laugh, and honestly, I didn't know whether to laugh right along with him.

A thought came to me suddenly, and I asked, "Does my dad know?"

"Nearly all my employees know, Julia. Most are happy, or they're at least okay with the situation. If not, I can use mind control to make them forget."

"Mind control. How does that work?" I asked warily.

"A seasoned vampire can manipulate someone's thought process to make people think that something we suggest is the thing they should be doing or thinking. How successful a vampire is at mind control is usually determined by their age and power."

When Alex had finished speaking, he looked away from my line of sight. As if he knew what question I would ask him next and that I wouldn't like his answer.

"Alex, have you ever used mind control on me?"

"Yes, I've used mind control on you. And on others when in your presence."

He still didn't look my way, which was starting to annoy me. I thought he might have done it at the hospital when he got the nurses to bring Megan to me, but I wanted to hear it from him.

"You need to know another fact because it concerns what I'm about to tell you, but you must promise that you'll talk about this with no one else. So make that promise, Julia."

"I promise, Alex. I mean, who would believe me anyway?"

"Very well," he replied. "It's about our blood. A vampire's blood can heal certain ailments and injuries if we get it to people on time. So, when your dad called to let me know about your accident, I drove to the hospital and waited with your parents until you came out of surgery. I gave you some of my blood to aid your recovery, just enough so they wouldn't get suspicious of you healing from your injuries inhumanly fast. When you came around, I used mind control on the nurses to get them to bring your baby to you, and then I used it on you to make the experience more pleasant than it would have been."

"What do you mean, more pleasant?" I asked. "Wait, don't answer that. I don't want my memory of that day to change. It's all I have."

He leaned over the table to grab my hand, but I pulled it away from his grasp.

"Did you give me more of your blood when you visited me afterwards? And did you use mind control on me then?"

"Yes, to both those questions, Julia. I needed to help you heal."

"Why?" I asked. "Because my dad asked you to?"

"No. I couldn't stand to see you in pain. I couldn't do much about the emotional pain you were going through, but I could take away the physical pain. So I did what I had to."

"I needed the physical pain," I yelled. "Yes, sometimes I wished it would go, but soon after, I would welcome it. Being in physical pain made the emotional pain easier to bear."

That was it. The floodgates were open again, and I really didn't want to cry in front of anyone anymore. They all give me that look that's a cross between pity and *'I'm going to run away now because I don't know how to deal with you and your tears.'*

Alex knelt before me and pulled me in for a hug. "I'm sorry. I just wanted to help you in any way I could—to make your life a little easier. I didn't know that you used physical pain as a coping strategy. But that's not a healthy way to deal with emotional trauma, Julia, so I'd do it again without hesitation."

He reached over to his jacket and took a hanky out of his pocket to dry my tears.

"Seeing you hurt makes me hurt, whether that's physically or emotionally. I want to help you heal from all your hurts now and always, and I promise I'll get you any help you need to be able to do that."

I didn't know what to say to that, so I linked my hands in his and held on like I was hanging on to life itself. Strange, really, as Alex had recently informed me that he was one of the undead. A quick thought came to mind.

"Are you dead?" I asked.

"What do you think?" he replied with a slight smile.

"Well, you don't feel dead," I said as I ran my fingers under his rolled-up sleeves. "Your hands and arms are cooler than mine, but they're not cold."

Alex nodded. "That's good to know."

"Is the rest of your body the same?" I asked innocently. Then I blushed to my roots and dropped my gaze, embarrassed at my question.

Alex lifted my chin, stroked my cheek and lips with his thumb and said, "One day soon, I hope you get to find that out."

Chapter Five

Julia

I didn't know what was wrong with me, but before I could think of the rights and wrongs of the situation, I leaned forward and kissed him full on the lips. He didn't kiss me back at first, and I tried to pull away, but he grabbed the back of my neck and held me close as he sealed his lips to mine in what seemed like a never-ending kiss.

His tongue invaded my mouth, sweeping the underside of my own. I shivered and groaned as he uncovered feelings and desires I'd kept buried for such a long time.

Alex stood, pulling me with him, his mouth never leaving mine. His hands trailed down my neck, caressing my back before grabbing my bottom and pulling me against his erection. I wished I hadn't worn a pencil skirt so I could wrap my legs around him and feel his hard length where I needed it most.

Alex slowed the kiss down and pulled back from me. "I didn't plan on kissing you like this tonight."

I stepped away from him, both embarrassed and disappointed. I'd felt something deep and primal in the lust that was building. Obviously, he hadn't.

"Julia, please don't think I don't desire you. I just wanted it to be special, so I could show you what you mean to me. I wanted to take you out somewhere nice, romance you a little—not nearly rip off your clothes and fuck you on the table."

Alex turned away from me, linking his hands at the back of his neck.

His words did something to me. It had been so long since I felt that someone truly desired me. When Gavin and I had been trying and failing to get pregnant, sex had become such a chore. We never regained a sexual or even a friendly relationship after losing Megan. So hearing Alex say he wanted to *"rip off my clothes and fuck me on the table,"* well, I didn't care what he was anymore because, despite all the emotional baggage I was carrying, he wanted me. That knowledge was heady, adding fuel to my raging hormonal fire.

I took the wine glasses and bottle and placed them on the countertop. With shaking hands, I unbuttoned my blouse.

"Do it," I said breathlessly. "Here, on the table. You don't have to rip off my clothes. I'm removing them myself."

Alex turned around, looking surprised but hopeful.

"Are you sure about this, Julia? We can take it slow and easy. I know things have been hard for you lately, so I don't want you to regret anything because you weren't ready."

"I am ready. Ready to not be an emotional wreck of a woman who will never be truly happy again. Please, Alex, even if it's only for tonight. Make me feel wanted."

With my last words, Alex stalked towards me and took my mouth in a hard, unforgiving kiss. He backed me up against the table, and even the thought of what we were about to do made me wet.

Alex growled into my mouth, his tongue duelling with mine for dominance. He unzipped my skirt, and it fell to the floor with ease. I stepped out of it and then kicked it away, and we still hadn't broken the kiss. I felt drugged and dizzy with lust, and when he lifted me to sit on the table, I was relieved.

Alex stepped back and broke our kiss. He looked me over from my chestnut brown hair to the tips of my knee-length, high-heeled boots. I became a little self-conscious and tried to join my unbuttoned blouse together over my stretch-marked tummy.

"Don't hide yourself," Alex commanded in a throaty voice. "Every inch of you is beautiful, and I'll spend forever showing you that if you let me."

Alex slipped my blouse off my shoulders and unclipped my bra, all the while gazing into my eyes with a look that told me this would be everything I needed and more.

Before he could touch me again, I reached out for the buttons on his shirt. I wanted to feel his skin against mine, all of him. Alex pushed my hands away and laughed as he ripped his shirt open, buttons popping off as he did so.

"At least I got to rip some clothes off," Alex remarked, chuckling as he tossed it to the side. I laughed until he bent and took my right nipple in his mouth, and then I groaned loudly. It was bliss to feel him lave his tongue over my full breast, pulling and tweaking the other. After scraping his teeth on my sensitive nipple, he swapped and tongued my left breast while using his fingers on the right, building my need for him even more. I couldn't help the gasps and moans coming out of my mouth as I lay on the table, having my breasts worshipped. But I wanted so much more and wasn't too proud to beg for it.

"Please, Alex, I need you inside me," I told him while pushing up so I could unzip his trousers. To my embarrassment, I realised the wetness from my sex had seeped through the lace of my knickers and onto the fabric covering his zipper.

"I'm sorry," I murmured, dropping my hands and looking away from the evidence of my arousal on him. Alex wasn't my boyfriend. For all I knew, this was a one-night stand.

"Don't ever be sorry about something like this, Julia. Seeing how wet you are from what we're doing turns me on more than I've ever known, and I'm so hard I ache."

His words were sending me over the edge, and my embarrassment disappeared. "Please, Alex. I need you."

As soon as the words left my mouth, Alex pulled off my knickers, spread my knees apart, and thrust his tongue as deep inside me as it would go while strumming my clit with his thumb. I detonated from the inside out, a powerful orgasm that left me crying out his name.

Alex pulled me up to the edge of the table, unbuttoned and unzipped his trousers, and then pulled them down with his boxers, exposing his cock to me for the first time. It was long and thick, and I sat up to touch it.

Alex shook his head and guided his cock towards my entrance. He thrust inside me with deep, hard strokes as he leaned over me, sucking each breast into his mouth until both nipples stood proud, wet, and wanting more.

"Put your hands over your head and hold on to the edge of the table," he commanded while placing my boot-clad ankles over his shoulders. "I want to watch those beautiful tits bounce while I fuck you."

I felt more wetness flood over his cock, loving his dirty talk. Then he let go, thrusting so hard the table was moving across the room, making loud noises against the hardwood floor. I drowned out those noises with my screams of absolute ecstasy. It was everything I needed, and when Alex stroked my clit in rhythm with his thrusts, I orgasmed one after the other.

Alex threw his head back and groaned. Then I felt a gush of warmth as he came deep inside me.

Chapter Six

Alex

Once Julia's breathing became steady, I lifted her from the table and kissed her softly. She wrapped her arms around my neck and held on tight—as if she never wanted to let go. Then she sighed contentedly.

I never wanted this perfect moment to end, so I kept kissing her and holding her close. Pretty soon, however, my cock began pulsing inside her as I became hard again.

"Oh," giggled Julia. "Again? Already?"

"Yes," I replied as I unzipped her boots and removed them, kissing each bare foot as it was revealed. Then I kicked off my shoes, trousers and boxers and walked towards my bedroom, keeping my cock buried inside her.

I wanted to keep her in the moment, not regretting what we'd done. If I gave her space, she might put a voice to the worries I was sure were racing around her head. So as soon as I set her on my bed, I began kissing her again. Then I made love to her like I'd wanted our first time to be.

Julia tried to get me to up my pace by pushing her hips up to meet mine with quick, jerky movements, so I stopped, took her face in my hands and looked at her while I spoke.

"Julia, let me love you nice and slow. I've wanted you for so long. Allow me to savour this special moment; I promise I'll make it good for you."

She nodded her response, but I saw tears form in her eyes as she bit her lip to keep from crying. So I did the only thing I could do at that moment—I kissed her, pouring all the love in my heart into that one simple act.

When I moved again, I ground the base of my cock into her clit, eliciting long, deep moans from Julia as her tears were forgotten. I felt the familiar throbbing tingling feeling in my groin, warning of my impending release, so I picked up the pace a little while keeping to the same grinding rhythm. She dug her nails into the lower half of my back and shouted, "Oh God! Alex, don't stop!"

When I felt her sex contracting around me, I was done for, and after four more deep thrusts, I was coming too, each pump draining my energy but leaving me wanting more, like an addict.

"I have to use the bathroom to get cleaned up," Julia announced, bringing me back to the moment. I gave her a quick kiss, then pulled out of her body, leaving a trail of sticky wetness running down her thighs. It pleased me to see my seed running out of her like that. Like I'd marked her as mine for always.

I took her hand in mine. "Come with me; I'll run you a bath."

I consider a bathroom a place of luxury where one can relax and chase away the stresses and strains of life, so I'd chosen the mid-grey tiles and warm lighting carefully, as well as the Jacuzzi bath. When we entered, rather than her being impressed, I heard Julia mumble, "Alex, I need to pee."

"Okay," I replied, letting go of her hand and walking towards the bath.

"Erm, Alex, I, oh shit. I've got to go now before I pee myself," she declared, sitting herself down on the toilet and proceeding to pee loudly. I laughed when I saw how embarrassed she'd become about the situation. Julia wouldn't meet my gaze as she said huffily, "You, Alex Staithes, are no gentleman." I laughed even harder when she added, "And you kept your socks on for sex."

I looked down and could see that I had indeed forgotten to take off my socks, but in my defence, I'd been a little preoccupied at the time. Julia's cheeks reddened further when I reminded her of this.

Despite it being highly amusing, I needed to stop all the embarrassment so she wouldn't go running. So I stepped out of the bathroom to give her a few moments to compose herself.

When I returned to the kitchen to retrieve Julia's clothes and boots, I realised I hadn't even closed the curtains or locked the door.

Once I'd locked up, I carried her clothes into my bedroom and went back to the kitchen for the wine. I plated up some cheese and crackers along with a few grapes, so we'd have something to snack on. I'd consumed a full bag of blood earlier, so I was okay as far as that side of me went.

Chapter Seven

Alex

When I entered the bathroom, I found Julia relaxing in the bath with the Jacuzzi setting bubbling away.

"This is lovely," she mumbled, lying back with her eyes closed.

"I brought us some food," I informed her, holding up the plate. "And more wine."

I set the glasses down along with the plate on the wide, tiled area around the side of the bath, then I changed the lighting so that only the floor lights surrounding the bath were lit. This made the room appear more tranquil, despite the bubbling noise.

"Move up so I can sit behind you," I told her while getting in as quickly as I could before she could protest.

"Alex, how come you can eat food and drink regular drinks?" Julia queried. "I thought vampires could only drink blood."

"Obviously, as a vampire, blood is essential. Without it,

we just wouldn't function. But that side of us that lets us exist as human also needs sustenance. It also depends how old we are. A newly turned vampire will require a blood feed maybe two or three times a day, but one such as myself—who's been a vampire for many years—can take blood as little as three times a week and be okay."

"How long have you been a vampire?" she asked.

"That's quite a difficult question for me to answer," I replied truthfully, handing over her glass of wine.

"I was born Aðalbrandr, meaning noble sword, by the way," I said, flexing my hardening cock against her bottom, "over 950 years ago near a small coastal town in Norway.

"My mother was a beautiful Viking noblewoman named Brisafreya, and her Viking warrior husband was Brandr. My sister, Freya, was born ten years later.

"They groomed me from an early age to be like my name suggests: a warrior with brute strength and bravery. My mother, however, always cautioned me to use my head more and join the rest of the noble families in a sort of council—unlike Brandr—and to think about other things, such as keeping our people warm and fed.

"I had two uncles, Gamall and Sebbi. Gamall and my mother were twins and shared an interest and belief in what they would later term as witchcraft.

"In Viking culture, it wasn't frowned upon for women to practice witchcraft, but men were ridiculed if they were found doing so. Instead, men were classed as shamans and used to call upon the gods to send a good harvest, or for safe passage when setting out to sea.

"Sebbi wasn't a relative as such, but more like a close friend to my mother. He was by her side constantly, especially if she seemed worried or ill, and he comforted her whenever Brandr would be with one of his mistresses. Or after yet another one of their fights. You see, Brandr wasn't good to the women in his life. It had only taken a week or so for my mother to get pregnant with me, and he was away in battle for most of her pregnancy, which spared her his wrath. I remember them arguing a lot when he was home, and he used to make her cry often.

"When I was born, and Brandr knew he had a son, he demanded a feast that lasted for a week. I was told many years later that he'd taken another mistress during that time, and he'd kept her for years. She died after having an argument with him in which they'd fought. He was going to be tried for her death but was pardoned when they needed him in an upcoming war with neighbouring lands.

"When Freya was born, he didn't want to know. Brandr hadn't wanted a girl, just more sons. It used to break Freya's heart when he ignored her, and he would make my mother take her from the room when he came in. I hated him more with every passing day.

"Sebbi and Gamall had both been father figures for Freya. In fact, she had them wrapped around her little finger." Thinking about my sister as a carefree little girl always made me smile.

"When Freya was about nine years old, Sebbi and Gamall left for England, along with Brandr and around forty other men from ours and the surrounding villages. Sebbi had informed them that England offered a better climate where they could grow plentiful food, unlike Norway and its harsh winters. Brandr had been on several successful raids along the North of England's coastline so he could back up some of Sebbi's claims.

"They were to build a settlement in which they would create homes, then some would sail back so they could bring us to this better place when the weather was mild, as this made for safer travel for the women and children.

"They returned two years later, but Brandr wasn't with them. Sebbi addressed the village councilmen, telling them Brandr had been killed in battle and died as a warrior. Everyone but me believed him."

I took the body wash from the shelf and poured a generous amount into my hands, then proceeded to wash every inch of Julia I could reach.

"Why did you think he lied?" she asked.

"It was the look he gave me when he spoke; it was different to the one he gave the others. I'd seen that look before between him and my mother, and I knew right then that Sebbi would play an even bigger part in our lives than he had previously.

"Later that night, I went to speak with my mother about it and heard familiar noises. You see, I was twenty by then, and being strong and handsome, I'd caught the eye of many of the lonely village women while their men were away. I'd been having sex with quite a few of them every chance I could get, so I recognised the sounds. But they were ones I hadn't expected to hear from my mother and Sebbi together. I didn't confront them; I just left Mother's hut as quietly as I could.

"A short while later, Sebbi came to find me. He said he knew I'd found him making love to my mother, and he wanted to explain a few things to me. My mother followed him moments later, looking much happier than I'd seen her for many years. Sebbi said that he was both mine and Freya's father, not Brandr, as we had been led to believe. He also said he was a Born Immortal, and Freya and I were too. I asked what that meant, as I was confused by what he was saying.

"Sebbi explained the meaning of vampire, the need to drink blood and the strength and speed that his kind had. He then revealed his fangs, and his eyes changed colour. I grabbed my sword, pulling my mother behind me. Sebbi spoke calmly, saying that he would never hurt me, my mother, or Freya, and despite still being wary, I believed him. He also said he was going to take us all back to England, where he'd lived many years before coming to Norway. He said he'd readied a place for us, and we would sail as soon as the moon was full, which was seven nights from then.

"Over the next seven nights, Sebbi told us all about his kind. How he could change humans by draining them of their blood, almost to the point of death, then feeding them his own blood. He said Born Immortals were more powerful and could walk in daylight. Although direct sunlight drained their strength.

"Sebbi insisted I would know when the time was right for me to take my first swallow of human blood. At that time, my body would stay as it was and never age, and as long as I drank blood regularly, I would heal quickly from any wounds. Freya and I—being of his blood—had never been ill a day in our lives. We didn't know what it was like to suffer from a cough or fever, but I had a few battle wounds and knew about pain and healing, so that part of being a vampire appealed to me."

"I don't understand something, Alex. Wasn't your mother human?" Julia questioned.

"Yes, she was, and I know what you're going to ask. How was she able to become pregnant to a vampire?"

"Yes, I mean, I don't understand how someone who is one of the undead can have living sperm. And, Alex, if you do have living sperm, we've had unprotected sex. Twice."

"As far as I'm aware, my lovely Julia, a Born Immortal can only reproduce with a human woman after he Blood Bonds with her. It's the giving and receiving of a small amount of blood from each other at the same time—usually during sex, as it heightens the potency of the blood. It changes the body at a cellular level, which then enables the human female to become pregnant.

"By Blood Bonding with a vampire, whether Born or Made, you are entering into an unbreakable bond. Something that has more meaning and worth to the immortal than a human marriage ever could. As long as the human continues to take the vampire's blood, he or she will never age and will have the same long life as the immortal one," I told her.

"What happens when you stop loving the one you Bond with?" she asked in a soft voice.

I turned her head so she met my gaze.

"Julia, when a vampire falls in love and Bonds with a human, both the love and the Bond last forever."

I let the meaning of what I'd just said wash over her for a moment before I smiled and handed her more food. When we finished the plate, I retrieved a couple of towels from the rack, and we stepped out of the bath to get dry.

When we went back into the bedroom, I noticed that the time was now 11:15 p.m., and as I didn't want the night to end, I asked Julia to stay with me.

At first, Julia declined, but then she asked if I would continue with my story if she stayed, so I agreed. Julia sent both her mum and dad a text message to say she'd had too much to drink while celebrating her new job and was staying the night here in my spare room to sleep it off. I then texted Maggie to let Nik and Josh know I wouldn't be back in tonight.

Julia glanced at the bed and asked, "Do you have anything I could sleep in?"

"My arms, hopefully," I replied. I winked at her, then went to get her a T-shirt from my wardrobe. To make Julia feel more comfortable, I put my boxers on, and we lay facing each other on top of the bed.

"How long did it take to sail to England?" she asked.

"Six very long days," I replied, the memory of that journey still fresh in my mind after all these centuries.

"In our last two days at sea, we hit a storm that overwhelmed even the strongest men who were rowing with us. We tried and tried to gain the upper hand, but we were tossed and thrown about like leaves in the wind. Inevitably, the ship listed over to a point where we began taking on water.

"My father, Gamall, and I were rowing with about thirty men, each trying to gain control of our oars. Others were trying to get rid of the water we were taking on when a few of them were swept overboard. None of us knew what had happened until my father howled out as if in agony. You see, through the powerful Bond he had with my mother, he felt the very moment she went overboard. He leapt out of the confines of his seat like an animal and ran the length of the ship faster than was humanly possible. Despite everything we tried to do, we could save none of the fifteen men and women who went overboard that night, my mother included."

I gave myself a few moments before I carried on with my story, the guilt of not being able to save her still heavy on my soul. Julia placed her hand on mine and said how sorry she was. I linked my fingers with hers and carried on with the story of my life.

"Hours later, the storm broke, and we were slowly

getting back on course for Bretland, as England was then known. My father and Freya were inconsolable and clung to each other in their pain and grief. It was down to Gamall, Frankke and I to organise getting ashore. We decided to moor the ship in a cove, take the small rowboat we carried and transport everyone to shore in that. Some of the strongest men we had with us went first so they could make sure it was safe, and they came back steadily over the next few hours to bring everyone else. Frankke, Gamall, my father, Freya, and I were the last ones to step ashore that night—to what is now known as the pretty fishing village of Staithes in North Yorkshire."

"Is that where your surname comes from?" she asked.

"Yes. I took the name Alexander because it wasn't unlike Aðalbrandr—my Nordic name—and Staithes because it's where I first stepped foot on English soil."

I hadn't said my Nordic name for a while, and it seemed strange to keep hearing it again.

"We made our way to the settlement, weathered, weary and heartsick for those who were no longer with us. During that terrible storm, we'd lost wives, mothers, husbands, sisters and brothers, so the mood was low between all of us for many months.

"Freya was the only thing that kept my father going. The once pleasant Sebbi became moody and aggressive in his dealings with everyone else, myself included. Gamall tried different types of witchcraft to help him, but nothing seemed to lift his spirits at all. Then one day, a cart carrying two men pulled up outside our settlement. One of them was my father's brother, who was named Eadgar, and the other was Eadgar's Born Immortal son, Colton.

"Eadgar and Colton were a ray of light in our dark, grieving world, and we began looking forward to a future in our new land. Sebbi came around slowly, and we eventually became a family again.

"Colton was about to take a wife so he could start a family when he became a vampire, making his children Born Immortals like him. I wasn't so sure that life appealed to me anymore. I knew I had a lot to learn about being an immortal and hoped that Sebbi would provide more information now that he was getting back to himself again.

"Eadgar and Colton taught us how to make a living on the land we'd acquired, as the soil here differed from what we'd been used to. They gave us the means to purchase cattle and tools. It was apparent that there was wealth in his family, but Sebbi didn't want to go back with them to the east of Yorkshire, even though they welcomed all of us, including Gamall. They left us about two months later and made us promise to visit them soon.

"Freya grew into a beautiful young woman who was like my mother in looks, with her grey eyes and pale blonde hair. Freya had everything she desired because my father spoiled her every chance he could. From the best dolls the woodcarver could make when she was a child, to the pretty jewellery that was made locally. You'd have thought this would have made her a spoiled brat, but that couldn't be further from the truth. She was so kind to everyone, and she loved the young children of the village. Freya would gather them around her and make up stories of magical worlds with strange creatures and handsome heroes. Everyone adored her.

"When she was nineteen, Freya came to speak to me about being a Born Immortal. Freya said she didn't want to become a vampire because she wanted to be a wife, a mother, and then a grandmother. Freya also said she'd spoken to Father about it, but he was insistent she take the blood and became a true immortal as soon as she could, like Colton. Freya said she'd asked if she didn't take the blood, would she grow old and die like normal humans? Father had gone into a rage, saying Freya wasn't like other humans, and even without the blood, she would age more slowly than her husband and children. He'd said that when she died, she would die alone because all her family would have long since gone.

"I told her I'd seek out Eadgar and Colton and ask what would happen to us if we didn't take the blood and become vampires, so we'd know one way or the other.

Father had been trying to persuade me to take the blood for months, but I refused to do it until Freya did, so neither of us made him happy.

"I asked Freya what had prompted these thoughts. She told me she'd fallen in love with Tobias, who was Frankke's son. Tobias was a strong, handsome young man. At twenty-two, he was only three years older than Freya, and he worked as a woodcarver. I remember her taking my hand, placing it on her belly, and telling me she was going to have his child. I was angry that she'd let him make love to her without the marriage ceremony, but she said I'd lain with many women without being married, so I couldn't judge her or be angry with Tobias. But this was my sister, the sweet Freya, so of course I was angry.

"Then I thought of my father, who'd been travelling with Gamall for the last two months, and I knew the situation could get a lot worse. So I arranged for her marriage to take place in two days' time while praying that my father wouldn't return beforehand.

"Freya looked beautiful, and they made a wonderful couple. You could see that Tobias thought the world of her. Their love was so pure and real that it made me want the same for myself. My father came back the day after the wedding and was furious. Even more so when he scented the pregnancy on her. At first, he wanted nothing to do with Freya, but she was his precious daughter, and he couldn't stay angry with her for too long.

"When her baby daughter was born, Freya named her Brisa after my mother. Sebbi was thrilled and spoiled her even more than he had Freya. She was adorable, and we all fell madly in love with the beautiful little girl, who was such a happy child.

"Father kept trying to persuade me to take the blood, and I ignored him at every turn. Eadgar and Colton had gone to Ireland for a while, so if I wanted to speak to them about it, I'd need to travel, but I didn't want to leave Freya and her family.

Time moved on as it always does. I made sure through the various trading we'd built up that our village had suitable homes for everyone and that we had enough food for winter.

"Freya had informed my father that she wouldn't take the blood. She wanted to have more children and be a normal mother to them. Tobias was against her becoming a vampire because he didn't want her to be different to them all. This made up my mind for me, too, and as Father knew I would only take the blood if Freya did, he stopped asking me about it.

"When she was twenty-seven, Freya became pregnant again. She used to take Brisa and spend two evenings a week with my father and Gamall at their home on the edge of the village. More often than not, I would join them after my work was done—a kind of family tradition that we tried not to miss. It was during one of those evenings that our lives changed forever.

"On that fateful night, Freya had arrived alone without Brisa for the first time. Brisa had been tired after playing out all day in the sun, so she'd stayed at home with Tobias. Father went into a panic and kept asking where Brisa was. Freya assured him she was all right and was probably sleeping by now. But he left us and ran the mile to Freya's house. We all followed in the cart, fearful as to what our father's instinct had told him.

"Freya's house was on fire and had been for some time. Our father lay on the ground outside—his body charred and burned. Freya leapt from the cart and ran towards her burning home, screaming for Brisa and Tobias. It took all the strength I possessed to keep her from running into the fire. The dread I felt in the pit of my stomach told me that my niece and brother-in-law were already dead.

"Gamall went to my father and gathered him up onto the back of the cart. Keeping Freya in my arms, I placed her on the seat beside me and headed back to my father's home, while men from the village tried to prevent the fire from spreading. The smell of my father's burned flesh and my sister's wailing despair still haunt my dreams today."

I let out an exhausted sigh as Julia put her arms around me and held me close.

"I don't know what to say, Alex. There are no words to comfort you when you lose a child like that. Freya must have thought her life had ended that night. I know I did when I lost Megan. But she lost Brisa and Tobias on the same night."

"She lost more than her daughter and husband on that night, Julia," I stated, continuing with the painful story.

"By the time we got back, I heard my father speak to Gamall in a gravelly voice, asking where Freya was and thanking him for giving him so much of his blood. Gamall stumbled off the cart but was caught by one of the men they employed to work the land, and they carried him inside.

"Father tried to take Freya from me, but I wouldn't let him. Pushing him aside, I carried her as quickly as I could to the nearest bed. When I stood back, I could see blood appearing on the front of her dress, and I yelled for my father or for anyone to help me. Father came in shirtless; his skin had already healed from his burns but was still black with smoke. He dropped to the floor beside Freya, pierced his fangs through his wrist, and told Freya to drink from him. She shook her head, keeping her mouth closed, but all the while, more blood was appearing on her dress and down her legs."

I shuddered when I thought about the rest of what had happened that night.

"Freya pushed up to grab her knees, screaming as she went, and I heard Anya—the woman who kept house for my father—say, 'She needs to push; the baby is coming.' Freya was only five months along, so I knew the child couldn't survive, but her body was trying to birth the baby, anyway. I removed her clothing and undergarments as quickly as I could, tears streaming down my face, and in what seemed like no time at all, Freya pushed a baby boy into the world.

"It was heartbreaking. You could see through most of his skin, but he was a perfectly formed yet tiny baby. Father couldn't hear a heartbeat, but we wrapped him in a woollen cloak and handed him to Freya. She said in a weak voice that his name was Tobias, like his father, and I was to make sure both he and she would be buried alongside her husband and Brisa in the new Christian way her husband had favoured.

"My father pushed me aside, took hold of Freya, looked into her eyes and demanded that she live. But her eyes closed, and her head shook from side to side. When the placenta came away, it was in bits. Anya told us that she had seen this before, and it was so bad that the mothers had never lived long afterwards.

"I kept telling Freya I loved her and that I would find her in the next life, but she'd lost consciousness by then. Even though she was a Born Immortal with a quicker healing ability, I knew this was too much for her to come back from. And she wouldn't want to live without her family.

"In the next instant, my father grabbed Anya and sank his teeth into her wrist, savagely tearing a deep gash through her skin. I knew what he was about to do, and I tried to stop him, but he threw me across the room with such force that I heard four of my ribs break as I hit the thick wooden wall, and my shoulder was dislocated. I looked over at Freya and saw that my father was forcing Anya's wrist over her mouth and was working her throat by rubbing and squeezing it, forcing her to swallow. Anya was screaming, so my father used mind control on her, telling her that she wanted to do this for Freya and that she felt no pain. Anya calmed down and immediately became quiet and compliant.

"I struggled over to the bed, but physically I was no match for my father, even without my injuries. A Born Immortal has more strength than a normal human, but when you take the blood and become a vampire, the strength and powers you gain are immense, and I have yet to see them rivalled. So I just sat back and watched as he made Freya swallow the poor human woman's blood. Eventually, Anya swayed, and that's when Father removed her wrist from Freya's mouth. He bit his own wrist and bid Anya drink from him so that she wouldn't feel the effects of the blood loss.

"On that very night, I saw my father for the monster he truly was, and I knew I could feel no love for him anymore. But my sister would now become a vampire, and I hoped she'd be the same thoughtful, loving woman she'd been before she experienced all that loss. Because I knew that whatever Freya became, she would now be it forever.

"'Freya will sleep for a day or two, and when she awakens, she will be truly immortal: a vampire with the need to feed on blood as well as human food.' Father spoke those words so normally. Like the scenes from the last hour hadn't happened. 'She will not want to do this on her own, my son, so will you take the blood and join her in this life everlasting?' he questioned with hope in his voice.

"'Freya will never forgive you for this, Father. You have done a terrible thing this night,' I told him, my voice laden with sorrow. I said I would join Freya in her immortal life, but only she would have my loyalty, for he did not deserve it.

"I left the room and went in search of Gamall to tell him all that had happened, and to ask for his help in gaining my immortality.

"The next day, with the help of the villagers, I buried the baby, Brisa, and Tobias, as Freya had requested. Then I went with Gamall to my home where I drank his blood, and at thirty-seven years old, had my last human sleep."

Chapter Eight

Alex

Julia was sobbing quietly in my arms by the time I'd finished recounting my story, and I could have cried right along with her. Instead, I held her close and found comfort in her embrace.

"I am so sorry for all that your family suffered, Alex. How on earth did you carry on? How could Freya survive such an ordeal?" she questioned through her tears.

"Julia, of the many things I've seen and known over the centuries, what stands out most is the inner strength and power of females. It's something that will prevail above all else. Even if it takes some time to emerge and show itself, it will always be there. Men have more physical strength and power than women of equal stature, but that's where it ends regarding the dominant of the species. Human men are emotionally weaker than women, and they find it harder to empathise with people than women do. That's why I have a lot of respect for all the women in my life."

"All the women?" Julia questioned. I could tell she was a little put out by this remark, and maybe a little jealous, too. Hopefully.

"Yes, all of them," I affirmed before explaining my statement.

"Freya, of course, but I'll tell you more of her story later. Then Maggie, well, she's just an angel, really. She looks after Josh, Nik, and me like a mother hen, constantly reminding us about things we forget and making sure we're okay. Maggie has done that for over thirty years while looking after her husband and three children. Then Daniel and Keeley—her nephew and niece—when their mother passed away. And lately, her elderly mum and in-laws, all while holding down a full-time job.

"Then there's Gina. She's in charge of our cafeteria and cleaning duties, even in our cottages, so you can see how much we trust her. She's worked for us in different capacities for about fifteen years now. During that time, she's brought up two children and had quite a few health problems, yet she still carries on. Gina is unhappy but has stayed in a loveless marriage. She's spent all these years working at keeping her family together, but she's unloved by her ignorant husband. I mean, how many men would be so selfless as to stay with someone like that? Everyone knows what the situation is, and we all tell her to think of herself, but Gina never does."

"How do you know all that about her marriage, Alex? It's quite personal, and I don't think you should be sharing it with anyone," Julia admonished.

"Gina is a lovely woman. I'm sure you'll become friends because everyone gets on really well with her. You just can't help it. Anyway, I caught her and Nik arguing a few months back. He's had a thing for her for a long time, but she seems to think he's just winding her up. She's always carried a bit of extra weight, and I know she's been trying and failing over the years to get rid of it. But Gina hadn't had much success until recently, and Nik was telling her that she should stop losing weight and exercising because she's getting rid of all those curves he likes."

"Wow! Nik was so out of order. What did Gina do?"

"Well, to be honest, Gina let rip about all the things she hated about him, which apparently was a lot. She went on forever about him being a man whore who objectified women and loved himself more than others. She said he was messy and always threw his dirty clothes on the floor—unlike me and Josh, who put them in a basket—and he told stupid jokes which people didn't laugh at anymore."

"What did Nik say to all that?" asked Julia.

"He didn't say anything; he just grabbed her, then kissed her."

"What did Gina do when he kissed her? I thought you said she was married?" Julia remarked.

"She kissed him back at first, but then she broke off the kiss and backed away. Nik told Gina she should leave her husband and live with him. He said he knew they'd be good together, and her kids were older now, so she didn't have to stay for them anymore. Gina burst into tears and ran over to the other building. I followed her, not wanting to see her upset, and that's when I heard her telling Maggie what had happened. Gina said that she knew Steve—her husband—didn't love her, and that she hadn't loved him for a long time. But if she left him now, she'd be admitting that all she's worked so hard for over the years had been for nothing, and she was worried about what it would do to her children and her mum. Gina also said the only way she'd be with someone else would be for love, and she didn't think Nik was capable of it."

"Do you think she's right?" Julia asked hesitantly.

"Well, you know Nik and how he is. But I've got to be honest, Julia, it really shook him. He looked lost, not his usual confident self at all. He said he knew I'd heard everything and thought I was about to warn him to keep away from the staff. But I didn't.

"I asked him if he loved her. He told me he'd loved her for years. So I asked him if she knew, and Nik said she must. I suggested that maybe he needed to prove it to her. And she was right; his jokes were stupid."

"I hope that whatever Gina does, she finds happiness," Julia murmured as she stroked my chest hair.

"I hope so, too," I replied, looking into her eyes.

"There is another strong woman in my life, Julia, and that's you."

"Me?" she scoffed. "Why me? I'm not strong."

"I think you are. The way you demanded to see Megan, even when the staff at the hospital told you no. How you dealt with organising the funeral when you were in so much physical and emotional pain."

"That wasn't all me, though, was it, Alex? You helped me get Megan in the hospital, and both my parents and in-laws helped with the funeral."

"Do you think it makes you weak to admit you need help? Or to accept the help that's offered? I sometimes think that's harder than doing things yourself."

"Yeah, well, I wasn't strong enough to stick it out in a loveless marriage like Gina has, so you're definitely wrong on that score."

"Gina only stayed for the sake of her children. I'm not saying that's right, but I can see the strength someone would have to possess to make that kind of sacrifice. If Megan had lived, would you have stayed with Gavin for her sake, even if you were unhappy?"

"Yes, I would." Julia sighed, looking down at her hands.

"I think the right course of action is for someone to leave and not put up with any bullshit. No one should, male or female. But it isn't easy for a woman because she has the desire to please and make things right for everyone. It's deeply embedded in her feminine soul. That's why women are the stronger sex because most men only want to please themselves."

"Does this include you, Alex?"

I took a deep breath and looked away from her before saying, "I am a little selfish, Julia. I've wanted you since I saw you with your father at that Christmas party fifteen years ago. And although I know that you probably need to be by yourself for a while before you jump into another relationship, I want you to be mine.

"I'm not just talking about sex and a few dates here and there; I'm talking about commitment and love. I've been on this earth for so long, and in all that time, I've never wanted to Bond with a woman. Don't get me wrong; I've had casual relationships. Some have lasted several years. I could never commit to them as my heart was never truly in it. But then one dance with you and I knew why I could never love another in all those years. You were meant to be with me, Julia, and to hear you say you are all mine… That moment can't come soon enough for me."

She was quiet for a long time, and I wanted to break the silence but not overwhelm her, so all I said was, "Come on, it's late now; let's go to sleep." And with that, she rolled onto her side with me lying behind, my hand on her scarred hip, reminding me how close I'd come to losing her.

Chapter Nine

Julia

What was I supposed to think about tonight's revelations? Alex had given me a lot of information to process, but I couldn't think clearly enough for my mind to work. There was no way I'd be falling asleep until I'd truly come to terms with all the facts.

Okay, Alex was a vampire who had been around for centuries, yet I wasn't frightened of him. I believed him when he said he wouldn't hurt me. All the sorrow he'd told me of—well, I can relate to that, and it made him seem more human to know that he still feels so raw from it. But to know that he wants a relationship with me, one that requires love and commitment… I just wasn't sure what to think about that.

Alex said when a vampire falls in love, they love forever. I thought the love I had with Gavin was forever, but look at us now. God only knows what, or who, he was doing, and

I'd just had sex with a vampire. Great sex, too. I haven't had orgasms like that in years. If ever, in fact.

I thought Gavin was good in bed because he nearly always made me come—at least in the early years of our relationship. And because he was my first, I had no one else to compare him to. But Alex really knew how to play my body. As if we'd been together for many years.

It felt so familiar being with him. I should have been shy or held back a little; instead, I was begging him to get inside me. That's just not like me—to be so demanding, I mean. I never was with Gavin.

Maybe this was a new me? An improved version of me. A sexy, demanding, throw caution to the wind and just go for it, version of me.

Yes, I think I'd love to be that kind of person—someone who gets what she wants in life. A strong woman, like Alex said. I could definitely go with that. Maybe I should do something outrageous like bungee jumping or parachute out of a plane... Perhaps not. Heights usually make me vomit, and I wouldn't want to catch that on the way down.

Still, I suppose I could start slowly and build up to the new me. I had a new job now and money in the bank. I could get some new clothes and maybe a new hairstyle too.

Alex turned and let go of my hip, pulling me out of my thoughts.

I had him, too, or I could have if I wanted. I rolled over and ran my fingers down his chest to where the sheet pooled at his waist.

God, he had such an impressive body. It was muscular without being too big or bulky. He lay in bed at the side of me, naked, apart from the boxers he'd put on for my benefit. But he didn't need to do that for the new me. So maybe I should help him remove them...

"What do you need, Julia?" Alex asked in a husky, sexy voice.

Now was the time for the new me to take a stand and tell him, "You, Alex, naked and hard." But instead, I said, "Erm, I haven't brushed my teeth tonight."

Damn! Damn! Damn! Where had the new me gone? It was there on the tip of my tongue to tell him exactly what I wanted, but then it disappeared in favour of good oral hygiene.

Alex flicked a switch and turned on the light over my side of the bed, then held out his hand.

"I think I have a spare toothbrush that Gina got me for my travel bag. I'll get you that."

We began brushing our teeth together at his large bathroom sink, him with an electric toothbrush, me with a manual one. I watched to see if he brushed his fangs. He must have noticed because he smirked and said, "Yes, I do brush my fangs, but not all the time. Only if they've been used."

I nearly swallowed some of my toothpaste and instantly went to spit it out. *He means used them to drink blood,* I thought. Those visions from earlier of him licking my neck crept into my mind, making me warm in some very rude places.

Suddenly, his eyes seemed to bore right through me. His nostrils flared, and I remembered him telling me he could scent my arousal. But I was fully clothed then.

I wasn't wearing any underwear at all now, so there'd be no hiding the effect my wicked thoughts had on my body this time.

I put the toothbrush down and let him lead me back to bed. Gathering my courage, I went towards the side where I had lain before; Alex followed with need and intent in his eyes. I stopped him and asked if he'd turn out the light. I was all for being the brave new me, but not with the light on.

As soon as the light went out, however, I took hold of his boxers and pulled them off. Then I lifted the T-shirt over my head and went towards him.

I began by placing lazy kisses down his torso, giving each nipple a quick flick with my tongue as I passed. I could hear his breathing getting heavy, and it spurred me on. The muscles in his belly flexed as I moved lower, kissing and licking around his hips, enjoying the feel of him below me.

I moved slowly, from one hip to the other, but before I could get there, his cock twitched at the side of my face, stopping me in my tracks. I took a deep breath in, smelling his body wash from earlier—a scent that was totally male. After placing a gentle kiss on the tip, I took him into my mouth.

I worried he was too big, and I wouldn't be able to make it good for him, but the sounds that were coming from Alex spurred me on. It was a real turn-on, knowing he was getting so much pleasure from what I was doing.

I licked him from root to tip and back again, stroking and laving his balls when I got near. Then I took him in my mouth again, this time taking him as deep as I could without gagging. He grabbed my hair, thrusting gently into my mouth, groaning loudly.

After freeing my hair from his grasp, I straddled him as quickly as I could, taking his thick, wet cock deep inside me on the first slide. I rode him hard and without pause, crying out his name within less than twenty seconds, shocked at how quickly my orgasm had hit.

I slumped forward on his chest, trying to catch my breath. I was aware he was still hard inside me, so I began riding him again to help him find his moment, but he stilled my movements and kissed me.

It was slow and dreamy at first, and I felt cherished and wanted. Then the kiss changed, causing my sex to throb around him. It made me moan into his mouth through his kiss, and I felt myself growing wet again.

Alex rolled us over, pinned my arms above my head, and hammered into me without stopping. Hard, deep, fast, and I felt an orgasm building again. I was about to come when he flipped me over, so I was on all fours. He fed his cock back into me, slowly this time, and began a rhythm that drove me mad with sheer frustration because my orgasm was so near. Alex purposely kept it out of my reach by changing the speed or angle of penetration, showing me he was in charge of my body. He pulled me upright so that my back was to his front and sat back on his heels, his cock still inside me.

"Who owns your body tonight, Julia?" Alex asked in a rasping voice.

"You do, Alex. But please, let me come; take this ache away for me," I answered, desperate for release.

"I want to possess you every night. I want to be inside you, body and soul." He licked and kissed my earlobes, then nuzzled and kissed my neck. I knew what I wanted—what he wanted—and I gave voice to the thoughts before I could stop myself.

"Bite me, Alex. Taste my blood."

Alex paused. Nuzzling my ear, he whispered, "Are you sure you want this, Julia?"

"Yes, I want this. I want to know how it feels to let you drink from me. I need to know if I can do this."

Alex began moving inside me again, slow and deep, building into the same rhythm that had me begging for release. He kissed and licked my neck, the anticipation of what he was about to do bringing me closer to the edge. I felt his fangs slide into my skin, delivering such a sharp sting of pain that I cried out in panic. But then he sucked my blood into his eager mouth. A pleasure like no other I have ever felt tore through my body, throwing me into a powerful orgasm that had me moaning so loud for so long I could barely breathe. Alex reached down and rubbed my clit, sending more orgasmic sparks through my body. With every pull he made at my neck, the ripples of pleasure carried on until, finally, he let go and roared out his own release.

Alex turned my face to his and kissed me, whispering sweet words of love and pleasure. I could taste my blood on his lips; it didn't bother me, though. Nothing bothered me at this point. The euphoria I experienced still coursing through my veins.

He picked me up and lay me down on the bed, then he brought a wet towel and cleaned the stickiness between my thighs before getting in bed beside me and kissing me goodnight.

Chapter Ten

Julia

I woke up a little disorientated, unsure of where I was until I heard Alex singing along to the radio in another room. Needing to use the toilet, I left the bed and made my way to the luxurious bathroom. I felt a little sore, but it wasn't unexpected considering my activities last night.

I checked my neck for any sign of bite marks, but there was nothing there. It was almost like it had never happened.

Needing time to get my thoughts together before I saw Alex again, I decided on a shower. As the warm water flowed over me, I tried to think about what to do and say when I left the comfort and safety of the bathroom.

I suppose the first question would be, what's next for us? Do we date? Do we take it slowly? Because I have to say, what happened last night was the complete opposite of slow. Do I bring all this up if Alex doesn't? Or should I just be the new me and go out there and not worry?

On finishing my shower, I decided to let the new me reign

for a while and just go with the flow. After getting dressed—minus my knickers—I left the bedroom to find Alex.

My handsome Viking vampire was in the kitchen putting some bacon under the grill. He was singing along loudly to the Drifters' song, "Saturday Night at the Movies." Hilarious just wasn't the word for it. It made me laugh out loud, so he flicked water at me when he washed his hands.

"I can't believe you're laughing at me when I'm cooking breakfast for you," he said in a totally fake sad voice. The equally sad effect pout he tried to pull off made me laugh even harder. I was grateful for the humour of the situation because it helped get rid of the awkwardness I was feeling. After all, this morning-after thing was unfamiliar to me.

The next song was "Save the Last Dance for Me," and Alex quickly pulled me into his arms for a dance. I was surprised by how good he was, twirling me around and then pulling me back close to him. He moved his hands over my back and down to my bottom while the song played. Then he paused and said, "You, my lady, have no underwear on."

I laughed again and replied, "You, sir, have roving hands, and if you'd been more of a gentleman, you wouldn't have said anything about my lack of underwear."

"Oh, what I could do to you now, Julia. I swear my mind is working overtime with all those dirty thoughts," he said while lifting my skirt.

"I think we had enough of that sort of exercise last night, if you don't mind," I admonished, trying to pull out of his arms.

Alex tugged me nearer and whispered in my ear, "I'd like to lift you up on the counter, spread your legs and worship every bit of what I find in between."

What could I say to that? I felt the heat rising through

my body as he leaned in to kiss me. Then my stomach grumbled loudly. Alex gave me a chaste peck on the lips. "My lady is hungry," he said, "so I will feed her first. How do you like your eggs?"

"Scrambled, please. And, Alex, I'm a bit...tender in certain places this morning, so although the worshipping sounds like heaven, I'd rather wait a while, if you don't mind."

There, I said it. I was blushing from head to toe, admitting my lady parts needed recovery time. But after going without for so long, I think they'd been overworked.

Alex stood back, took my face in his hands and asked, "Did I hurt you last night? If I did, I'm truly sorry. I can make you feel better if you'd allow it. My blood will help you heal; you'll only need a drop, and your...tender parts will feel much better."

"I'm not sure, Alex. Maybe some rest and cranberry juice would be okay," I told him, unsure about any more blood stuff going on.

"Don't worry about taking my blood, Julia. It won't harm you. You've had small amounts before to help you heal, remember?"

"No!" I answered sharply, looking away from him. "You used mind control on me, so I *can't* remember."

"Well, from this point on, you do have a choice," he said, gripping my arms. "This time, you get to say what happens. Now and always."

"What about Bonding, Alex? I mean, you drank my blood last night, so what if...?"

"Don't worry about that. To Blood Bond, you'd have to drink from me at the same time as I drink from you. It usually happens during sex and would take more than the single drop of blood I'm offering now. So, will you at least consider it before you leave?"

"Yes, okay, I'll consider it."

"Good. Now let's have the extremely late breakfast I'm aiming to cook for you."

Alex was right; it was late. I hadn't checked my phone for the time, but the wall clock said it was 2 p.m. My interview had been at 5:30 p.m. yesterday, and I'd been with Alex since then.

"I slept well," I stated. "I rarely sleep that well anymore."

"So did I. And I very rarely sleep well, either. Must be something we did," he said, grinning.

We ate in relative silence, although I did compliment him on his cooking. When we finished, he poured me a cup of tea, and I asked him, "Where do we go from here?"

He sat back and sighed. "You know what I want, Julia. What I said last night wasn't just sex talk. I meant every word."

"But, Alex, we hardly know each other. How can you be so certain about me?"

"I recognised you as mine; I can't explain it any better than that. Our kind, both Born Immortal and Made, talk of having a Fated one or mate. Our Fated one is someone who we know is meant to be ours. We don't always fall in love with them immediately, but it will happen. Once we meet them, we just know that while they are on this earth, there'll be no other for us."

"This is all new to me, though. You can't just expect me to... I don't know. I need to get used to it, Alex. To *us*."

"I loved being with you last night. And how you gave yourself to me; how you trusted me with your body and your blood. I want that always," Alex professed. He had such a sexy voice. In fact, Alex was the whole package. How did I get so lucky? I wanted to reach out and touch him, though I didn't. Instead, I asked, "How was that for you? My blood, I mean. Because let me tell you, Alex, I've never experienced a feeling like it."

"It was perfection. Your taste, your pleasure, and your trust... It was amazing. Like nothing I've ever felt before. But we need to stop talking about it. If I get any harder, my cock won't fit in my trousers. And you can't do anything about it because you won't take my blood to help you heal," he said, shifting in his chair.

I took a deep breath in and hoped I wasn't making a big mistake when I said, "Okay, I'll have a drop of your blood."

Chapter Eleven

Alex

I circled the table and pulled Julia towards me. She was nervous, and I didn't want her to feel that way around me. Wanting to settle her, I coaxed, "You can help me wash up, and if you do a good job, I *might* let you have some of my blood."

She smiled and muttered, "Slave driver," as she followed me to the sink.

Julia relaxed as we began our task. Now and then, I pretended to inspect her work, so she flicked bubbles at me. It made me think of how it could be for us as a couple, doing ordinary domestic things together every day.

I had an idea how to get her to take my blood, so I said to her jokily, "Now, my dear lady, because you have done such a good job, I shall reward you with a kiss." As I leaned over to kiss her, I extended my fangs slightly and bit my lip until I tasted blood. I watched as Julia closed her eyes and kissed me and saw the moment she tasted my blood when her eyes shot open, and she tried to pull away.

I held her face in my hands and carried on kissing her passionately. Before long, she was kissing me back with equal fervour, the taste of my blood forgotten.

I pushed Julia against the wall and pulled her skirt up to her waist, wanting to take her hard and fast. With the way she was pulling my T-shirt out of my jeans and running her hands around my back, I knew she had the same thoughts. Just as I was about to strip her naked, there was a knock at the door.

Julia took her hands out from under my T-shirt and straightened her skirt. The moment was lost, and I wondered when I would get the chance to kiss her like that again.

There was another knock, then the handle turned and in walked Gina with her arms full, closely followed by Nik.

"Hi, Alex, I've brought your dry cleaning from Mr Singh," Gina said, dropping the items over a kitchen chair. Then she turned and noticed Julia. "Oh, it's Julia, isn't it? George's daughter. I haven't seen you for years. Maggie said you'd be taking over from her in the offices."

"Yes, I start Monday night," Julia confirmed.

"Well, that means you're free to come out with us ladies from work tomorrow night. We go uptown once a month, then end up back in the village for the last hour of the disco at the Red Lion. We always have a great time, and it will be good for you to meet everyone."

"That would be great, Gina, thanks. Though I could do with getting something done with my hair before I go out. Can you recommend somewhere in the area?"

"Yeah, I'm going tomorrow to Cathy's in town. I can give you her number if you like. They do beauty therapy there, too. I was thinking of getting a spray tan if they can fit me in," Gina said enthusiastically.

Personally, I didn't think that Julia needed to change anything about herself, but she had a genuine smile on her face, so I said nothing. Unfortunately, Nik wasn't so smart.

"Why the hell would you get a spray tan? Won't it be weird when one day you're pale and the next day orange?" he asked with a smirk.

Nik did not impress Gina with his outburst. She folded her arms across her chest and replied, "It will look natural, not orange. Anyway, what's it got to do with you, Nik? This is what ladies do when they're going out."

"Gina, when you lot are on a night out, you're certainly not ladies. And now you're corrupting poor Julia."

"Poor Julia? Maybe it will be me doing all the corrupting, Nik," Julia remarked.

I laughed as Nik thought of a comeback, which seemed to take a while.

"I think I'll invite myself on this night out then and—"

"Oh no," cut in Gina. "It's ladies only. No men allowed."

"That's a shame," replied Nik, "because I'm picking Sergei up later."

"Sergei!" squealed Gina. "I've really missed him, Nik. I haven't seen him in months. Oh, you'll just adore him, Julia. He has a sexy Russian accent and has that tall, dark and handsome thing going on. He makes me laugh, and he always seems to wind you up, Alex."

"No, he doesn't," I argued. But he wound me up big time. And what was with the tall, dark and handsome thing? I hoped that wasn't Julia's type. I may be tall and considered handsome, but I'm fair-haired.

"He says he's bringing you some real vodka this time," Nik replied, and I groaned inwardly.

Nik, Sergei, Gina and vodka are not the best combination.

"Julia, the soundest advice I could ever give you is to keep away from those three when there's vodka involved. Sergei's special Russian vodka, especially," I said in a warning tone.

Julia gave me a defiant smirk.

I quickly tried to think of a way to make sure she'd be okay on this night out, so I offered to be their taxi home, telling them I would bring the twelve-seat minibus from work.

My offer was eagerly accepted. Nik gave me a sympathetic look before tapping me on the back, saying, "Alex, you are a very brave man indeed."

I asked what he meant, but he shook his head and laughed.

"Well, I'd better get on with my work, or my bosses will be mad," Gina remarked with an exaggerated sigh.

"Yes, or I might start cracking a whip on your sexy arse," replied Nik.

"You wouldn't dare, Nikolas Harding," Gina admonished while walking out the door.

"Wait up, Gina," yelled Julia as she grabbed her bag. "If you're heading back to the compound, I'll go with you."

This was it! Julia was leaving, and we hadn't arranged to see each other again, apart from me driving her home on Saturday night with everyone else.

I followed them out of the door, and before Julia could climb into Gina's golf cart, I turned her around and kissed her lips.

To my surprise, she kissed me back, but I could feel the

heat from the blush on her cheeks. I don't think Julia expected me to do anything in front of Nik and Gina, but it didn't bother me who knew about my feelings for her. That was something she was going to have to get used to because there was no going back to *just being friends*. After stealing one last kiss, I whispered, "I'll call you later." Then I stepped back and waved as she and Gina left.

"Well, Alex, care to explain what just happened there?" Nik asked.

"Nik, if you need me to explain what a kiss is, then you've led a very sad life," I replied.

"Alex, you know what I mean. Josh and I know she stayed with you last night. What's going on with you two?"

"That's between me and Julia. I don't want to discuss it right now, so I'd appreciate it if you'd let it go. And don't discuss it with anyone else, either."

Nik put his hands in his pockets and sighed.

"Have you told her what we are yet? I know you went further than kissing her, Alex, because I could scent much more than that."

"Yes, she knows what we are, and as for the rest... well, again, that's mine and Julia's business. For now, anyway."

"Look, Alex, I'm only asking because you've always been discreet with women. I've never seen you kiss anyone in public, and you've never brought a woman to your home. I think it's about time that at least one of us settled down and found love, so if that's what's going on here, I'm pleased for you. For both of you."

"Thanks, but what about you, Nik? When are you going to get your girl?"

"When she's brave enough to end her marriage, that's when I'll get my girl. How sad is that, eh? All I have right now is a bit of playful banter and plenty of bickering, and I don't know if I can take it anymore. Maybe I should go back out to Russia with Sergei and Gregor for a few weeks, just as a break from it all. I can finish up some business while I'm out there."

"Whatever you want, Nik. Just run it by Josh so he can set up transportation. You could try to track that prick, Ivan. Gregor said he fucked off to Germany and left them in the shit again. I was thinking of refusing his business next time he wants to use us."

"Sergei tried tracking him, but he seems to have gone under the radar."

"That reminds me, Nik. If you take Sergei out to the Red Lion, try to keep him and Gina under control. You all nearly got arrested last time. If it wasn't for mind control, they'd have locked you up."

"Alex, if we end up going, you can come with us. After all, you are the designated driver, God help you. You're either very brave or very stupid for volunteering."

"What do you mean? What can be so bad about taking a bunch of women home?"

"Alex, just remember that most of these women rarely go out and will have been drinking from as early as seven in the evening until, well, if the Red Lion has one of its famous lock-ins, then it could be two in the morning. The women sing loudly, shriek like banshees, and shout about hating men before declaring how much they love you for taking them home. Then cock talk."

"Cock talk?" I queried, getting a bit worried.

"Yeah, they talk about who they think has a big cock, and if they don't like a bloke, or if he's being moody, they always say it's because he has a small cock. Then they need to pee, one after the other, and, Alex, you know it's not like when we go. A drunken woman squatting down for a piss is not a pretty sight, believe me. Especially old Moira from the canteen."

"You're joking! Old Moira, the lovely granny who brings us the cupcakes?" I asked. Nik nodded, his face ashen.

"But then comes the vomiting."

"Oh God, they don't, do they?"

"Yep, and it's always advisable to take at least two buckets."

"Oh fuck! What have I done? I only volunteered so I could see Julia again. I'll try to get out of it and just see her at the pub. Why didn't you say something, Nik?"

"You'd already volunteered, my friend, so what could I do? If you drop out now, they'll sing about your small cock on their way home."

"But I haven't got a small cock," I said while subconsciously adjusting my package.

"It doesn't matter what size you are. You'll have disappointed them, Alex. And though I'm sure you impressed Julia last night, she'll probably be drunk and will join in with the rest of them."

"I could ask Josh if he wants to take them."

"He won't do it, Alex. You didn't see him the last time he volunteered because you were in Ireland with Finn and Freya. He was in shock for days. He said he thought his black skin was going to turn white with the horror of it. I wouldn't have thought anything could take down a big vampire like Josh. But driving our female staff home after a night out just about broke him."

Chapter Twelve

Julia

I couldn't believe Alex kissed me in front of Nik and Gina. We'd only just got together last night. Kissing me in front of people was like announcing that we had something more. Maybe we did? Alex had certainly made his feelings clear last night, and this morning.

When I thought of last night, I couldn't help but smile. It was the most erotic night of my life. That's one word I could use to describe it. Thrilling, sexy, orgasmic, hot, and many more would follow if I allowed myself to carry on. Gina pulled me out of my daydream.

"Sooo... You and Alex. How long have you been seeing him?"

"Gina, you've already seen him kiss me, so I don't mind telling you, but I don't want this to go any further. Not yet."

"No worries on that score, love. We all have secrets to keep."

"I've known Alex for a while, and he's been a good friend to me since..."

"I know what happened to you, Julia, and I'm so sorry. You don't have to say anymore if you don't want to." Gina put her hand over mine after pulling up behind the loading yard.

"Thanks, Gina. It's hard to talk about. I'll just skip that part because I always end up crying. Anyway, as I said, Alex has been a good friend, listening to me talk and…just being there for me. It wasn't until after my interview last night that it became anything more. All I know is we went to his home and sat chatting, then he told me he was a…" I didn't want to say anything in case she wasn't aware of what they were.

"A vampire?" Gina questioned.

"Sorry, I didn't know if you were aware."

"Yes, I've known for years. I donate blood through the work's nurse. As do other employees."

"Well, I wasn't in the know until last night. And I admit I found it hard to believe at first. But after a while, it didn't really bother me, which sounds strange, I know. But Alex is such a nice person, and I know he wouldn't hurt me."

"He is nice, Julia, and *really* good-looking. He's also tall, hunky, and basically an all-round sexy guy. But that kiss he just gave you… I could tell it meant a lot more than, *'I'm glad you spent the night with me.'*"

"I don't want to move too fast, though, Gina. I've not been separated for that long, so I don't want to launch myself into a new relationship. What would everyone think of me if I did that? It just felt so right with him last night, and part of me feels tempted to go straight back to him now."

"No one knows what you need more than you. So my advice, for what it's worth, is to do whatever you want.

Especially if it makes you feel good. There's only you that can live your life, not anyone else. So don't worry about what anyone thinks. I know that's easier said than done, but the longer you worry about something, the more barriers you put up against it. I know I have, and now it seems just too late for me."

I put my hand on her shoulder and gave it a light squeeze. "Gina, it's never too late. Not for love or anything else. I know there's something between you and Nik, so why don't you act on your own advice? Maybe we can both find what we need. Who knows?"

"I'm married, Julia, but it's not worth the paper it's written on. Steve and I loved each other in the beginning. When I had my daughter, things were great between us. Then two years later, after having my son, our relationship went downhill fast. But he's been a wonderful dad, worked hard all his life, and he's never raised a hand to me in anger. It's more than a lot of women have. But as far as our love life goes, there hasn't been one for years. Many, many years. And believe me, I've read all the magazines that tell you how to spice up your love life and get your marriage back on track. You can't force something that just isn't there anymore. I know this sounds stupid, but if he was a bad man and he hurt me physically—God forbid—it would make it easier to leave. But he's a good man, just not good at being a husband."

My heart went out to Gina. I could tell how much the situation was costing her emotionally.

"Nik is great, though, Gina. And maybe he's the one who could give you all the loving you've been missing out on all these years."

"Nik doesn't love me; he just acts like he does. I've worked here a long time, and I've seen the women he's taken to bed. Young, slim, good-looking women. So what on earth would he want with me? A short, overweight forty-three-year-old with two grown-up kids," Gina stated.

"Why are you putting yourself down? You're a very attractive woman, Gina. Maybe you should give him a chance to prove himself?"

I let out a sigh, debating whether I should say anything.

"I've been told that his feelings for you are real. But it's up to you what you do with that information," I said.

Gina went quiet until I broke the silence by asking for her mobile number so I could get the details for tomorrow night. I told her how much I was looking forward to it and that I hadn't had a girl's night out in ages. She said she'd make sure it was one to remember. I gave her a hug, said goodbye and left to get my car.

Chapter Thirteen

Julia

I kept thinking about Gina as I drove home. I thought how sad it was that she'd spent all those years without love and affection from her husband, just because he was a good father and a good man. Gavin was a good man and would have been a great father, too. But before I left, we couldn't be in a room together without arguing.

Would I have stayed? When Alex had asked me, I said yes, but after speaking with Gina, I just don't know anymore. She seemed so sad yet resigned to her fate. She also didn't have a lot of confidence in herself, and I could empathise with her there. My confidence had plummeted since the accident. That's why for this night out, I was going to treat myself and make some changes to my appearance. Then I could go out and feel like the new me. The Julia I wanted to be.

When I pulled into the driveway, I saw my mum through the kitchen window, and I knew I couldn't put it off any longer. It was time to face the music about my night with Alex. I felt like a teenager waiting to be told off for being out too late, but when I opened the door, all Mum said was, "Cup of tea, love?"

I sat down at the breakfast bar and waited for Mum to speak.

"So, when do you start work?" she asked, not looking at me while she made us both a cuppa.

"Monday. Which is good because I've been invited out tomorrow night with the girls from work."

Mum finally turned to look at me. "That's great, love. I've heard about their nights out, and I'm sure you'll enjoy it."

"I hope so," I replied, wanting to keep the conversation light. "I'm thinking of having my hair done tomorrow if I can get booked in. Gina from work said that Cathy's in town is a good place to go."

"Yes, it is. You can have all sorts done there, too, like manicures and facials. I don't think it's expensive," Mum said.

"I hope she can fit me in for a cut and maybe some highlights. If it's not too late, I could even get a spray tan. Although, I think you're supposed to leave it on overnight, so maybe not."

"You could try to get in tonight for a spray tan; it opens late on Thursdays and Fridays. It's where I had mine done before we went on holiday last year."

I rang the number Gina had given me for Cathy's and asked if they had any appointments free. I booked in for a spray tan at 6 p.m. and for hair and nails in the morning.

"I could do with some new clothes, too. Do you fancy going shopping with me tomorrow afternoon, Mum?"

"Julia," she replied with tears in her eyes, "I would love to come shopping with you."

I put my arms around her and asked, "What's wrong, Mum?"

"Nothing, love. I'm just so glad to see you making plans to go out and enjoy yourself, as well as taking care of your appearance again. We couldn't seem to get you out of your pyjamas or even brush your hair last week. So hearing all this today, knowing you want to have fun again, it's wonderful."

I suddenly felt so selfish for all the worry I'd put my parents through since the accident.

"I'm sorry, Mum. I know you've been worried about me, but I feel much more positive about my future now," I told her truthfully.

"Can I ask if that has anything to do with Alex Staithes?" Mum had finally broached the subject.

"Yes, I think it does," I replied, blushing but not avoiding her gaze.

"Do you want to talk about it?" she asked as she sat down next to me.

I didn't know what to say at first. Did I want to talk to my mum about the wild night of passion I had with my soon-to-be boss? Not really, but I wouldn't hide what had happened from her, either.

"I went back to Alex's home after the interview. We were talking and drinking wine and hadn't realised it was so late. I decided to spend the night with him rather than get a taxi home."

"You mean sleep with him? In his bed?"

"Yes, Mum, I slept with Alex. In his bed. And yes, we had sex. More than once, if you must know. And it was bloody fantastic every time."

We both sat there blushing profusely after my declaration. But just when I thought she wouldn't carry on with the conversation, she said, "I'm glad to hear it. It's good to know there's someone who can make you smile and your eyes sparkle. I assume you know what he is?"

"Yes, he told me last night he was a vampire. Freaked me out at first, but I wasn't afraid of him."

"Alex is a good man before he's anything else. He came all the way to Birmingham as soon as your dad called him after your accident. He was so good when you woke up after having some of his blood. And with Megan, he was amazing. He got you exactly what you needed because your dad and I were in bits. I was a complete wreck when I saw you and learned what had happened. I know Megan was your child, Julia, but you are mine. Not only were you physically hurt, but you were so emotionally hurt that it tore my heart in two. I should have insisted I bring Megan to you, but the doctors advised against it. Thank God for Alex."

"His sister lost her daughter when she was only eight years old, and her son was stillborn on the same night. It was due to a house fire in which her husband also died."

I will never forget the sad story he told me about Freya's family. My heart went out to both of them for what they'd endured that night. Mum sat with her hand over her mouth in shock.

"Oh, that poor family. What a terrible thing to happen to them. It's like something you see on TV. How do you ever get over something like that?"

"Alex says that the inner strength and power in females is something that will prevail above all else."

Mum placed her hand over her heart and smiled. "I think I could fall in love with him."

I knew where she was coming from with that statement.

The longer I'd been away from Alex, the more I wanted to be with him. I knew it was wrong and I should give it time, but I couldn't wait to see him again. Obviously, my mum wasn't bothered, which was one of my concerns. An excuse to hold back my emotions. But tomorrow, I'd be the spray-tanned, hair-highlighted, perfect-nailed me, and *she* wouldn't hold back at all.

Chapter Fourteen

Julia

I looked in the mirror and hardly recognised myself. Normally I wore little make-up, but the new colours I'd bought made my blue eyes seem much brighter.

Chelsea—the hairdresser—had done a brilliant job with my hair, which was usually a dull chestnut brown. Now I had three different coloured highlights through it, ranging from copper to golden blonde, and the spray tan brought the lighter colours out.

Mum helped me choose a cobalt blue shift dress that ended mid-thigh. I thought it might be a bit too short, but it hid my tummy, and Mum said it made my legs look longer. With a pair of black patent heels and a black-and-blue patent clutch bag, I was ready for my first girl's night out in years.

Mum and Dad were sitting at the breakfast bar with a cuppa, discussing where to go on holiday next year. When I stepped into the kitchen to get their opinion, everything went quiet. Dad put down his cup and came to stand in front of me. Taking hold of my hand, he twirled me around like he used to when I was a little girl as he said, "Bloody gorgeous, love. I can't believe this is my Julia. You look like one of them supermodels."

"Laying it on a bit thick there, Dad," I said as I kissed his cheek. I was certainly no supermodel, but it was nice to see the proud look he had on his face. Mum was the same. I hugged her and thanked her for going shopping with me.

"Will you be coming home tonight, love?" Mum asked, noticing the overnight bag I'd dropped at my feet.

"No, I'm going back to Alex's tonight," I replied sheepishly. I'd avoided speaking to my dad about Alex since I got back yesterday. I wasn't too sure what he would say about me spending the night with someone I wasn't in a committed relationship with, even at thirty-four years old. But he didn't look at me any differently.

"I can't believe he volunteered to drive those women around on one of their nights out," he said. "I've never taken Alex for a fool until now."

"What do you mean, Dad? I think it's sweet that he's driving us." I wasn't sure what Dad was getting at.

"Oh, you'll find out soon enough. These ladies' nights out are legendary. They make us men look like choirboys. And from what Josh said, the poor driver has his work cut out getting them all home safe."

"Well, I'm sure he'll cope," I insisted. I saw Alex pull up in the minibus, so I kissed Mum and Dad goodnight and went outside.

Alex got out of the vehicle and stood stock still when he saw me, his mouth gaping open.

"I brought an overnight bag. Should I keep it in the front with me?" I inquired as I walked towards him.

He hurried forward, took my bag and placed it on the front passenger seat floor before turning to take my hand and helping me into the vehicle. He watched me buckle my seatbelt without saying a word.

"Is everything okay, Alex?" I asked, worried that I'd offended him somehow. "You said you wanted me to stay with you when you called me last night."

I thought his silence meant he'd changed his mind.

He closed the door and went around to the driver's side. After he'd buckled his seatbelt, he finally turned to me and let out a deep breath.

"Julia," his voice sounded husky but controlled. "You look absolutely stunning tonight. You're a beautiful woman anyway, but to see you now, like this, I want to take you back to my place and make love to you all night long. I wanted to kiss you when I saw you just now, but I was afraid if I did, I wouldn't be able to stop. And I don't think that would have gone down well with your parents, who are peeking through the curtains at us."

"I appreciate you giving my confidence a boost, Alex. And let me tell you, in those black jeans and T-shirt, you look even more gorgeous than you normally do, so we make a good pair tonight."

Alex took my hand and kissed it before saying, "We make a good pair always, Julia, not just tonight."

Maggie—who was our first pickup—came out looking as perfectly groomed as usual. She was going on sixty but didn't look a day over forty. Maggie was always so well put together, and tonight was no exception. She wore a black and red bodycon dress with black high-heeled boots and a black jacket. She was so pretty and feminine; I could only wish to look that good at her age.

Next was a lady called Moira, who Maggie informed me worked in the canteen on Fridays. She was at least seventy, with pure white hair and sparkly blue eyes. Moira promised to make me some cupcakes to celebrate my first week at work.

After collecting Moira, we picked up Gina. Alex was shocked when he saw her. I'd met her at the hairdresser's earlier, so had already seen her transformation. Gina had gone from shoulder-length strawberry-blonde hair to a baby blonde pixie style, cut into the neck at the back with a little length on top. She wore a black pencil skirt with a vibrant pink blouse that showed off her ample cleavage, and super-high black stilettos that made her legs look long and lean. Gina looked stunning but blushed from head to toe when everyone in the minibus told her so.

I asked her what her husband had thought about her new style and colour. Gina said he hadn't noticed, although her son and daughter said she looked great, and at least ten years younger.

Gina had told me that her husband wasn't a bad man, but I didn't necessarily agree with that. Even if they were friends and not lovers, he should have noticed such a drastic change in her appearance. She said she'd lost over twenty-six pounds in weight over the last three months by going to the gym and doing kickboxing. I think Gina should be kick-boxing him out the door.

Next came Maggie's niece, Keeley, who was a beautiful blonde with blue eyes and a model figure. She wore black skinny jeans with a white chiffon top and cami, and the same super-high heels that Gina wore. But to be honest, this girl could have worn a black sack and still looked fabulous. Keeley said her daughter was staying with her ex's parents this evening, so she could get drunk tonight if she wanted to.

Moira and Maggie both gave a cheer, and Gina held Keeley's bag while she buckled herself in.

Just then, an Adonis of a man came out of Keeley's house and asked Alex if he could hitch a lift into town with us. He was tall, exceptionally good-looking, with a broad muscular frame, and if I hadn't had my own sexy guy sitting by the side of me, I might have been drooling just then. His name was Daniel, and I found out he was Keeley's twin brother. He kissed Maggie on the cheek and told Moira she was looking gorgeous tonight. Moira blushed and promised him cupcakes next week. Then he turned to Gina, did a double take and said, "Bloody hell, Gina, you look as sexy as fuck! Oops, sorry, Auntie Mags and Moira. But Gina, you really do look good."

Gina kissed him on the cheek. "Thanks, Dan. You've just made my night by saying that."

Maggie introduced us, telling him I was starting in the office on Monday night and that I was George's daughter.

It turned out that my dad was Daniel's supervisor at work, and he told me funny stories about their time in the loading yard.

There were three other women, Jean, Ami, and Joanne, who were meeting us in town. They'd been to a party for the new women's underwear and sex toy chain, Silk & Tickle.

Maggie started talking about a new vibrator they had advertised called "*The Big Boy,*" which had seven different speeds and came with a free tingle lube. Daniel shouted,

"No, Aunt Mags, you can't talk about stuff like that in front of me." Then he covered his ears, shouting, "La la la."

Alex shook his head and seemed to shrink into his seat, and I laughed so hard I cried. I could tell already this was going to be one hell of a night.

Chapter Fifteen

Alex

Julia looked like a goddess tonight. My goddess. I told her earlier that she looked beautiful, but she didn't believe me. I was already thinking of the ways I was going to prove that to her later. If I hadn't seen how much Julia was looking forward to this night out, I would have turned the minibus around and taken her straight home. If I could last that long.

There were many places in our little village of Barrowfield where I could pull in and take her right there and then in the vehicle without anyone seeing us. We could have had sex facing the beautiful Pennines, but I was a gentleman and kept my hands to myself.

The journey to Rothley became so awkward when someone mentioned one of those sex-toy parties. Maggie, of all people, started going on about a new vibrator that came with free lube, and I wanted to disappear. I'd worked with the woman nearly every night for over thirty years, and she was like family, for God's sake. I did not need to hear her talk about sex toys of any sort, and if I wasn't driving, I would have put my hands over my ears like Dan.

Gina looked so different that you wouldn't even think it was her. I couldn't wait until Nik saw her later at the Red Lion. She told Julia that her husband hadn't noticed her new look. I think Gina should dump the ignorant prick and get someone who really appreciates her.

I dropped them all off at a bar called Pip's and arranged to pick them up outside a pub called The Station two hours later. Grabbing Julia for a quick kiss before she left attracted wolf whistles from Dan and Moira, although it didn't seem to bother Julia. I watched her walk into the pub arm in arm with Gina and couldn't help but send thanks to whichever god had seen fit to make her mine.

Just then, I had a feeling I was being watched. I turned around, but even with my perfect, immortal vision, I could see no one. I also couldn't sense if it had been human or vampire, but there was something vaguely familiar about them.

Turning a full 360 degrees, I tried again to see what had brought this uneasy feeling my way, but I could see nothing. I tried to pass it off as my overprotectiveness regarding Julia, but I had been on this earth long enough to know I shouldn't just dismiss it.

Still feeling wary, I pulled out my phone as I climbed into the minibus and called Josh. As always, he answered on the first two rings.

"No, Alex, I'm not swapping driving duties with you tonight, not even if you gave me a million pounds and your share in the company."

"Calm down, Josh. I'll not rope you into the designated driver nightmare I've got going on. But listen… I've just dropped them off in Rothley and had the strangest feeling I was being watched. It's really set me on edge. I sense they're familiar, but I can't tell whether they're human or vampire. Though if I was to guess, I'd say vampire, as they were gone before I could find them."

"There aren't any other vampires about other than us and the Russians. Nik and Sergei are here with me, and Gregor is visiting with Freya over in Aldbrough. Finn isn't coming over until January, but I'm sure you could sense if it was him, anyway."

"It definitely wasn't Finn or Patrick. Just put some feelers out and see what you can pick up. If we have an unknown vampire in our town, Josh, we all need to be aware."

"Leave it with me, Alex; I'll call you if I find anything. Are you coming back here until it's time to pick them up?"

"Yeah, but I'm going to have a look around first, just in case I can find anything. I'll see you in about twenty minutes."

"Alex, don't let the ladies catch you. They might think you're keeping an eye on them, and that would make them angry. Maggie is scary when she's angry."

"Maggie's fucking scary when she's describing a new seven-speed vibrator called *'The Big Boy.'*"

"No fucking way, Alex. That's just wrong."

"Yep, and she said it comes with tingly lube, too," I laughed.

"I don't want to hear any more, so I'm hanging up."

I heard the dial tone and laughed again. After searching around for another ten minutes without success, I went straight back to find Josh, Nik, and Sergei.

Chapter Sixteen

Josh

Alex arrived at my cottage about twenty minutes after I'd hung up the phone. I could tell he wasn't the same guy that had left here earlier tonight to pick up Julia and the rest of the ladies from work.

Since his night with Julia, he's had a spring in his step; like he has a new purpose in life. But now he was subdued, and I knew that whatever had occurred tonight had really got to him.

"Did you pick up any trace of whoever was watching you?" I asked, already knowing the answer because of his behaviour. He was pacing the floor and tapping his lip with his thumb, obviously trying to make sense of what had occurred.

"I picked up nothing, but I'm sure it was a vampire. The speed at which they disappeared ruled out a human. The odd thing is, I sensed a familiarity, but for the life of me, I just can't place them."

"Perhaps you are sensing danger all around because of your female—this Julia I am hearing of. Maybe you worry she will leave you for a sexy Russian vampire named Sergei," said the teasing Russian.

"Fuck off, Sergei," Alex replied.

This wasn't the time to rile Alex up. He was strung too tight.

"Have you had any blood recently? If there's a threat out there, you need to make sure you're alert and firing on all cylinders, so it might be best if you have a bag of blood before you collect them."

"The last blood I had was Julia's," he replied, a smile now appearing on his face. Good. I hated seeing my best friend and brother so on edge. In truth, I was thrilled that Alex had finally found his special someone, and I wished him all the luck in the world. As far as I was concerned, I owed the man my life. And if there was a threat, I would do my best to make that threat disappear.

"Josh told us about Maggie's cock talk," said Nik.

"It was more vibrator talk," Alex corrected.

"Fake or not, it's still cock talk, and I've got to say it doesn't bode well for you if they started it before the drinks were flowing."

Alex shrugged his shoulders. "Well, you and Sergei are going to the Red Lion later, so you must want to hear it. And I can't wait until you see Gina."

"Why, what's she done?" Nik asked, his curiosity piqued.

"I won't say too much, just that she looks so different, and she had Dan Saunders nearly tripping over his tongue on the minibus," Alex teased.

"She wouldn't fucking look at Dan, not when she sees me, anyway," Nik joked. But Nik was easy to read, and I could see he was itching to get to Gina.

"We should go now to see my Gina," Sergei said, getting up from his chair.

He thought the world of Gina, too, and they had a lot of playful banter and heated discussions, which drove everyone mad. Nik and Sergei were great friends, as well as cousins, and Nik knew Sergei would never make a move on Gina, so he allowed him to be near her. That wouldn't happen with anyone else.

"They have another hour before I pick them up and bring them back to Barrowfield. Have you let the staff at the Red Lion know they're going in tonight?" Alex asked.

"Yes, they know."

I owned the Red Lion and several other small businesses around Barrowfield and Rothley. If it were left up to me, I'd buy the whole place, but we were still expanding Night Movers, and I was happy to purchase the odd home or business every now and again.

The pub was doing well, considering that a lot went out of business during the recession. There was a disco with karaoke tonight, but sometimes we had a live band on Saturday nights. The pub was also known for its after-hours lock-ins, but this happened less and less over the years. I trusted my staff to decide when to do it.

No one in the village knew I owned the pub, just a few of the bar staff and Alex, Nik, and Gina. I wanted to keep it that way.

"I'm going to take Julia's bag over to my cottage before picking the ladies up. Who wants dropping off at the Red Lion?" Alex asked, heading towards the door.

"Sergei and I are going, so we'll wait for you in the minibus. Josh, are you coming with us?" Nik prompted.

I didn't want to go, to be honest. A quiet night in suited

me more these days. I like to have fun as much as the next person, but every weekend seems pretty much the same when you've been on this earth as long as I have. But for some reason, I found myself saying, "Yes, I'll go."

Chapter Seventeen

Alex

After dropping Josh, Nik and Sergei off at the Red Lion, I made the ten-minute journey into town to pick the ladies up. None of them were outside waiting for me, so I parked the minibus and went inside to look for them.

They were at the bar with shots lined up in front of them. Keeley was counting back from three, two, one before they all downed their shots and slammed the glasses on the bar. Julia turned towards me with a big grin on her face.

"Here's my Alex," she said, obviously a little tipsy. All the ladies made a grab for me and peppered my cheeks with kisses. When I reached Julia, she planted a big wet kiss on my lips, winked, and said, "My kiss was better."

I laughed and asked her how many drinks she'd had. Julia shrugged, then kissed me again. I liked the kissing, and also her not being bothered about doing it in public. But realistically, the booze probably helped with any inhibitions she had.

Bitten and Bound

It took twenty minutes to get the ladies to make the three-minute journey to where I'd parked the minibus. Between them all going to the toilet and trying to get more drinks before they left, I was amazed it hadn't taken longer.

The noise level in the vehicle was horrendous, with lots of shouting and laughing at decibels I'm sure exceeded safety regulations.

My eyes kept drifting towards Julia, who sat beside me. She was twisting in her seat so she could see the others in the back. Her dress had ridden up her thighs, and it was impossible not to imagine running my hands up and down them.

From her handbag, Joanne pulled out a light-up dildo she'd won at the sex-toy party she'd been to.

As a vampire, my night vision was perfect, yet a human could've seen that thing from miles away as it changed colour from green to blue, then purple, then red. I thought it was disturbing, but the ladies howled with laughter, and even more so when Moira grabbed it to show how to give the perfect blow job. The way her white hair and face glowed from green to blue was the stuff of nightmares, and when I saw the familiar sign for the Red Lion, I was relieved beyond measure.

Josh and Nik were standing outside the pub with Sergei, who was smoking a cigarette. They came forward and helped the ladies out of the minibus, complementing each of them as they got them out. When it came to Gina's turn, Nik helped her down from the vehicle, twirled her around and spoke to her softly.

"You look stunning, Gina. The hair, the tan, the clothes,

they all really suit you. Promise me you'll dance with me later."

Before she could answer, she was picked up and twirled around by Sergei. Gina hugged him and laughed before getting him to put her down. Nik took her hand in his, and the terrible threesome made their way into the pub, leaving me and Julia outside alone.

I pulled her close and held her while I looked into her eyes. The tan made her blue eyes sparkle like sapphires, and along with the colour in her cheeks and the smile she wore, I didn't think I'd seen her look this alive and happy for years.

"You look amazing tonight," I said before kissing her lips softly.

"I'm having such a good time, Alex, but I'm also looking forward to going home with you and getting you naked," she purred. I kissed her hard and pulled her as close to my body as I could get, glad that she was on the same page as me about later. But I could feel her sway and stumble back a little, the alcohol having an effect on her balance.

"I appear to be a little drunk," she declared. "I think I should have a glass of water when we go in, or I can see myself waking up with the hangover from hell tomorrow."

"Water it is, my lovely," I agreed as she grabbed my arm before heading inside.

Chapter Eighteen

Gina

Nik took my breath away. There was no point denying our connection anymore. The way he touched me when we were outside, and the words he said, were everything I wanted to feel and hear from a man. It just wasn't my man that said them. But truthfully, my husband hadn't been my man for years.

When I got back from the hairdresser's, he hadn't even given me a second glance. He just asked, "What's for dinner?"

Both my son and daughter said I looked great— younger, even, which was a real confidence booster. My daughter, Laura, is twenty-three and lives with her boyfriend in Rothley; my son, Jack, is twenty-one and still at home getting spoiled by me, although I think his girlfriend is trying to get him to move in with her.

I always thought I was keeping the family together by staying with Steve. For years, I tried my best to hide how unhappy I was. But I saw how Laura and Jack looked at my husband when he failed to notice my transformation today, and it shocked me to see the contempt in their eyes.

I hadn't loved him for years. How can you love someone who does their best to ignore you? What made the situation harder was having someone like Nik Harding making moves on me.

The man is utterly gorgeous. He's about six-foot-four with huge muscles, thick dark-brown hair, and the most beautiful chocolate-coloured eyes that set my soul on fire with just a look. I'd been in love with Nik for around twelve years, but I couldn't leave my family for him when my children needed me.

I also didn't think I was good enough for him. I mean, what would he really want with a short, plump mother of two, anyway?

I'd seen the women he'd dated, and let me tell you, I could never compete. But for some reason, Nik seemed to think he loved me and never gave up his pursuit. Looking at him in the low lights of the pub as he got me a drink from the bar, he seemed sexier than ever, and I wanted him so badly I ached.

I wanted what I'd seen in Julia and Alex over the last few days. I noticed how attentive he was—like when he held her while they waited for their drinks. How he kissed the top of her head when they squeezed themselves together to let someone get past. I'd spoken to Julia, who appeared to be wary of starting a new relationship. She thought it might be too soon after separating from her husband and worried about what people would say. But she didn't seem bothered anymore, and both of them looked as though they were in love. I saw the same look on Nik's face outside when he'd helped me out of the minibus, and that's what finally made me think it could work between us.

Nik caught me looking at him as he turned to hand everyone their drinks, so I tilted my head to the side, silently asking him to follow me.

My heart beat so fast as I walked towards the function room at the back of the pub. They only used this room for parties and various community events, but it wasn't in use tonight, so it was in darkness.

I opened the door, and Nik followed me inside. He closed the door behind us and came to stand in front of me. The light from the corridor shone through into the room, and I could see from the look on his face that it was taking a lot of restraint on his part not to speak or touch me. With a sigh, I stepped forward and took both his hands in mine. Being five-foot-three, I was still shorter than him, even in my heels, so I had to look up to hold his gaze.

"Can I stay with you tonight, Nik?" I asked, my voice hoarse with need. "I don't want to go home anymore."

He took my face in his hands as he gazed down at me. "If you stay the night with me, I'll make you mine. And know this, Gina, once you are mine, I'll never let you go."

"Okay," I whispered.

Nik kissed me like I'd never been kissed before. His lips were firm and relentless, parting my own so he could thrust his tongue inside my mouth, making me weak and tingly in parts that hadn't responded to anything in years.

Nik picked me up effortlessly. He carried me to a table near the glowing green exit sign in the corner of the room, gently laying me down on it, leaving my legs hanging over the side. He pushed up the stretchy skirt I wore until it reached my waist, exposing my black lace knickers. I was extremely glad I hadn't chosen to wear my Spanx; I would have been mortified if he'd seen them.

I'm not sure what I expected him to do next, but bending down and taking in the scent from my crotch and thighs took me completely by surprise. He licked and sucked at the lace covering my slit, and I nearly bucked off the table. Nik stilled me with a hand on my belly and a look that warned me not to move again.

I concentrated on his face, which glowed from the light of the exit sign, and the desire I saw there fuelled my own. He removed my knickers slowly, keeping his eyes fixed on mine. Then he spoke.

"I've fantasised so often about tasting, lapping and sucking on the juices I can force out of your sweet cunt—then turning my head to your sexy thighs and tasting, lapping, and sucking on the blood I can bring from you with my bite. Give me your permission, Gina. Let me taste every part of your essence."

Nik's words left me too stunned to speak. Seconds ticked by, and all the while, he kept caressing the inside of my thighs, getting nearer to my core. My eyes closed as his fantasy played out in my mind. Along with his touch, it was a potent combination.

Strangely enough, Nik tasting my blood wasn't a problem for me. I regularly donated at work, so this just seemed like another kind of donation, although a very intimate one.

The issue was…I'd never had a man perform oral sex on me. Even when we were first married and had a regular sex life, my husband never gave me oral sex.

We tried it once. Steve got no further than kissing the

inside of my thighs and then once on my clit before he told me he couldn't do it because he didn't like the taste of me there.

I'd read erotic romance novels where the man would gorge on a woman's *pussy*, as they call it in the books. I always assumed it was only there to sell those books, and men who actually wanted to do that were very rare indeed. But Nik was saying he'd fantasised about doing it to me.

I looked down at Nik and nodded my head, loving the sexy smile that came over his lips. Lips that were now kissing the space between the top of my thighs and my lower tummy.

I moaned at the throbs of pleasure he was creating around every female part of me, even without him touching them directly, and when he moved down to place kisses on my lower lips, a high-pitched gasp escaped me. My body tensed, anticipating what came next. He licked me from my opening to my clit and back down again with hard strokes. I felt even more moisture gather down there and wondered when it would make him stop.

He didn't stop.

Instead, Nik lapped up the wetness, groaning as if he'd tasted the best dessert ever. Instead of worrying about what was next, I relaxed and enjoyed the feeling of him worshipping the most intimate part of me.

He lifted my legs so that the back of my knees draped over his arms, forcing my legs apart and opening me up to him. Then he sucked and nipped at my outer lips before thrusting his tongue inside me. Nik hit a spot that intensified the pleasure coursing through my body. I threw my head back and let out a breathless, silent scream as I came, my hips undulating of their own accord as my body fought to keep the all-consuming, euphoric feeling of the first orgasm I'd had in years.

Before I could come down from wherever my body had seemed to levitate to, Nik pushed two fingers inside me, fastened his mouth over my clit and alternated between licking, sucking, and swirling his tongue around the swollen bud until I came again—the orgasm slamming into me even harder this time. Nik had me screaming and grabbing his thick dark hair, holding his mouth against me until the tremors subsided.

I felt his head turn as I ran my fingers through his hair, and I let out a small cry of pain as his teeth sank deeper than I'd thought possible into my thigh. But the pain quickly disappeared when I felt him take my blood to the back of his throat.

Nik groaned as if he felt both pleasure and pain at the action. But I didn't care about anything other than the need that was building inside me once more. Within seconds I began to orgasm again, his fingers still moving inside me, prolonging my pleasure until, at last, he let go of my thigh and lapped at the area he drank from.

Chapter Nineteen

Nik

I pulled Gina up from the table and kissed her softly. I knew she'd be able to taste herself. Maybe her blood, too. It made me feel powerfully virile and more alive than I've ever felt before.

I helped her put her knickers on, running my hands over her arse as I did so. Then I pulled out my phone and texted Alex to meet us out front. I wanted to take Gina home with me before she changed her mind. Ten seconds later, I got a text from Josh saying that he was heading out to the minibus.

I held Gina close and bent to rest my forehead against hers. We hadn't spoken since I'd tasted her, and I was worried about her lack of words.

"How are you doing, my love?" I asked warily. I didn't want her to regret what had happened because, for me, it was the best sex I'd ever experienced, even though I hadn't yet been inside her.

"I'm okay," she replied quietly, then sighed.

I didn't know whether it was a good or bad sigh, so I said, "I'm going to take care of you, Gina. Whatever you want or need, just let me know."

Then I kissed the top of her head, picked her up and carried her out of the emergency exit.

Josh was already in the vehicle and had the motor running. He jumped out when he saw me approaching with Gina in my arms, concern clear on his face as he opened the door.

"Nik, what's happened? Is she okay?" he asked. Then he inhaled, scenting Gina's arousal on my face, as well as the scent of her blood. He looked at me questioningly but said no more.

We drove in silence, other than Josh tapping his fingers on the steering wheel. He kept flashing glances at me and Gina, watching me stroke the back of her hand that I held against my thigh. The connection seemed to soothe me and ease the fear I was having; the nagging doubt that Gina would get to my home and say she'd made a mistake and didn't want this after all.

A few minutes later, we pulled up outside my cottage. Josh said he'd tell the others that Gina wasn't feeling well, so she'd gone home.

"Thanks for that, Josh. And thanks for the lift," she said as I helped her down from the vehicle. They were the first words she'd spoken since we left the pub, and to my relief, her voice didn't sound anxious or regretful.

"No problem, Gina. I'm going straight back to the pub now. It was getting a bit rowdy when I left, and Sergei got

Julia to switch from water to vodka, which isn't making Alex very happy."

"That doesn't surprise me. Sergei's a persistent fucker when it comes to vodka," I mused, imagining Alex's annoyance with Sergei.

I got the impression that Alex only just tolerated Sergei, but the Russian was like a brother to me, and we were also the best of friends. Alex, on the other hand, was friends with Gregor, who'd gone to Freya's before coming here. Josh seemed to get along with everyone equally, just like Gina does.

I waved him off and took Gina's hand, leading her inside and towards my bedroom. I don't know why I felt so nervous. Gina had been in my home many times over the years. But after tonight, it would be her home, too, and I wanted her to love it as I did.

I switched on my bedside lamp and picked up the jeans and boxer shorts I'd discarded earlier. I wasn't sure why I closed the bedroom door as there was only us, but when I did, I heard Gina inhale, and she started to shake. I crossed the room to her, but she held up her hand to stop me.

"Why do you want me, Nik?"

"You know why."

"No, I don't. You're good-looking and so bloody sexy."

"So are you, Gina."

She shook her head. "I'm not some young bit of fluff, Nik. I'm forty-three."

"I was that age about 250 years ago," I replied.

Gina placed a hand over her lower belly. "I have a flabby muffin top from two caesareans."

"And you became the mother of two great kids who you love dearly. Oh, and for the record, muffins are my favourite," I declared with a wink as I stepped nearer. Gina huffed out a sigh.

"My hips and boobs are way too big for someone who is five-foot-three."

"Now you're just talking dirty," I said, pulling my shirt over my head. I closed the distance between us, put my hands on her cheeks and lifted her face so I could look into her eyes.

"I want you to be mine, Gina, and that's happening tonight."

"You wouldn't force me, Nik."

"I won't have to," I replied before kissing her. Just small pecks at first on each corner of her mouth, her eyelids, her nose, her forehead and then softly on her lips. She opened her mouth to deepen the kiss, and I removed her blouse, exposing her soft tanned skin.

Before I went any further, I put my arms around her and held her tight. What I felt for this woman ran so deep, I wanted to savour the moment and make sure she knew what she meant to me.

"I love you, Gina. I recognised you as my soul mate many years ago, and my love for you has grown even more with time. Now I wouldn't want to live my life without you in it. When we Bond and share our blood, it will make me the happiest person on this earth. We'll be able to sense in each other our love and happiness, anger and fears. We'll know when we're needed by one another. As you continue to take my blood, the Bond will grow stronger. You won't age or get ill, and you'll become stronger and fitter than you are now. As time goes on, we'll communicate telepathically."

"Nik, I love you too, and I want this, but I am anxious about what having a Bond will mean."

I couldn't look at her. For some reason, my eyes filled up with tears. I tried to say something, but I was too choked up to form words. This wasn't like me. I was a strong, immortal man, not a weak emotional fool.

"Look at me, Nik," she whispered. But I couldn't. I wanted her to see me as someone who would love and protect her, so I held her tightly for just a little longer.

A minute later, I felt her hands dip from my back down to my arse, then she moved them around to the front of my jeans until she reached the buttons. As soon as she popped the buttons undone, I felt my mood quickly change.

I stroked my fingers up and down her back, making her shiver. After unhooking the clasp of her bra, I slipped the straps off her shoulders, feeling the warmth and weight of her breasts against my chest. I stood back to look at them and felt her tense a little.

"You are exquisite, Gina, so womanly," I said, caressing her breasts. "It's like you were made to fit me. Your soft feminine curves will cushion my hard body as I thrust into you. Let me love you as you deserve."

Gina grabbed me and pulled me down for the hottest, most passionate kiss you can imagine—and believe me, I'd imagined plenty with this woman. She ran her hands across my upper back before venturing lower, the heat from her fingertips making me burn with need. Reaching the waistband of my jeans, she pulled them down, along with my boxers. My hard cock sprang free, slapping against my belly.

Gina dropped to her knees and took me in her mouth so quickly I didn't have time to stop her. She took me deep, angling her head so she could open her throat and take me further.

It was heaven, and it was also hell. As tempting as it was just to fuck her mouth and watch her throat move as she swallowed me down, that's not what I wanted right now.

I wanted to make love to her slowly or fuck her hard and fast. I couldn't decide which, but I knew I needed to be inside her. So I pulled her greedy little mouth away from my cock, lifted her into my arms and carried her to my bed.

I stripped off the rest of her clothes, and Gina groaned when I removed her heels. So I took each foot and massaged it thoroughly.

I love to see women in high heels, but I'm fucked if I know how they manage to walk in them.

Watching her ample breasts bounce as I moved her up the bed made my cock even harder. I cupped and shaped them, licking and sucking on her tawny-pink nipples.

Gina loved it. She held my head to her breasts as she writhed beneath me, panting and pleading for something, although it was unclear what. But I wouldn't be hurried. I was enjoying the tit play way too much and wondered what she would look like wearing nipple clamps.

She seemed to like hard pulls on one nipple while I sucked and bit the other, grazing them slightly with my fangs. Her breathing changed, along with the scent of her arousal, and before I knew it, Gina climaxed without me touching her sex.

I reached down and fed my cock into her slowly. Even though she was wet, she was so tight it almost hurt. I paused, pressing my thumb against the hood of her clit, moving it around in circles until I could feel more of her wetness coating me and I could slide in deeper..

"Are you okay, Gina? I can stop if you want."

I didn't want to stop, but I'd never hurt her.

Gina shook her head and mumbled that she would kill me if I stopped now.

I kissed her softly, rocking myself deeper until I was fully inside her. She wrapped her legs around me, and I moved my hands so that one was on her face, stroking her cheek, the other beside her head, helping me keep my full weight off her as I moved more forcefully.

She was gripping the cheeks of my arse, digging her nails into my skin, trying to pull me deeper inside her until she arched her back and came with a loud scream.

I continued in the same rhythm, wanting to bring her close to orgasm again before I claimed her as mine. As her soft moans became louder and more frantic, I whispered, "Bond with me, Gina. Be my woman, my love for always." She nodded her head between gasps and gazed into my eyes. In hers, I saw trust and love.

"I'm going to take your blood, Gina, and you must take mine, okay?"

"Yes, Nik, I love you so much. I need you... Please."

I lengthened the nail of my left index finger and pierced it into my neck as deep as I could go. Before I could tell her what to do, Gina struck at my neck and sucked hard, biting in further.

Fucking hell, this woman could bite. The sounds of pleasure coming from Gina as she took more of my blood triggered my own response. I bit down on the artery in her neck, drawing in as much of her blood as I could manage on the first pull.

There are hardly enough words to describe what happened next. Lights flashed in front of my eyes as waves of intense pleasure flowed through me. Gina let go of my neck, crying out my name over and over as she came, and it was almost as if every powerful sensation pulsed through me, too. It triggered my own release and, with it, a roar that was so loud I heard it in my ears long after I had stopped.

As we came down from the orgasmic high we'd just experienced, I sensed thoughts and feelings that weren't my own. Our Bond had taken, and it was Gina's concerns I could feel. It amazed her that sex could be that good, which made me want to beat my chest with pride. Yet she also worried I wouldn't want her now that we'd been intimate, when I wasn't so full of lust. I made my own thoughts and feelings clear, hoping that the Bond had worked for both of us and that she, too, could feel me in the way that I'd felt her.

From now on, we were one. Never would we belong to anyone else, and never would she starve for love and affection because, from me, it would be given freely and often.

"Wow, Nik, is that coming from you? I can sort of… sense you inside my mind…your thoughts and feelings. Is that really what you want?"

"Yes, you can sense me, and you are what I want. It's a done deal, Gina. You are mine, and I am yours. The sooner you get used to it, the better it will be for both of us because your worries are my worries now."

"I can feel it. Sense it."

"So stop doubting my love and need for you because it's something that will never change."

I was still inside her, my erection pulsing, raring to go, needing to prove to this woman that she was it for me. I thrust deep, then stopped, sending her all the lustful thoughts I'd had of every way I wanted to fuck her tonight. Gina tilted her hips, taking me deeper. Growling with satisfaction, I slammed into her over and over, my come from earlier easing the way.

There was no stopping me this time. No need to prepare

her body. She was as primed with need as I was and welcomed everything I had to give. I could feel her orgasm approaching, and her moans got louder, her nipples tight and hard against my chest.

This was it; what I had wanted for all those years—me and Gina with nothing but love between us.

When she cried out her pleasure, I felt the muscles in her cunt grabbing and releasing my cock in a rhythm that would have meant game over for me if I hadn't stopped for a minute.

After taking a few deep breaths, I rolled us over, placing her on top.

She sat up to ride me, a wicked, wanton look in her eyes. I watched her big, beautiful breasts bounce as she rode me hard, grinding herself into me. My woman was greedy for more, it seemed, as the friction of my pubic hair abrading her sensitive clit sent her soaring again, taking me with her this time, both of us feeling the pleasure we each experienced.

Bonding was definitely recommended.

Chapter Twenty

Josh

I arrived back at the Red Lion and parked the minibus as near as I could to the door. Those drunken women are hard to round up, and somehow I'd been roped into doing it again.

I was happy for Nik and Gina. They'd finally got together like they should have done years ago. Nik and I had been friends for so long; he was like family to me, and although I had only known Gina for about fifteen years, she, too, had become like family. She was the type of person that everyone immediately warmed to.

I always thought she'd be good when meeting with new clients. I'm sure she'd win them over with little effort.

Gina just had that way about her.

I got out of the minibus and sensed it immediately. Someone was watching. Definitely a vampire, but there was something odd about it, too. I couldn't discern if they were male or female or how old. Usually, those things we can detect. It helps us protect ourselves if we're attacked. But there was nothing of that sort to pick up on.

Alex said he could sense some familiarity about it, but I couldn't, which led me to believe that Alex had known this vampire before he met me.

As soon as I began looking around, whoever it was seemed to vanish. It could only be a vampire with that speed. But like everything else, where they'd been hiding was also a mystery.

I made my way into the pub, concerned about what we could be dealing with. Going straight to the bar, I motioned for my bar manager, Melissa, to join me.

"Mel, have you called last orders yet?"

"Just about to do it, Josh. Is everything okay? You look worried."

"Yeah, I just want this lot out of here," I told her, pointing toward the ladies from work, two of whom were about to start a karaoke song on stage.

"Mel, I don't want any lock-ins tonight. Give me a call later when you close. I want to make sure everything's okay."

"Josh, if there's something to be concerned about, I think I have a right to know," she stated.

The tough ex-army stance Mel showed when she was annoyed made me smile. She'd left the army two years ago, having been a medic with her battalion during two tours in Afghanistan. I gave her the job as soon as she interviewed, getting a sense that Mel would not only fit right in at this pub, but I could also trust her with my secret. She took the fact that I was a vampire surprisingly well, saying it wasn't the most fucked up thing she'd encountered in the last few years.

"Don't worry, Mel. This has more to do with the staff at Night Movers. Just call me later, okay?"

She nodded once in affirmation, then went back to serving customers. After a quick scan of the room, I made my way over to where Alex and Sergei sat. Keeley and Julia were on the stage singing Katy Perry's "I Kissed a Girl."

To say they were drunk was an understatement, as they needed to hold each other to stay upright, though surprisingly, they could still read and sing the words.

I was just about to tell Alex what I'd experienced outside, when at the chorus of "I kissed a girl," Keeley and Julia kissed each other on the lips before stumbling back, laughing. I looked at Alex and Sergei; their mouths hung open in shock.

Sergei turned to Alex and said, "I think your woman is a lesbian. I did not know this about her because she did not look like a lesbian. I am sorry, my friend. You should come back to Russia with me; I will find you a woman who likes men instead."

Alex scowled at Sergei, then stood to get Julia. I put my hand on his arm to stop him.

"Alex, you were right: someone was watching us. They were outside the pub when I pulled up, but they disappeared before I could see them. We need to get everyone home and figure this out because it's off somehow. I can't explain it, but it's like it was disguised."

Alex slumped back into his seat and shook his head. "How the fuck are we going to get them out of here safely while still watching out for whoever this is?"

"Mind control," said Sergei calmly, not the slightest bit bothered by the situation. "I was going to use it on the woman, Jean. Twice she grabbed my cock and squeezed, but not in a good way. So I thought I would compel her to keep those grabbing hands to herself—or to grab Josh instead."

"Don't you fucking dare, Sergei. I've got to work with the woman," I warned, covering my crotch and wincing. I'd been in the kitchen at work when Jean was kneading pastry dough, so I knew what her hands were capable of.

"Good idea, Sergei. You start with Moira and Jean, Josh can take Ami and Joanne, and I'll take Keeley, Maggie and Julia."

"I sense you do not like me, Alex, as you give me very loud women who like to grab cock. I am disappointed."

"No, Sergei, you have me all wrong," Alex assured him as he winked at me. "I've heard from Gregor that your mind control is stronger than mine or Josh's. So it makes more sense that you get the women who may be difficult to control tonight."

Sergei looked like he was about to argue, so Alex added, "Also, Keeley and Julia tend to vomit when they've had a drink, but if you want to swap, I have no problem with that."

"No," replied Sergei. "That will not be necessary."

Twenty minutes later, the deed was done. We were travelling along to Keeley's home when Julia suddenly yelled, "Stop! I'm going to be sick."

I pulled over as quickly as I could, and Alex opened the door. Julia leaned out and promptly threw up on the grass verge. This, in turn, set Keeley off. She opened one of the back windows and vomited all over the side of the minibus.

Sergei looked at Alex, patted him on the back and said in his heavy Russian accent, "I thought you lied tonight, my friend, about these women and their vomiting. But you did not. You are a good man, Alex. I respect you because of this."

Alex nodded, gritting his teeth, and I tried so hard not to laugh...

Chapter Twenty-One

Alex

I walked into the bedroom with tea and toast for Julia. She'd slept for about twelve hours after being drunk the night before, and I'd heard her stirring a few minutes ago.

Holding back her hair while she threw up in the toilet hadn't been my idea of fun, but I needed to take care of my woman. Afterwards, I'd put her to bed with a glass of water, two painkillers, and a drop of my blood.

She opened her eyes and groaned when she saw me. It wasn't the response I was expecting, so I kept quiet and waited for her to speak.

"I can't remember too much of what happened after we got back here, Alex, but I remember being sick and you taking care of me," she croaked. "So thanks. You are such a good guy, and I feel lucky to have you in my life."

"You are welcome, sweetheart. I'm just glad you enjoyed yourself."

I meant it. She was so carefree and had quite a few

laughs with the other ladies from work. I was happy for her. Julia needed to make more links to this village, as she'd lived away from it for so long.

"I got a text this morning," I told her. "Nik and Gina have Bonded by blood, so we have something to celebrate in our little family."

I was happy for them, but I also couldn't help feeling jealous. I'd planned to seduce Julia last night and thought I could talk to her about us Bonding, too.

"I'm so happy for them, Alex. Anyone can see they're meant to be together. Gina's still married, though. Wouldn't it have been better to wait for her divorce?"

"I've told you already that Bonding is more powerful and meaningful than marriage—and it lasts forever. The human ceremony means nothing more to us than a piece of paper, but the Bond means love, loyalty, and devotion for life."

I could tell she was thinking about this while eating the toast and drinking the cup of tea I'd made her. I knew how confusing it might seem and could sense that she was uncomfortable with it. I offered her another drop of my blood to help with the hangover; she accepted it today without pause, then settled down for a cuddle at the side of me.

"This is nice, having a lazy morning after a night out. It's been a long time for me. Funnily enough, I can't remember leaving the pub. I know I was singing, and I remember kissing Keeley, which seemed funny at the time, but not so much now. Then all I remember is hanging out of the van being sick."

"The kissing was unexpected but funny as hell. Although, the only person you should be kissing is me," I insisted before placing a chase kiss on her plump lips. "The thing is, we had to use mind control on you all to get you out of the pub, so that's why you can't remember."

I knew as soon as I'd said it that I should have kept my mouth shut.

Julia jumped up out of bed and yelled, "What the fuck, Alex? Why would you use mind control on us? We were all having a good time. So what if we were drunk? You had no right to do it." She grabbed her toiletry bag, stormed off to the bathroom, and slammed the door.

What was I going to say to her? I didn't know who was lurking out there or if they wished to do us harm. But I knew I wasn't willing to risk any of the humans last night, especially Julia.

I waited until I heard Julia stepping into the shower before I went to join her in the bathroom.

She was standing still, letting the warm water cascade down her back. I chuckled a little, seeing how white her sexy arse looked against her spray-tanned back and legs. I could tell she'd worn bikini briefs. I already knew there were no bra strap lines after undressing her last night. Her luscious, brown breasts looked so good I could have happily feasted on them for hours. But she'd been drunk, so I was a good boyfriend and put her in one of my T-shirts and tucked her up in bed.

I undressed and stepped into the shower behind her, my front touching her back. I wouldn't apologise, but she deserved an explanation.

"Julia, last night when I dropped you off in town, I sensed something. A presence. Most definitely a vampire, and it was close by. I went looking all around, but it had fled before I could even find where it had been. I couldn't sense whether it was male or female or how old, but it seemed familiar to me. Then, when Josh came back to the Red Lion after dropping Nik and Gina off at home, he sensed it, too, and believed it could be a threat to everyone. We'd already accounted for any vampire who had a reason to be in our area last night, and we knew it wasn't any of us. Plus, we'd have been able to scent each other.

"The reason we used mind control was to get you into the minibus and safely home as quickly as possible. You were all drunk, loud, and hanging back to dance. Also singing and grabbing Sergei's dick."

"I didn't, did I?"

"No," I growled. "Jean was Little Miss Grabby Hands last night. I would have lost my mind if you had done it."

She tensed in my arms, a little fearful after my outburst.

"Alex, are you still worried about this new vampire?"

"Yes, I am. When I meet a new vampire, I can normally sense their age. Obviously, it comes through as a rough estimate, but it's enough to gauge the vampire's strength, as that normally increases with the passing years. It's something that helps if we are attacked—to know whether to fight or flee. But Josh and I could sense very little about this vampire, almost as if it was hidden from us purposely."

"How could they do that?"

"With witchcraft, I suppose. Although I haven't seen it done successfully before."

"Witchcraft? Should I be scared?"

I didn't want her to be scared, but she needed to be aware of any possible dangers.

"To be perfectly honest, I'm not sure at the moment, Julia. But whatever I learn, I promise to keep you informed." I wouldn't let anything happen to her, but I couldn't be with her all the time.

Reaching for the shower gel, I moved her hair over one shoulder and poured the minty-scented gel from her neck down into the crack of her arse. Then I washed her back from top to bottom, feeling all the silky-smooth flesh under my soapy fingers, kissing along her shoulders and licking from her neck to her ears. When I got to her arse, I parted her cheeks and let my fingers slip between until she tensed.

"Shh," I whispered in her ear. "I won't do anything you don't want me to do. So just relax while I get you clean all over."

She nodded her head and let me continue. I massaged her arse cheeks, feeling their softness as I squeezed and kneaded. Then I dropped to my knees and soaped and massaged the back of her legs from thighs to ankles.

My cock was as hard as a rock, and when I turned her around to rinse her off, she licked her lips when she saw it. Still on the floor looking up at her, I picked up one of her feet and pressed my lips to it. Then I placed her leg over my shoulder and leaned her back against the tiled wall.

I rolled her outer lips between my lips and teeth, and she grabbed my head, trying to position me where she needed. I let her this time. I knew she felt I'd taken control of her when I compelled her at the pub, so I was giving up control to her now.

I thrust my tongue deep, enjoying the honey flavour of her cream on my taste buds. When she thought I had tongue fucked her enough, she guided me to her clit.

Julia gasped and looked down at me.

With me on my knees, my tongue lapping away at her clit and my finger gently stroking her entrance, she seemed like a goddess I'd been destined to worship. Again, I gave her control, or a choice, if you will.

"Does this feel good, sweetheart?" I asked, not stopping as my finger slid inside her.

"Yes," Julia gasped, closing her eyes and throwing her head back.

"Do you want me to stop?" I questioned, silently begging her not to say yes.

"No, Alex, don't stop."

The assault on her clit with my tongue and lips was quick and hard. I managed to find that sweet spot inside her with my finger, keeping the same strokes one after the other. She gasped and moaned as I used more pressure, then I fastened my lips to her clit and sucked, flicking her swollen bud with my tongue as I did so. Julia's orgasm happened so quick it surprised us both, and I felt every spasm against the finger I had inside her. Her legs seemed to give a little, so I stood and held her close, waiting for her to get her breath back before I kissed her gently.

"Come on, let me finish washing you, love," I said, grabbing the shampoo.

Julia didn't say anything, just turned and let me pour shampoo on her hair and massage it into her scalp. After rinsing it out, I took the conditioner and did the same. Then I grabbed the body wash again and continued to soap up the front of her body. Her breasts were just the right size for my hands, and I loved seeing her lovely, puckered nipples pointing straight at me—water rolling down each one, just waiting for my tongue to lap it away. Her breathing became quick, and the moans raspy from her throat as I sucked her nipples into my mouth, one after the other.

Julia pulled me closer and fisted her hands in my hair. She yanked hard, then angled my head so she could kiss me. Our teeth clicked together with the ferociousness of it, and my cock felt like it would burst.

"Fuck me, Alex. Fuck me hard and deep. And while you are inside me, bite me again. Don't hold back on either."

So I did as she asked and fucked her good and hard, pounding her against the tiled shower wall as she begged me for more. When I felt her orgasm approach, I bit into her neck and sucked hard, hearing her scream as she came around my cock, which in turn triggered my own release.

I extracted my teeth from her neck and lapped at the blood that ran down it. My saliva helped heal the bite marks, so I wasn't worried about anyone seeing them. But I was rougher than I should have been with that bite and worried what Julia's reaction would be.

After lowering her feet to the floor, I finally dared look into her eyes. What I saw there was the look of a thoroughly satisfied woman, and I couldn't contain my smile.

"I love it when you smile, Alex; you should do it more often. It suits you. You shouldn't be so serious all the time. You need to relax and have fun."

"I'm not serious all the time. I just like to make sure that jobs get done and that everything is ticking along nicely."

I was frowning, trying to think of how many fun things I'd done recently, but came up blank. Julia laughed as my frown increased, then kept on laughing. I laughed along with her as I shook my head. It was hard not to; her laugh was infectious.

"Come on, let's get cleaned up again and get out of the shower. The water's not that warm anymore."

To emphasise her point, she shivered a little, so we set about cleaning our bodies before the water turned colder.

Chapter Twenty-Two

Alex

I sat and watched Julia while she blow-dried her hair. The hairdresser had done a great job with the highlights, and as she dried it, you could see them more and more. With the highlights and the spray tan bronzing her face and body, she looked like a surfer girl with her hair all tousled coming out of the sea.

When her hair was dry, she put on face and eye creams, then slathered her body in a floral-scented lotion. A bit of mascara and lipstick later, she turned to me with a smile.

All in all, it had taken fifteen minutes, but I was enthralled with the entire process. She was surprised I didn't use any moisturisers or creams, but I told her immortals didn't need any. Julia said she was going to buy me some men's products, and I smirked as I opened my drawer.

Every year at Christmas, Maggie bought us men's facial products. As far as I knew, the others didn't use them either, and I had four unopened sets in the drawer.

Julia opened the first one she came across, then ordered me to sit and close my eyes. I did as she asked, and she patted something cool around my eyes, which actually felt good.

Julia explained it was an eye gel and should keep the wrinkles away. I didn't remind her I'd show no signs of ageing that weren't already present when I became a vampire. Julia then applied what she said was a daily moisturiser. I loved the way she touched me while she smoothed the creamy substance onto my face and down my neck. If Julia was to apply this to me every day, I would wear the stuff without fail.

When I looked in the mirror, I couldn't see much of a difference, but Julia said it gave me a more youthful appearance. When she started talking about treating me to a spa day, I quickly drew the line at that. No way was I going to be doing any girly stuff—no matter how much it would "destress" me. Making love to Julia for hours on end was a good stress reliever, and I told her so. She blushed and looked away. I could tell she was thinking of what we did in the shower.

I changed the conversation, letting her know that Gregor was coming tonight and was bringing my sister here for a few days.

"I would love to hear more of yours and Freya's story, Alex. The last part you told me was when you had become a vampire. What happened next?"

Taking her hand in mine, I led her into the living room, sitting her next to me on the two-seat sofa. I didn't want to tell her this next part of the story, but I also didn't want any secrets between us. I needed her to know what had made me the man I am today.

"After I awoke, Gamall fed me from his wrist. The thirst

for blood was incredible, and we had to call in another human so I could feed again. Mind control wasn't easy, and it took a few attempts to persuade the woman to let me take her blood.

"Gamall informed me that Freya had awoken only hours before me. She'd been out of it for nearly two days, and although she'd taken blood from both my father and a hunter who worked for him, Freya hadn't yet spoken.

"I noticed how weak Gamall appeared, and he suggested giving him some of my new immortal blood to help him replenish the blood he'd been giving me. Gamall was concerned about Freya and said Father kept trying to get her to say something, but she either wouldn't or couldn't talk. He encouraged me to go to her to see if I could help. So, when my need for blood was finally sated, I went to find her.

"When I went through the door at my father's house, I could find no one, not even Anya, the housemaid, so I went to the back of his home where the bedrooms were. I heard a woman sobbing in the room to the left, which was Father's bedroom. I pulled back the fabric from the doorway and found Anya knelt by the side of his bed with Freya's hand in her own.

"Freya looked as though she was sleeping, so I motioned for Anya to follow me. We went into the front room and sat beside the fire; a mouthwatering smell came from the cooking pot above it.

"Anya put her arms around me and cried, her tears soaking through my tunic. When I asked her what was wrong, Anya said she thought that Freya didn't want to live anymore, and she couldn't really blame her. She'd tried to tempt her with her favourite foods, but Freya shook her head when they tried to feed her. So I told Anya that I would go to her and see what I could do."

Thinking back to that day made my heart physically hurt.

"Freya's eyes were still closed when I sat next to her on Father's bed. I stroked away the hair from her eyes and spoke to her softly. The moment she stirred and looked up at me, she said, 'Oh, brother, what has he done to me? Why has he condemned me to this life?'

"I shook my head, not knowing the answer, and I remember leaning down to kiss her forehead before I spoke. Those very words and her reaction to them are deeply ingrained in my memories.

"'I have taken the blood, Freya,' I told her. 'I, too, am now immortal. You will not be on your own in this life. I love you, dear sister, and I will keep you safe from harm so no one can hurt you ever again.'

"Freya took me in her arms and cried for what seemed like hours. She only stopped when we scented Father enter the dwelling. He came straight to the bedroom and looked at Freya in my arms, then at me.

"'So, we are all as one now, my son,' he said proudly. 'You will make a good, strong immortal. Together we will become more powerful and will fear no one.'

"I didn't understand what he was talking about. Why should we fear anyone? It didn't make sense to me, but I didn't want to speak to him, so I said nothing and looked away. We waited for our father to go out again, and then Freya and I went into the front room to eat some of the rabbit stew that Anya had cooked. It was delicious as always, but somehow it tasted even better than usual, and both Freya and I complimented Anya on this. The woman fussed over Freya, pleased that she was now speaking at least, and she offered to make more of her favourite foods.

"Freya shook her head, looked into Anya's eyes, and in a clear voice, she said, 'Anya, you made sure I was fed and well cared for, and you agreed with my brother that it would do me good to take a walk outside.'"

"Mind control?" asked Julia.

"Yes, and Freya pulled it off first go. Not like me and my poor attempt. Freya then looked at me and said, 'I have no home now. Everything I loved or owned is gone, apart from you and Gamall. Will you let me stay with you, brother? I do not wish to be in my father's presence this night or any other.' I remember holding her in my arms and saying, 'Freya, whatever I have is yours, including my home. You can stay with me for as long as you wish, and you do not have to do Father's bidding ever again.'

"We left immediately, not wanting the confrontation with our father that was sure to happen if he saw Freya leaving with me. When we reached my home, Gamall was tending the fire. He got up and hugged Freya, tears streaking down his red cheeks. He pulled me over to them and hugged me, too. I wasn't used to displays of affection like that coming from Gamall, and I must admit, I got pretty choked up. Freya pulled back from us and said, "'Gamall, I need to learn everything you know about witchcraft and anything you found out from Eadgar and Colton about being immortal. I do not want my father to find out you are telling me about this. I will let him think he is teaching me all I need to know. When you come over to see me or I to see you, we can tell him it's so I can learn about herbs, potions and such.'

"Looking anxious, Gamall said, 'Freya, I am willing to tell you everything that I know, but if Sebbi uses mind control, he will compel me to tell him what we have been doing.'

"Freya replied, 'Do not worry. Before we part, I will also compel you, so all you'll remember is discussing potions.'

"'Freya, what's going on?' I asked. 'Why do you need to know all this?' I wasn't sure why this seemed so important right then.

"'Aðalbrandr, you are my brother, and you are loyal, noble, and good. I do not think you got these traits from our father. I do not trust the man who forced me to live life as an immortal, and neither should you.'

"'Freya, what our father did was wrong, but he loves and adores you. He was devastated by what happened to your family and tried to save them. You, above anyone else, have been his life. He would be nothing without you.'

"I wanted my words to reassure her, Julia, but she would not be moved on her feelings about him.

"Freya laughed a little and said, 'My brother, I love you, and I know that you and Gamall have a love for me that comes with no conditions. I cannot say the same for my father.'

"We left the conversation there, and I was glad to do so. I knew my father did wrong by forcing Freya to become immortal, but I also knew he loved Freya, and I remembered his charred body in front of Freya's house after he'd tried to save Brisa. I was torn between hating him for forcing Freya to become immortal and forgiving him for his selfish act of saving a loved one who did not want to be saved.

"Father came to my home later that night. He begged Freya to go home with him and Gamall, but she said she needed to be away from the home in which her son had died. Father went to her and held her close, whispering how sorry he was for the deaths of her children.

"'My husband also died, Father. Are you sorry about his death, too?' Freya questioned.

"'Of course I am, child,' he said. 'What do you take me for? Do you think I have no feelings? Think about this, Freya. You are my child, and I would have done anything to save you. Just as you would have done anything to save your own children. But somehow, that has made me a monster in your eyes. So tell me, daughter. How do we put this right?'

"'With time, Father,' Freya said. 'Just as with anything else. All we need is time, and then everything will be as it should be.'

"I thought this statement odd, as all would never be as it should be. Freya would never get her family back, and we would be on this earth forever. But Father seemed appeased by what she said and let her stay with me without any further argument.

"Months went by, one after the other. Freya and Gamall became inseparable and often took long walks around the village and beyond. They would stop and speak with everyone, and it was good to see Freya smile again. They practised their potions in my home and at Father and Gamall's.

"I'd often wondered why Gamall didn't have a home of his own with a wife and children. He insisted he was too set in his ways for a wife, although he enjoyed the company of women and liked to rut with them often. Gamall said he thought of Freya and me as his children, as we were blood to him, and he'd been with us throughout our life. He said he stayed with Sebbi at first to keep an eye on him after our mother died, and then because Freya lived with them and he could watch her grow up, child to woman.

"He told us that when Freya left to get married, he

stayed because he was used to being there and was too old to change. By now, he was sixty years old, and I asked him why he hadn't wanted to become immortal like us. Gamall reminded us that as he wasn't a Born Immortal, he would instead become a Made vampire, which would mean he couldn't walk in the sun as that would kill him. He said it was too late now because he wouldn't want to be a sixty-year-old man forever.

"The conversation made me want to know more about the differences between being a Born Immortal or Made vampire. So one day, while out hunting, I asked my father. He told me how to turn a human into a Made vampire by drinking their blood to the point of imminent death, then giving them our blood.

"Father seemed irritated as he said he'd told me all this before. I told him I'd forgotten, and I wanted to make sure I knew the difference in case I had to battle with one.

"My father said after the exchange of blood, the human becomes immortal like us, but they could be killed by driving a wooden or metal stake through their hearts and burning their bodies. He also said that if Made vampires were exposed to enough bright sunlight, they would die a painful death, burning slowly from the inside out. Although, after many years, they too can tolerate bright sunlight for a short time.

"My father told me that a Born Immortal could never be killed by any means, which was why we were far superior to Made vampires. I didn't question him further, and he offered no other information.

"One day, nearly a year after Freya's family died, Anya came to tell us that Gamall was gravely ill. We hurried to Father and Gamall's home, and the sight shocked us. Gamall was deathly pale, and his lips were blue. He was gasping for breath and holding his chest, but he smiled when he saw us. Sebbi was by his bedside, bathing his brow with a cloth. He looked at us both and begged us to convince Gamall to become a Made vampire.

"Freya immediately said no, and that we should respect his wishes to pass into the next world. But Father still looked at me to side with him and force Gamall to change his mind. I shook my head and dropped to my knees beside his bed with Freya.

"She moved Father's hand from Gamall's brow and kissed him gently. I did the same. We told him we loved him and would hold him forever in our hearts. Before we could say anything else, Gamall clutched our hands and then gasped his last breath.

"Father was both distraught and enraged that we hadn't begged Gamall to become a Made vampire. He began throwing furniture and other items around the room. I had to wrestle him away from Gamall's body, but he fought me like he meant to cause me harm.

"Freya yelled, 'Father, we need comfort from you today of all days now our uncle has left this life. So be a father to us, not a savage who beats his children.'

"This made my father pause, and he looked at Freya closely before saying, 'For a year, you have not wanted comfort from your father, and you suffered then over your losses. What makes you want your father now?'

"Freya just looked at him and said, 'It is perhaps, on a day like this, time to think about who is important to us. I know you will grieve the passing of your friend, Father, and I will try to give you comfort at this time.'

"'Daughter' was all my father said as he went to Freya and held her closely. I looked at them in that strange, surreal moment that I thought might never happen again. That's when I knew who held the most power in our family. She was the smallest of us all but had stopped us fighting with mere words.

"The villagers came together to build a funeral pyre befitting a noble Viking, and each left gifts with Gamall's body to take to the afterlife. As he was not a warrior, he would not go to the hall of Valhalla in Asgard, but to us, he was more important than any esteemed fighter, and I was touched by the love everyone in the village had for him.

"A week after Gamall's passing, Freya went out on one of her long daily walks. I'd been concerned about her strange behaviour over the last few days, so I followed her, staying far enough away that she wouldn't be able to scent me.

"Freya met a man from our village who was considered a great warrior. I watched as she spoke to him and nearly fell over with shock when she fought with him. I knew she wasn't in immediate danger because she was stronger than any human, and I was impressed with her fighting skills.

"The way she threw him, pinned him, and then jumped away to let him get to his feet again was so quick and practised; Freya must have been doing it for some time. When the fighting finally ended, Freya hugged him, then fed from his wrist. I waited until the young man got onto his cart and left before I joined her.

"'Freya, what is going on? Why do you need to learn to fight? I will always protect you. And anyway, we cannot be killed. Father told me,' I said, making it clear how annoyed I was that she thought she needed to learn how to fight.

"'Yes, he told me the same. Did you believe him, Aðalbrandr?' Freya asked.

"'Why would he lie to us, Freya? It serves no purpose,' I replied.

"'Why indeed, brother?' was her only reply.

"I couldn't understand why she was doing it. A woman should never need to fight. She kept home and made babies. Although thinking about that statement, I could see why Freya had chosen a new path. I wondered whether Gamall had known about her learning to fight, but I knew he must have.

"When we got back to the house, Freya prepared our meal. She asked if I would sharpen the axe because it was becoming blunt. I did as she asked, then chopped more wood for the fire. I changed my tunic before we ate and found Freya covering up the woodpile with a blanket. I joked that she didn't have to keep the wood warm, and Freya laughed along with me, saying it was nice to cover it up as it made the room look pretty.

"Father came round as he had done every night since Gamall's death. We sat and ate a hearty meal, and then Freya got up to clear away our dishes.

"The next thing I knew, Freya was standing behind our father, asking him why he had compelled someone to set fire to her home. Father spun around to face her and denied her accusation. But she persisted, questioning him about that night, and then she pushed him so hard he fell to the floor.

"I felt like I was watching all this from a distance and in slow motion, but when Father leapt back up to Freya, I ran to grab him. He cried out in pain, and his legs gave way as Freya pulled her hand away from his chest, blood covering her fingers. She shoved me out of the way and pinned Father to the floor, pushing a long metal tool further into his chest.

"'This tool belonged to my beloved husband, who you murdered! It is fitting that I use it to help you meet your end,' she told him.

"'No, Freya,' Father wheezed. 'You cannot do this. I cannot die. I am immortal.'

"'You can die, Father. I know what I have to do. You killed my husband and children. It isn't right that you get to live a long life while they are cold and dead in the ground,' Freya declared, sobbing.

"'I didn't mean for Brisa to die. I loved her. She was the blood of my blood. I tried to save her; you know this, Freya,' my father said, struggling to take a breath.

"'But she is dead, Father, and by your hand. Why did you do it? Why did you kill my family?' Freya screamed.

"'Your husband was stopping you from becoming immortal. He would rather you face death as an old woman instead of life still young and beautiful,' Father gasped.

"'But I would have rather faced death as an old woman, having known true love, family, children and grandchildren than the immortal life you offered. I did not want this, Father. Now I have to mourn the loss of my family forever.'

"With that, she stood and lifted the blanket off the woodpile, revealing the axe I'd sharpened earlier.

"'No,' I yelled while making a grab for the axe. But she kicked my hand away and lifted the axe into the air.

"'Aðalbrandr,' my father choked, 'stop her, son. She does not know what she is doing.'

"'Oh, I know exactly what I am doing, Father. I rendered you weak with a stake to your heart, and now I shall cut off your head before I burn you until there is nothing left. I studied well with Gamall this past year. Colton had told him how a Born Immortal who had taken blood could be killed. I used mind control on each of the unsuspecting villagers to find out what they were doing the night the fire started, and I found the one you had compelled. I did not kill the man; it wasn't his fault he had to do your bidding,' she said as she raised the axe.

"'Freya, think what you are doing. Do you want to live with your father's death on your conscience? Once done, you cannot take this back,' I warned.

"'How well I know this, brother, for I live it every day, even though it is not what I wanted. But I cannot carry on knowing that my father murdered my family. If I do not do this, then you must promise that you will end me,' Freya cried.

"'No! Freya, I could never do that. I only chose this life because Father made you take the blood. I cannot live it without you,' I declared.

"'He took the choice away from both of us that night; he knew what you would do when I had taken the blood. I bet you tried to stop him,' she said.

"'Yes, I did try. I knew you would hate him for it,' I admitted.

"'Well, now you know everything I hate him for, so you must understand why I have to do this. Please, Aðalbrandr, help me finish him.'

"I glanced at my father, who had blood pouring from his mouth. Then I looked at Freya and nodded my head.

"She removed his head with two swings of the axe, then quickly moved it from his body. Freya took the same blanket she'd covered the woodpile with and asked me to help her wrap his body in it. She told me we needed to burn him until there was nothing left but ash, so I picked up his body and carried it to the cart.

"I hastily tethered the pony to the cart while Freya placed Father's head in a basket and covered it up. She went back into the house to bring a burning torch of wood. Freya dropped it into a metal cone attached to our cart, as we would need it to start a fire. Then we went far enough from our village so that they wouldn't see the fire burning. We were lucky that the weather had been warm and sunny, so the ground was dry. After fashioning a small pyre, we placed Father's head and body on it, although we kept the two parts separate.

"Freya lit the blanket and basket surrounding his body and head, then the kindling underneath. We watched as the fire raged on into the night, and all that was left of my father were ashes."

I stopped talking at that moment. The same sickening feeling washed over me every time I relived that terrible night. I still couldn't believe I played a part in my father's death, and I wondered if Julia would be appalled by my story.

She touched my face and kissed my lips.

"You're still traumatised by what happened that night, aren't you, Alex? How did you face each other after all your father's remains had gone?" she asked.

"It was hard for me to look at Freya, but when I did, I noticed she was shaking. She took hold of my hand, begging, 'Please don't hate me, brother. I could not live knowing what he had done and not seek vengeance for my family. But now he is gone...and I don't have the peace I thought would come to me.'

"I took Freya in my arms and held her tightly. She was sobbing and shaking, but I could find no words to comfort her. So I held her until she stopped crying, put her in the cart beside me and set off for home.

"Before we got there, Freya asked me to take her to where her family was buried, so I steered the pony in that direction and took us where she'd asked. When we got to their grave, Freya jumped down from the cart and walked over to the mound. It had flattened out over the year, and the wildflowers Freya and Gamall had planted were growing in abundance.

"Freya dropped to her knees and touched the ground, wailing so loudly I thought she might wake the village. She clawed at the earth, screaming, 'I need you to come back to me, my loves. I need to feel you in my arms.'

"I ran up behind her and pulled her away from the earth before she could dig any deeper, then held her arms to her sides, stopping her from moving.

"'Please, Freya, you cannot do this,' I shouted. 'They are gone, and you have to leave them in peace. You must let them go. Not in your heart and mind, though. You can keep your memories of them, and I can keep mine, but you must let their bodies rest undisturbed.'

"'I cannot,' she cried. 'I need to be with them. They were my life, and without them, I have nothing.'

"'You have me, dear sister, and I have you. You are my only family now. Please do not leave me. I need you to survive this life. I chose it because of you, so you would not be alone,' I sobbed. 'Do not tell me what I did was in vain.'

"Freya turned and grabbed my shoulders before saying, 'I don't know how to do it, Aðalbrandr. I don't know how to live without reason.'

"'I will be your reason, Freya. We must live this life he forced us into and be good and honourable people.' She sagged in my arms, and I lifted her onto the cart and took her home.

"We talked on the way. Freya told me how her need for her and Gamall to discover precisely what started the fire that night enabled her to find out about our father. Although, she'd had her suspicions about him, anyway.

"Freya told me how Gamall had informed her of everything he'd learned from Colton; how he was worried that she wouldn't be strong enough to finish our father when the time came. So they organised for a good, strong warrior to spar with her in fights. He taught her how to fight with fists and weapons, and she gained more strength every day.

"Gamall had been reluctant to see his friend die, even though he hated him for causing the death of Freya's family, so he made her promise not to do anything until he'd passed away.

"I told her she could have come to me with what she knew, but Freya said she didn't want to taint me with her deception and actions. Also, Freya thought I'd have tried to talk her out of it, and she was right. I would have done...at first.

"I realised that Freya hadn't taken the time to grieve over the loss of her family, seeking revenge for them instead. I knew if Freya were ever to be happy again, she would first need to grieve the loss of her husband and children and the life she lived before. I would help her because no matter what she had done that night, she was my sister, and I loved her more than anything."

Julia was silent for a moment, but her gaze never left mine when she finally spoke.

"I think if I were Freya, I would have done the same. She lost everything, and then your cruel father took away her choice by making her immortal. If the driver who'd crashed into me had lived, I could have sought him out and killed him. Years in and out of prison hadn't reformed him. He didn't deserve to live after he caused Megan to die. I'm glad he's dead, but I would have liked him to suffer," Julia told me.

"It's not so easy to kill, Julia. It changes you, and the memories haunt you, whether you kill for revenge or not."

"Have you killed many people, Alex? You've lived a long life, and you're a powerful vampire. There must have been people who've crossed your path that you fought with," Julia asked hesitantly.

"In 1743, I was at the docks in Liverpool waiting for the fabrics to come in from the Far East. At that time, slave trading was big business, and I happened upon an area in which slaves brought in on a ship from Africa were being paraded on a platform.

"A man was wielding a long whip, which he cracked against the wood, making the slaves and everyone around him flinch at the sound. Black men and women of various ages were sold to the highest bidder. A few women were topless and looked so young and fragile. Two men appeared to have been beaten and were full of infected sores. One of those men collapsed and was dead before he hit the platform. It was horrifying to witness.

"A man who looked as if he worked for the one in charge of the auction threw the dead man into a large crate. The other slave was swaying as if he, too, was going to fall. The man asking for bids went to kick the sick slave into the same crate, saying that he was ready to die anyway so no one would bid for him. Before his kick made contact, I leapt onto the platform and said I would buy the slave. The auctioneer was shocked and asked if I was ill in the head for wanting a slave that wouldn't last the day, and the crowd that had gathered laughed at me. But I threw him some coins, and he gave me leave to take the poor man.

"I took him back to the rooms I rented when in Liverpool, but the landlady protested vehemently at his presence. I compelled her with mind control to stop her dispute and to send for a doctor.

"I brought him water to sip and set about cleaning his

wounds. I thought he was too far gone for my blood alone to heal him, but I needed to know if there was any chance of saving him so he could live a mortal life.

"He looked to be in his mid-twenties and should have had a full life ahead of him. The doctor said the infections in his festering wounds would soon finish him, and there was nothing he could do.

"He'd gone past the stage of fever and had turned cold. So I sent the doctor on his way after compelling him with mind control into thinking he had saved the man.

"I patted my chest and said *Alex* repeatedly, trying to get him to understand my name. Then I pointed at him, and he weakly touched his chest before saying something like *Jesuwa*.

"To me, it sounded like Joshua, so I patted his chest and said, *Joshua*. Then I looked into the man's eyes and asked him if he would like to live forever. Of course, he couldn't understand what I was saying, but he nodded his head. I bit into his wrist and drank his blood, his frightened eyes never leaving mine as I did so.

"I didn't need to drink for too long as he was near death anyway, so when I heard his heartbeat falter and get to the last few intermittent beats, I bit into my wrist and gave him my blood.

"The next evening, he roused a Made Immortal, or vampire, as common folklore likes to call us. Joshua was thirsty for blood constantly, and with the language barrier, it was hard to get him to understand that I had to bring it to him.

"During that time, I used mind control to get the local prostitutes to come to my rooms and feed Joshua their blood, although I paid them well for their service. It took nearly a week for the blood lust to calm enough to transport Joshua with me safely back to Yorkshire."

Julia put her hand on my arm and asked, "Is this Joshua York you're talking about? Josh, your friend and colleague?"

"Yes, it is. Each of us has a story, Julia, human or not."

"Carry on, Alex," she encouraged.

"We stopped regularly on the way back, making sure he was well-fed on both blood and healthy foods. When Freya saw what I had brought with me, she was astounded. We'd never discussed turning a human before, and it shocked her that I'd done so. I explained what had happened, and Freya immediately took him into her arms and held him, whispering soothing words that visibly calmed him.

"Over the next few months, Freya taught him how to speak English. She also taught him to read, write, and basically everything else he would need to know to help him get by in life.

"Joshua told us about his home in Africa. His family was poor, as was most of his village. They shared a small parcel of land and had an ox to help them plough. He worried that without his help, his family would struggle to work the land.

"Unfortunately, as Joshua was a Made vampire, he wouldn't be able to survive in a sunny climate anymore, so he wasn't able to return to his family. At twenty-five years old, he became part of a new family—a brother for Freya and me.

"Often Joshua would wake up in a panic, crying out words in his native tongue. He said the horrors that he and the others had experienced on the ship would come back to him in his dreams. Josh was severely beaten for trying to stop the rape of a woman who had been captured. She came from his village and was a sweet, kind young woman who was going to be married to his friend.

"They'd set a few of the captives to work below deck, cleaning duties mainly, and it was during that time that two of the guards had grabbed the woman and forced her down to the floor before they raped her. She screamed and tried to stop them, but her movements were restricted because she was still in shackles.

"Both Josh and another captive leapt on the guards and tried to stop them, but they couldn't do too much as they were in shackles, too.

"Several guards pounced on them before tying them to a pole, where they were whipped and beaten. The lacerations from the whip became infected and would have caused Josh's death if I hadn't saved him.

"The woman was brought back below deck later and was unrecognisable. They had beaten her so badly that they'd broken her jaw, cheekbone, and all her fingers. Her eyes were swollen shut, and she was bleeding from her mouth and ears. Because she was naked, they could also see that she was bleeding from every orifice.

"Because all the captives were on shorter chains, no one could go to help her. So all they could do was listen to her whimpers and tears until, later that night, the whimpers stopped. Her body was discovered the following day by the guards bringing water. The captain came down and became angry and beat the guards. Probably because he'd lost the money she would have brought when sold. They went away and left her body below deck for a while, and when they came back, she was wrapped in cloth and taken above deck to be disposed of.

"After he was done telling us about his nightmares, I knew I couldn't rest until these men were punished. Freya suggested finding out when the ship was next due back in Liverpool so we could bring the men to justice.

"The whole issue of slavery was bad enough, but to treat another human that way was deplorable. And while these men were alive, their brutal actions would continue.

"At that time, it was seven nights' travel to Liverpool, as Joshua could only travel at night. So we planned our journey well in advance, and when we finally reached Liverpool, I went about my business as usual.

"During the daytime, I purchased fabrics and other items from the trade ships so no one would become suspicious about why Freya and I were hanging around.

"When the ship came in, we stayed until the crew and guards came onto the docks. I recognised one of the guards from the auction, but I couldn't identify anyone else. Although seeing him was enough to assure me it was likely to be the same crew, it had been almost a year since I'd rescued Joshua.

"Joshua was always treated equally by Freya and me. He was our family as far as we were concerned, but for this to work, he had to act like our slave. It didn't matter that he was finely dressed. Many people considered it a sign of wealth to dress their slaves in fine attire.

"We perused the local taverns and whorehouses until we found the same men who had raped the woman Joshua had told us about. We lured them to the back of a slaughterhouse, which was a fitting place to end them.

"It would have been easy to break their necks or slit their throats, but Freya suggested a punishment befitting their crime. So Freya and Joshua handed them a knife each, and then Freya used mind control on them, telling them to cut off their cock and balls.

"The men screamed as they were doing it, but Joshua

kept up the mind control that Freya had started and encouraged the men to carry on. He used mind control again to help them remember the woman they had raped and left to die.

"Eventually, I decided I had seen enough and used my claws to slit their throats. When death finally claimed them, Joshua collapsed on the floor and wept. He cried during our walk back to the rooms, and Freya immediately started to mother him, drying his tears and putting him to bed. Then she let her own tears flow, but I couldn't comfort her.

"I felt sickened and couldn't stop pacing, so I went out to a tavern and drank until I felt warmth seep into my cold mind—letting the prostitute I purchased change the thoughts in my head to pleasure, not death.

"We left Liverpool the next morning, and none of us have spoken of that night since. Joshua and I dealt with enough scum over the years that needed a swift exit from this earth, but we usually just used mind control to screw them over and take their money and property instead.

"We gained property and businesses all over England, but we always preferred Yorkshire. We have homes in North, East, and West Yorkshire, as well as here in South Yorkshire, where our main business is run. Freya came to live with us for a time near where we are now.

"She was always trying to do her best for the families surrounding where we were living in Barnsley. Women and children were working in the mines, as well as men. And many children didn't live long enough to become adults. They died in accidents, from poor nutrition and lack of sunlight, or from backbreaking work—all common occurrences for poor mining families.

"Freya used to go to the poorest areas with baskets of fruit, meat and bread to help feed the families living there.

They called her 'The Angel' because she was so kind and generous and always made time for the children. She'd tell them stories as she used to in our village when she was still human. And, of course, when you see Freya, you will also see why the children thought her an angel. So, as you see, we were not always killers in our past."

"I can't wait to meet her," Julia said.

"She will love you, Julia, and you will love her."

"What about Gregor? What's he like?"

"Gregor is a very serious man who doesn't trust easily. He has a good business mind, and he, Sergei and Viktor head a similar business to ours in Russia, as well as being involved in oil and gas. We've been friends for centuries and opted to merge part of our business some time ago. As well as doing our supermarket jobs, we are also the go-to transportation service for vampires, both Born Immortals and Made."

"Wouldn't it be just as easy for Born Immortals to travel by planes, like regular passengers?" Julia asked.

"Yes, you are right in theory. We can walk in daylight, although it still makes us slightly weaker than doing the same at night. But we still need valid passports and other travel documents. While this was easily forged a few years ago, with all the terrorist activities in recent years, obtaining a passport and remaining under the radar while you get through customs is becoming nearly impossible. The technology we have now makes it easy for someone to trace your background with a few taps on a keyboard.

"Joshua is a technology genius, but he's found it extremely hard to hack into our passport agency this year. And every year onwards will be the same. In view of this, Gregor and I decided to purchase planes.

"We have people who work at Doncaster Airport and

Leeds Bradford Airport, so we can get landing slots and keep the planes there until we use them again.

"Gregor has secured us three airports in Russia, two of which are in Moscow and the other in Kursk. We have the use of two airports in Germany, giving us access to both the east and west. We are currently working on airports in Sweden, Norway, France and Spain, but from what I'm told, it will only be a matter of weeks before they grant us permits.

"We're already able to use every ferry port in the UK and Ireland due to our legitimate transport business. Remember, they are used to us moving produce and other goods between the UK and most other European countries, but with the planes, this will become much quicker."

"Wow," she exclaimed, both surprised and a little impressed, I hoped, with this rapidly expanding side of our company.

"Will I be dealing with any of this, Alex?"

"I hope you will, but to be honest, Julia, our foreign partners aren't happy to use humans in this part of the business. Although, they seem to accept that Maggie can handle it. All our Russian partners are fond of Maggie. She was younger than you are now on her first journey with us to Moscow. Sergei got her drunk as hell on the first night, and it took two days for her to recover, even with my blood. Gregor has a lot of respect for her. He bought her a car for her birthday, which had her husband wondering what was going on, I'm sure," I said with a grin.

"He sounds very generous."

"You don't know the half of it. Gregor has a... well, I'm not entirely sure what he feels for my sister. He treats her like a princess and brings her diamonds and other expensive jewels every time he comes over. And he always visits her first before us."

"Do you think he's in love with her?" Julia asked.

"Yes, but maybe not as one would be in love with a Bonded mate. You'll know what I mean when you see him with her. We're having a meeting later to discuss the vampire presence as well as business."

"Will Gregor mind me being there? If he doesn't like humans other than Maggie knowing his business, he might not want me around," she remarked.

"You're going to Bond with me, Julia. Gregor will know this, so he won't object to you being there."

She was quiet for a moment, and I could tell she was carefully planning what to say next.

"Alex, do you really want to commit to a lifetime with me? I'm nothing special, and I can't understand your feelings for me."

I put my arms around her and spoke to her softly.

"I think you do understand, Julia. I think you recognise I am yours. That scares you because it's unfamiliar to you as a human. But if you trust me and trust the feelings you have for me, everything we could be to each other will make sense."

"Every time I'm with you, Alex, and especially when we make love, I feel even more connected to you than before. It's like falling in love, but it's more intense, and that's what scares me. I feel it wash over me, and for a moment, I can't breathe. But then I fight it because it's too soon to feel this way. It should be something that develops steadily over time, not within days."

"So, you're falling in love with me?" I prompted. Julia nodded her head.

This was good, more than good. I needed to act on it before she protested again.

"Falling in love with you was easy, Julia. It was letting you go that was hard. I won't let that happen again. I believe in fate and destiny, as do most immortals. After all, we live so long and see so much it becomes easier to recognise. And when we do recognise it, the need to act is strong. Tell me you'll Bond with me, Julia, and soon, so we can begin our life together."

"I need to speak to my parents first," Julia said. "I assume you'll want me to live here with you?"

"When we first Bond, we'll find it hard to be apart from one another for very long. The need for sex will be constant, and so will the need to share blood. It will calm down eventually. As the Bond takes, we'll be able to sense each other, our feelings, thoughts and needs. It's something I look forward to more than anything," I told her truthfully.

"Next weekend, then. I want to get my first week at Night Movers out of the way before I have a sex marathon with my boss," Julia said with a giggle.

I couldn't believe what I was hearing. She was going to Bond with me next weekend. This was what I'd wanted to hear for years, but for some reason, I couldn't speak. I couldn't move, either. I just stared at her, grinning like a loon, which set Julia off giggling again.

"Marathon sex, you said. I'll hold you to that, Julia, so be prepared."

I received a text telling me that Freya and Gregor had arrived.

"Come on then, my lovely. It's time to meet your new family," I told her. Then I kissed her on the tip of her nose and led her over to our offices.

Chapter Twenty-Three

Julia

I'd agreed to Bond with Alex. There was a voice in my head telling me I was doing the right thing by Bonding with a kind, handsome, and very sexy guy. Then another voice was telling me I'd lost my mind by committing to someone over 950 years old who'd drink my blood on a regular basis. Although, when that happens during sex...well...let's just say it's not a hardship.

We made our way over to the Night Movers' compound hand in hand, with Alex humming a T. Rex song that had been playing on the radio before we left the cottage.

The warmth in the office was so welcome after being out in the chilly October air. Josh, Sergei, Gregor and Alex's sister were already there.

Gregor was over six feet in height, had short brown hair and piercing blue eyes. He had an intimidating air to him, and when he smiled, I felt relieved for some reason.

Freya was stunning. She had beautiful long blonde hair

and pretty grey eyes, much lighter than Alex's. But you could tell that she and Alex were siblings. Alex introduced us, and Freya hugged me before saying, "I've been looking forward to meeting you, Julia. Alex has told me so much about you."

"I have news for you, Freya. Julia has agreed to Bond with me," said Alex proudly.

Cheers went up, and Alex was pulled away from me, with all the men in the room shaking his hand.

"Oh my God! I'm going to have a sister," Freya squealed, hugging me again before whispering in my ear, "Thank you, Julia. You will make my brother complete."

Then Gregor embraced me, too. "Julia, it is so good to meet you, finally. I am happy for you and my friend. This is great news—first Nikolas and Gina, and now Alex and Julia. There must be something in the water," he declared in subtly accented English.

"Then we should not drink this water, Gregor," Sergei said. He winked, then kissed my cheek.

Josh grabbed me about the waist and swung me around with ease, which made me feel as light as a feather.

"Welcome to the family, Julia. I finally have a sister that won't torment me," Josh declared. He placed me on my feet in front of him.

Freya laughed. "I don't know what you mean, Joshua Bubbles," she said.

"You see what I mean, Julia. My other sister keeps picking on me."

"Why do you call him Joshua Bubbles?" I asked, puzzled by the name.

Freya opened Josh's desk drawer, revealing two bottles of children's bubble makers. She took one out, opened it, and blew through the bubble ring.

"Keeley's daughter calls him that because he keeps these in his desk for her for when she visits. It's so cute the way she says it."

Freya laughed, but she was also gazing fondly at Josh.

"I think it's sweet," I said, tapping Josh on the hand.

"She's such a lovely little girl," replied Josh. "I can't understand why her father wouldn't want to see her."

"He is not a real man. A real man treats his woman and children with love and respect and would never abandon them. We should find him and kill him," said Sergei in all seriousness.

"Sergei, it is not our way to kill a human who does not physically harm another," Gregor admonished.

"Well, *I* think he should be held accountable!" Freya stated.

Gregor stroked Freya's hair while he spoke. "What would you like me to do to him, my Freya?"

I could see the relationship between Gregor and Freya that Alex had spoken about. He looked at her with utter devotion. I knew Sergei didn't mean they should kill Keeley's ex. At least, I hope he didn't. But I thought that if Freya requested it, Gregor would do anything she asked.

"Will you all just cut it out!" Alex let out an exasperated huff and rolled his eyes. "I agree that Keeley's ex *is* a prick, but it's not up to us to handle it. Keeley is a wonderful mother, and Daisy wants for nothing. Her ex's family love Daisy, even if he doesn't. Freya, I know you adore Keeley, but you have to keep out of this."

"Alex, it's hard to do that. I've known Keeley since she was a little girl coming to visit her Aunt Maggie. When her mum died, and they came back to live around here, I used to take her shopping, and we would sit and chat for hours. She had so much potential, and now she's working part-time, cleaning and cooking here. She went to college and got her A-level in business studies. Why can't you employ her in the offices? She would be an asset to any business," Freya argued.

"She was working part-time at the job she does now while she was at college. We offered her employment in the office, but she went to university. She got pregnant halfway through her studies, so had to leave. When she came home, she asked for her old job back and hasn't requested a change since," replied Josh.

"I will employ her, Freya. The structural renovations at Rothley Manor are nearing completion. Keeley can come and work for me; she can be my assistant in England. You will speak to her, yes?"

"Thanks, Gregor. You are my hero," Freya said sweetly, hugging Gregor and kissing him on his cheek. He beamed and stroked her hair.

Nik came into the office and was immediately enveloped in hugs and handshakes, congratulating him on Bonding with Gina.

"Where is my Gina?" asked Sergei. "I miss her."

"She's in the cottage with her kids. They came over earlier, and we talked to them about our being together. I had to reassure her son that this was a new thing between us, although I'd loved her for a long time. They both said Gina should have left their father years ago; they knew she was unhappy. I told them they'd be welcome in our home anytime they want to come by and see their mum."

He ran his hand through his dark, wavy hair and sighed. For someone who had just got everything he wanted, he seemed really stressed.

"What did her husband say when she told him?" asked Josh.

"Gina phoned him this morning to say she'd left him, and do you know what he said? The miserable fucker said, 'Oh, okay,' then he asked her if she'd ironed his work clothes. I wanted to go round there and rip him to pieces."

Everyone was appalled, especially the two Russian men. I think Alex and Josh kind of expected it.

"Anyway, her daughter brought a few things to the cottage for her, and Gina seems happier with some of her own stuff around. We'll collect more later in the week."

"I will buy her anything she needs," Sergei declared. "She does not have to go back home and see the man who made her unhappy. You tell her Sergei will not see her cry. Or we could kill him."

"Sergei, just give it a rest with this killing shit! Julia will think we're barbarians," an annoyed Josh yelled from across the room.

"Whatever Gina needs, I'll be the one to buy it. She's mine now, and anything she wants, she gets from me," Nik said. "By the way, Alex, I'll need to see Grayson as soon as possible, so I can put Gina's name on everything I own. And to fast-track her divorce."

"He'll be here on Tuesday with the new contracts, so call him tomorrow and let him know what you need. I need to see him about my assets, too." Alex looked over at me and smiled.

Gina came into the room looking radiant, if not a little sad. She went straight to Nik, which seemed to calm him down. He held her head and kissed her softly, mouthing the words *I love you.* This was not the Nik I was used to. The muscle-bound tough guy was so protective and loving towards Gina, and their love was a beautiful thing to see.

One after the other, everyone in the room descended on Gina, offering hugs and congratulations.

Gregor kissed her cheek, congratulated her, and placed a black velvet box in her hand.

"For you, Gina. A gift to celebrate your Bond with Nikolas."

The box carried the name *Holden & Sons*—an exclusive jeweller based in York.

Gina opened the rectangular box and gasped. "Gregor, this is beautiful, but it must have cost a fortune. You shouldn't have spent all that on me."

"Gina, it is beautiful jewellery for a beautiful woman. When a couple Bond, it is a wonderful thing. It should be celebrated and honoured. Come, let us see how it looks on you."

Gregor fastened the prettiest diamond and gold tennis bracelet I had ever seen over Gina's wrist. As she moved her wrist around, the diamonds caught the lights of the office, reflecting coloured prisms around her arm and hand.

"Thank you, Gregor. I'll cherish this forever," she said. Then she threw her arms around his neck and burst into tears.

Nik went towards them, thanked Gregor, then took Gina from his arms and sat her on his lap.

"Sorry, everyone, I seem to be overemotional today," Gina remarked as Nik kissed her tears away.

"Alex and Julia have decided to Bond next week," gushed Freya. "It's so great to have all this love around us."

I smiled at her warmly. Our news had delighted Freya more than I'd hoped. Gregor, Josh, and Alex all gazed at her with love and affection. She seemed truly happy, and it occurred to me that Freya and true happiness may not always go hand in hand.

"We need to discuss business, then we can go out, drink,

and celebrate all this Bonding," boomed Sergei's voice from behind us.

"We should be ready to submit our initial proposals and building plans to the council by the beginning of next month, all being well," Josh stated while tapping something into his computer.

From the rest of the conversation, I found out that Night Movers and its Russian counterparts had joined forces to open a new supermarket on the outskirts of Rothley. This would be good news for the people of Barrowfield, as they would no longer need to travel ten miles to the nearest one.

It was great to get a gist of what my job would entail, although this was quite an informal gathering. Alex and Gregor were leading the meeting, with both Sergei and Josh throwing figures into the mix.

As intimidating as Gregor could appear, I found that Alex could more than hold his own against him. I have to admit, it was a serious turn-on to see the man I was going to commit to in business mode, and I wondered how I would keep my hands off him during my working week.

Nik didn't appear to have much input at all; he couldn't take his eyes or his hands off Gina. It wasn't long before he stood, made his apologies, and carried Gina out of the room.

"It's the Bonding," explained Alex. "The urge to be alone with each other—to make love and share blood, is so powerful in the first few days. It helps the Bond strengthen and grow." Everyone in the room nodded and murmured their agreement.

Would it be like that for me and Alex when we Bonded? I had to admit it was making me a little anxious. But Alex was smiling at me and what I saw in his eyes made my fears melt away.

I was falling for him in a big way, and his feelings for me were clear and true. He loved me, and as bizarre as it seemed for someone to love me after such a short time, I was happy knowing I meant that much to him.

Josh took a call from his mobile and jumped up from the desk immediately.

"It's Phil Jones—one of the night drivers. He stopped the lorry because there were sheep in the road, and someone set fire to the trailer."

"Is he okay?" asked Alex. "And where did it happen?"

"Yeah, he's fine," Josh said while grabbing his car keys. "He's on the road between Barrowfield and Rothley. He's already called the fire brigade. Phil thinks whoever did it used some sort of accelerant because of how quickly it took hold. He's given up trying to get the sheep through the gate and has gone into the field himself. He's worried if the fire brigade doesn't get there soon, the fuel tank will blow."

"Oh fuck! What did we have in the trailer?" Alex asked as he looked at Josh's computer screen. After a few clicks, he printed off two copies of the delivery invoice, which showed the full contents of the trailer.

Looking through it quickly on his way out of the door, Alex told Josh it was mainly canned foods, although there were also cleaning products that could be flammable, so they would need to give a copy to the fire brigade. The contents were supposed to be going to a supermarket in Staffordshire, and the trailer had been full.

Everyone in the room followed Alex and Josh out of the door. Alex turned to me and Freya, telling us to stay where we were. Gregor agreed.

"We're going with you, Alex," Freya told him adamantly.

"No, Freya. It's too dangerous. I don't want either of you hurt."

"What the hell, Alex? You don't get to decide what I do. I'll keep Julia safe, don't worry."

Alex looked at us both and shook his head before bending to kiss me.

"Just stay far enough back, please."

"I will. But that goes for you, too," I said as we rushed along together to the cars. We could already hear the sirens as we neared the vehicles. Josh called Nik to let him know what was happening and promised to update him when we reached the scene.

Gregor insisted that Freya and I get in his car with him, so Alex and Sergei climbed into Josh's SUV.

Chapter Twenty-Four

Julia

Fire lit up the small village of Barrowfield and its surrounding countryside by the time we arrived, and the police and fire brigade had cordoned off a large area around the burning trailer. When Alex explained about the delivery invoice and the potentially flammable products, they led him to the nearest fire engine, where he spoke to someone in charge.

Phil Jones was sitting with the paramedics, an oxygen mask covering his nose and mouth. Josh went straight over to ask what had happened.

I heard him say he was driving down the road when he came across ten sheep in the middle of it, and the gate to the field was open. He left his hazard lights on and went to herd them through the gate. Phil had got five sheep back into the field when he heard a *whoosh* and saw the back of the trailer go up in flames, so he ran back to the lorry's cab to get his mobile phone to call the fire brigade.

Phil was shaking his head, saying he should have taken the phone with him when he got out. Josh told him he'd done a brave yet stupid thing by returning to the cab because nothing was more important than his life, and we were all happy that he was safe.

I felt Freya tense up beside me before glancing around warily.

"Gregor, do you feel that? Can you scent anything strange?" she questioned.

"Yes! It's another vampire, and they are close."

As quick as a flash, Freya took off to wherever she thought the vampire was. Gregor spat out, "Foolish girl; it could be a threat!" He shouted Sergei over to stay with me before he took off after Freya.

I wondered if it was the same one Alex had mentioned this morning, and I must admit, I got a little freaked out about it. I yelled for Josh and explained what Freya had said before she left, so he called Alex to let him know.

Around ten minutes later, Alex, Freya, and Gregor came towards us, and all three looked puzzled.

"I'm going to stay and sort out the removal of the trailer and cab. It'll probably be late by the time I get back, Julia, so Freya can stay with you at the cottage tonight," Alex said wearily.

"No, it's ok, Alex. I'm going home tonight. I've got some things I need to discuss with my mum and dad."

I knew Alex wasn't happy about it, but he didn't argue. He just nodded his head and walked away.

When I thought about explaining what Bonding with a vampire meant, I decided it wasn't a conversation I wanted to have with my parents. Not without Alex with me, anyway. It was easier to tell them I was going to move in with him.

They were worried it was too soon, but they didn't object. To be honest, it wouldn't have made a difference, anyway. He was like an addictive drug to me, and I craved his presence.

Alex called me later that night. He sounded exhausted and was also extremely worried. The police thought vandals had started the fire in the lorry trailer, but it seemed pretty obvious that the mystery vampire was the one to blame, although he couldn't tell the police that. Apparently, Freya had also thought she recognised the scent, but like Alex, she just couldn't place it. They needed to find the vampire, and soon, before someone associated with Alex, Freya, or the business got hurt.

We decided I'd move in with Alex on Wednesday, which left hardly any time to sort out the things I wanted to take with me.

Most of the items I had from living with Gavin were still in boxes, so transporting them wouldn't be hard. But I hardly wanted any of those things. They were reminders of a past I wasn't yet ready to revisit—one of sadness and failure—and I wanted to look forward to a future filled with hope and love.

Excitement had replaced the anxiousness I'd felt before about rushing into a new relationship. I was lucky to have been given a second chance at love, and I was determined to take it.

Chapter Twenty-Five

Julia

Monday brought fog and rain to our little Yorkshire village, and everyone was talking about the lorry fire. Mr Singh from the post office had taken it upon himself to find out as much information as possible to help with the police enquiry. This meant that my popping in for a few stamps took forever, as he'd found out I was starting work at Night Movers. I thought Mr Singh might have missed his calling in life. When I left the shop, I felt as though I'd been quizzed by an overzealous detective.

When I got to work, my dad was already there and came up to the offices with me. Alex was nowhere to be seen, which I was grateful for. I didn't want my dad to be asking him questions about us moving in together while we were at work.

Maggie got me settled and went through some basic health and safety stuff, like where the fire escapes were and where the alarms were situated. The incident yesterday had

shaken them; it was the first time the company had experienced sabotage of any sort.

My shift was 6 p.m. until 6 a.m., Monday to Thursday, with Friday, Saturday, and Sunday off. I was grateful for the long weekend due to what Alex and I had planned.

The job was much harder than I thought it would be. Due to the trailer fire, Alex had organised extra drivers to follow the lorries from the Barrowfield depot for ten miles, and the logistics of that had everyone busy.

Maggie was patient with me and seemed happy to have another woman in the office with her. Josh and Nik were in and out all evening, helping with the additional security measures, and Alex didn't come in until after midnight. He looked so stressed, which made his grey eyes appear darker than usual. But as soon as he saw me, he smiled and let out a tremendous sigh.

"Hi, Alex. How are you?" I asked, trying to look as concerned for him as I was. But I couldn't stop a huge smile from spreading across my face.

"Much better for seeing my beautiful woman," he said, giving me a look that told me he was thinking of doing anything but work with me tonight.

He made my knees weak, my cheeks flush and my breathing quicken. I reacted to him like a teenager with a crush on her favourite rock star, and it made me want more —from him and from life itself.

"Well, Alex, now you're here, I can take off for my break if that's okay?" Maggie picked up her coat and bag.

"Yeah, Mags, I'll stay, and Nick and Josh will be back soon. By the way, the lads in the yard said they're serving a spicy curry in the canteen tonight."

"Alex, don't tempt me. Not now I'm back on my diet again."

Alex groaned before telling Maggie, "Don't replace the proper biscuits with those low-fat ones again, please. It was like dunking cardboard in my tea."

Maggie laughed and gave me a wave before she closed the door.

"Honestly, Julia. Don't eat the biscuits if she's changed them," he said, going over to the place where the tea and coffee-making facilities were and looking through the cupboard.

Josh came into the office, closely followed by Nik.

"I'll have a cup of tea if you're making one," said Josh. "It's getting cold out there now."

"I was checking the biscuits," Alex replied as he filled up the kettle.

"Oh, fuck no," said Nik, making his way over to Alex and grabbing the biscuit tin. "Maggie better not have swapped the biscuits again," he whined. Nik opened the tin and began sniffing a biscuit before deciding it was safe to eat.

"Was everything all right on the roads?" Alex asked, making his way over to my desk.

"Not a peep or sheep." Josh smiled, but it didn't quite reach his eyes, and the worry in them was plain to see.

"Have you had any more luck identifying the vampire?" I asked. The kettle had finished boiling, so I got up to make the tea.

"No, and it's grating on my nerves," Alex grumbled. "Josh, Nik, and our Russian friends felt no familiarity, but Freya and I did. So that tells us whoever this vampire is, they're likely to be pissed off with either me or Freya. I'm assuming it's me because Freya hadn't experienced this vampire before. And it must be from our past before Josh because he didn't have the familiar feeling that Freya and I had."

"You told me that only Born Immortals can walk in the sun, and each time you sensed something, it was dark. So do you think it's a Made vampire?" I enquired, trying my best to understand all this vampire stuff.

"Not necessarily. Although we do have deliveries leaving the depot in the daytime, so they'd have their pick of lorries if they could be out in daylight. But it would be easier for someone, anyone really, vampire or not, to get away without being seen at night."

Josh leaned forward and spoke to me directly. "I'm a Made vampire, and after I reached my two-hundredth year, I found I could be in the sun for a couple of hours without it harming me. I feel exhausted, and I need more blood than I would normally have to get me fighting fit again. I couldn't risk more exposure than that, but a Made vampire who was much older than me could stay a lot longer in the sun."

"So we can't narrow it down to one or the other, then?" I asked, understanding their frustration.

Nik took a drink of his tea, then said, "Alex, we know it's at least 271 years old, whichever type of vampire it is. Because that's how long Josh has been with you. We know it didn't come here through our transportation, so at some point, it could have been exposed to daylight for travel purposes. So I would say, if it's a Made vampire, it's probably over five hundred years old. Unless, of course, it has a human who can bring them here, like in the old days."

"Or it could be a Born Immortal," Alex said with a sigh, covering his face with his hands.

"Can you think of anyone you've had a major disagreement with recently? Or someone you've known for centuries who would want to harm your business?" I asked. Though I knew everyone else must have asked him those questions.

"Vampires tend not to keep a feud going. If it was a major disagreement, then it would be sorted one way or another, but it wouldn't last for centuries."

The way he said *one way or another* made me wish I'd never asked the question. I knew he meant that one of the parties would be dead. I tried to keep up with the conversation, but after that, I kind of shut down. I was in a room with three vampires who were big and powerful; I felt small and inadequate in their presence.

After a while, I heard, "What do you think, Julia?" which interrupted my thoughts.

"I'm sorry, Alex. I kind of had a blank moment there. What were you saying?"

He came over and knelt beside me, asking, "Are you okay, sweetheart?"

"First night shift I've ever worked. I think I'm flagging." I wasn't totally lying, but I didn't want Alex to have anything else on his mind.

"Welcome to the vampire shift," Josh said as he bared his fangs and laughed. I tensed in my seat. It was the first time I'd seen anyone other than Alex bare their fangs, and it unnerved me.

"Put them away, Joshua Bubbles," Alex ordered, smirking at Josh's subsequent frown.

"Piss off, Alex. Only my little Daisy can call me that," Josh said as he opened up the little plastic bottle.

"It's like working with school kids!" Nik declared while trying to avoid the bubbles that Josh was blowing his way.

Maggie came back to the office with a sandwich and immediately yelled, "Joshua York, put them away!"

"Aww, come on, Mags, lighten up. It's only a few bubbles," he said, blowing them over to her desk.

"I swear to you, Josh, if any of those bubbles get on my monitor screen, you're doing the cleaning. You put too much washing-up liquid in those bubble bottles."

"But that's how you get the best bubbles," Alex insisted. Josh and Nik nodded in agreement.

"Julia, why don't you take your break? I'm sure you've earned it having to put up with these numpties."

Alex grabbed my coat. "Good idea, Mags. I'll take Julia for a quick bite to eat while you stay with the numpties."

"I included you in the numpties, too, Alex."

He laughed and shook his head while helping me into my coat.

"Now, you know I'm your favourite, Mags, and don't deny it."

Nik folded his arms across his chest. "Bullshit, Alex. We all know I'm her favourite."

"You're both wrong, you know. It's so obvious that it's me. But it's okay to be jealous," Josh declared with a smug grin.

Maggie rolled her eyes and sighed. "See what I have to put up with, Julia? They don't pay me enough to work here, I swear."

Chapter Twenty-Six

Alex

I took Julia back to my cottage and offered to make her a quick stir-fry. What I really wanted was to throw her on the bed and bury myself balls deep inside her. But she was feeling tired on her first night shift, and I wouldn't add to that.

We talked about work and what Julia had been doing in the office with Maggie. I got the impression she found the amount of paperwork overwhelming. I reassured her we were busier than usual because of the fire.

Gregor and Sergei had reluctantly flown back to Moscow. They'd wanted to stay and help identify the mystery vampire, but I didn't want to involve any more people in this than necessary.

Freya stayed on because she also sensed some familiarity and was determined to find out who they were and what they wanted. She was currently staying with Josh at his cottage because Julia was moving in with me on Wednesday.

That seemed to be the only thing keeping my head together.

I'd spoken to the farmer whose sheep were on the road, and he told me that the gate had been securely fastened. He'd passed the area two hours before the incident, and the sheep were definitely in the field when he left.

I looked all around the vicinity of the fire in the daytime to see if I could find any clues, but once again, I came away with nothing. This was the Yorkshire Pennines with plenty of rocky outcrops in the hills and dales. It made for a beautiful vista but could easily hide someone if needed. Still, I could scent nothing.

Julia seemed even more out of sorts as the minutes ticked by. When I asked her what was wrong, she said, "Nothing's wrong; I'm just tired." But I knew it was a lie. I felt a little helpless but didn't push her, and we ate our stir fry in silence. She tried to clear the table after our meal, but I placed my hand on hers to stop her. She took in a breath and looked down at our joined hands.

"What's wrong, Julia? And don't tell me it's nothing this time."

She took another deep breath, then looked up at me. After a tense silence, she came around the table to stand in front of me.

"I know I'm technically at work, but I also want to...you know."

Was I getting this right? Did Julia want to fool around with me? I cupped her face in my hands and kissed her before saying, "Why don't you show me what you want?"

Julia pulled her sweater over her head and removed her bra before pulling my head down to her breasts. I didn't need any further instruction. I began licking and sucking on her breasts, drawing her nipples into my mouth. Julia let out an almost pained cry and panted, "Alex, I need you."

I was hard as granite and had us naked within seconds.

When she dropped to her knees and took me in her mouth, I forgot all my worries completely. I tried hard not to grab her hair and pull her forward so I could plough deeper into her mouth, but I failed miserably. She was just too tempting, and all too quickly, I felt that tingling sensation rising inside me.

Although I'd have loved nothing better than coming hard in her mouth, I knew my woman needed something more. So after one more pump of my hips—well, maybe two or three—I pulled her head away, dropped to the floor, and laid her flat on her back with her legs wrapped around my neck.

If I thought her mouth was heaven, I was so wrong. Her tight, wet sex was so heavenly I could hear angels singing every time I thrust deep. I had only been inside Julia for about ten seconds before she came.

Apparently, giving me a blow job had really turned her on.

I was such a lucky bastard.

The kitchen floor wasn't the best place to fuck, but the pure spontaneity of what was happening blew my mind. When Julia's next orgasm came, I was right behind her, and the noises coming from me were twice as loud as hers.

I lowered her legs and collapsed on top of her. Both of us were panting, and sweat rolled from my forehead into my eyes.

"Now there's nothing wrong," she said.

Chapter Twenty-Seven

Julia

The week was rolling on quickly. Before we knew it, Wednesday had arrived, and along with Gina and my parents, we moved most of my belongings into Alex's cottage. It was mine now, too, as Alex kept saying. But I couldn't get my head around that just yet. Not while everything between us was still so new.

Mum loved the cottage, but I was so glad that Alex wasn't around while she was giving it such a thorough inspection.

I left the boxes in one of the spare bedrooms and said I would go through them at the weekend, which gave me an excuse to say I was busy. Alex said we wouldn't be able to stay away from each other when we first Bonded, so I didn't want any surprise visits from my parents.

Gina and I stayed behind on the pretence of getting ready for work, but I couldn't wait to question her about her Bond with Nik.

"Right, Gina, spill the beans," I demanded. "What made you finally get together with Nik?"

"It was a mix of everything. I felt so good on Saturday after I left the salon. When I got home, my kids were dead impressed with my new look, and when my daughter asked my ex... Wow! It feels so good to say ex when I talk about him. Sorry, Julia, where was I? Oh yeah, she asked him what he thought about my new look, and he wasn't the slightest bit interested. He just asked if I was cooking something.

"I wanted to cry, and I could feel the tears welling in my eyes, but when I glanced at my kids, they seemed disgusted with their dad. I saw them share a look—kind of like, *'He's such a bastard to treat her like that,'* and it was a big wake-up call. They knew he didn't love me, and the look they gave me after that was one of sympathy. I couldn't have that, Julia. It was then I decided I wanted what you had with Alex. Even if it was just for one night, I needed someone to act like I was his reason for being. When we got to the Red Lion, and I saw Nik gaze down at me, I knew I could have that forever."

"What was the actual Bonding like? I mean, you had to drink his blood, too. Weren't you worried?" I queried.

"We were a little preoccupied, to be honest. I mean, you do know that you Bond during sex?" she asked, blushing.

"Yeah, sorry, Gina. I didn't mean to pry."

I felt the heat from my own blush all over my face and neck.

"What I meant to ask about is the connection you get... you know, the whole *'I can sense your feelings and emotions.'*"

"Well, it's fantastic in one way. I can sense that he loves me so much it takes my breath away, and whenever he tells me he thinks I'm beautiful or sexy, he really means what he says. That's done wonders for my self-esteem. And when we're having sex, I can feel his pleasure rolling through me, too."

"Wow, really?"

"Oh, yeah, and believe me—sex with Nik is like nothing on this earth. I didn't know it could be like that, Julia. I'd only been with Steve, and I hadn't had sex for years before the night I Bonded with Nik, so I suppose I'm not the best judge. But, *oh wow*! It's perfect."

"I know what you mean. I thought I had a pretty good sex life when things were okay between me and Gavin, but with Alex, it's on a different level, and I can't seem to get enough."

We both burst out laughing, and it took a while for us to compose ourselves.

"There's just one thing with the Bond that's a downer, Julia. You can't hide your emotions. Unless there's a way to do it that Nik hasn't told me about. So if you feel weepy for any reason, they're there to dry your tears, which isn't a bad thing. But when I thought I saw a spider in the bathroom and I was worried it had run up my bathrobe, I didn't even get the chance to scream. Nik nearly broke the door down to get to me. He was scared that something awful had happened. It freaked us both out, to be honest. It was like he thought I'd met Norman Bates in the bathroom, not a spider. As our Bond progresses, Nik said it'll be easier to determine the other's emotions."

"Do you regret the Bond? I mean, you could have just lived with him instead."

"No, I don't regret Bonding with him, Julia. I just regret not doing it sooner."

"I've fallen so hard for Alex," I admitted. "I can't imagine a life without him."

"It's great to be us, isn't it?" Gina said with a smug look on her face, and I wholeheartedly agreed.

I didn't get to see Alex until later that evening. He'd been on a business trip to Norfolk, then went straight to meet Freya at the home that Gregor was having renovated outside Rothley.

There were some issues with the building works that needed to be sorted. Josh said he didn't think it was wise to leave Freya alone with a builder who insisted she wouldn't understand any of the plans because she was *"just a woman."*

Freya told the builder she understood perfectly well how she could dispose of condescending men's bodies without anyone finding out.

By the time Alex walked in, Maggie and I were so busy sorting out the next week's shipping and import papers I could only give him a quick wave from my desk.

He went out of the office for about half an hour, and when he came back, he had a strange look on his face. I couldn't decipher what it meant, so I left my desk and went to stand next to him.

"What's wrong, Alex?"

"I went to the cottage to get changed, and your things are there. Clothes and boxes and stuff."

"I'm sorry. I meant to sort it all out, but I didn't have time before my shift."

Was he annoyed at having to share his space after all these years? I should have sorted more boxes out, but Gina and I had got chatting and the sorting kind of stopped.

"Why would I be annoyed? I finally have you with me every day and night. It's what I've wanted for years. Seeing your things with mine... It's finally all real, and the only thing missing is the Bond. I've hoped for this for so long. I can't wait until we walk into our cottage together later."

Our cottage. It seemed so strange to hear him keep calling it that, but that's what it would be from now on. It was only a couple of weeks since I'd considered putting a deposit on a home of my own. Now here I was again, sharing a home, my life, and my love. I went up on my tiptoes, kissed his cheek and whispered in his ear, "I love you, Alex."

He looked down at me with glassy eyes, took my face in his hands and said, "I love you, too, Julia. I need to take you home and—"

"Sshh." Placing my finger over his lips, I added, "Later, Alex. We have company." My eyes darted over to where Maggie sat staring at us.

"Sorry, Mags. I forgot where we were for a moment," he said.

"No problem, Alex. It's good to see you so happy and in love. It wasn't something I thought I would see in my lifetime. For you *or* Nik. We just have to get Josh and Freya sorted now."

We ate in the cafeteria with my dad. He'd been quite worried about me rushing into things with Alex, but everyone in there could tell that we were in love, and I saw my dad's worries begin to fade the longer he watched us.

Alex and I didn't go to the cottage until our shift finished at 6 a.m., and although I was exhausted, I wanted to make love with him as a proper living-together couple. We said very little to each other beforehand, just washed and kissed each other in the shower. Then we dried off, got into bed and held each other for a few minutes.

When he kissed me again, it was gentle and unhurried, and we made love the same way. Every second of it was utter bliss, and when I came, I thought the world had stopped turning, only to spin out of control until the ripples of pleasure finally eased.

We didn't move position, with Alex still above me, staring into my eyes as he told me he loved me. He made love to me again, saying the words over and over, and I said the same in return.

It was perfect and sweet, and I have never felt more loved and cared for in all my adult life.

Chapter Twenty-Eight

Julia

Before we went to work, I called in at my mum and dad's bungalow to collect a few things I'd forgotten the day before. It was an excuse to see my mum and to arrange for us all to go out for a meal together the weekend after. Alex was going to treat us to a night of dinner and dancing at a converted stately home near Barnsley.

Mum and I sat down with a cup of tea, and from out of nowhere, she said, "I had a phone call from Gavin's mum yesterday."

"Oh, is everything okay?" I asked, wondering why Mum had such an unrepentant look on her face.

"She wanted to let me know that Gavin is seeing a lovely girl who works in the office with him. She's the daughter of one of her friends, apparently."

"Is it Katy from accounts?"

"Yes, I think that was her name."

"Wow! She's only twenty-one," I said, looking at Mum

and wondering why she couldn't hold my gaze. "What did you say to that news, Mum?"

"I told her you'd moved in with your boyfriend. I said you were both very much in love, and I thought you'd get married to Alex as soon as your divorce came through," Mum replied sheepishly.

"Okay... What did she say to that news?"

"Well, she sounded shocked and annoyed, and I'm glad. I can't stand the woman. Never could. She was always trying to get one over on us—always looking down on your father and me because we weren't as well off as they were. I'm glad we have nothing to do with them anymore. I also might have mentioned that Alex was a multi-millionaire and owner of Night Movers."

"I'm sure she knows who Night Movers are, Mum. They're in a similar business, after all."

"Are you mad at me for telling her about you moving in with Alex?"

"No, not at all. And before you ask, I'm not upset that Gavin has a girlfriend, either."

"She said it was a bit sudden you moving in with him, but I said you'd been seeing him for a good while. I didn't specify a date, though. I don't know if she'll contact you or if Gavin will."

"Mum, it's got nothing to do with any of the Laytons, so don't worry about it," I told her as I placed my hand on hers.

"Gavin doesn't contact me now because we don't have anything to say to each other anymore. I don't wish him or his family any ill will, but if I never spoke to any of them again, it wouldn't bother me," I said truthfully. "When they phoned before, it used to upset me, and I'd cry after I'd spoken to them. You have to give yourself time to grieve during an amicable divorce because you're losing people who've been your family. But as time moves on, you start to think and feel differently. I hope Gavin finds love like I have. He deserves to be happy the same as I do."

"I'm so glad to see you like this, Julia. You were in such a bad way when you came back to live with us, and we were so worried about you. I suppose we have Alex to thank for that."

"I can't deny that Alex helped save me from the depressive state I'd fallen into. But I also think I was ready for this change in myself. It's like I'm a new me—someone who embraces change and looks towards the future instead of clinging to the past. I didn't like the person I'd become, so it was time to change. Alex just hurried it along."

"Do you get along with everyone else at Night Movers?"

"Yes, I do, very much. They're like a big family. Gina has been great, and I get on well with Josh, Nik, and Freya. And the two Russians, Sergei and Gregor."

"Ooh, I met Gregor at one of the work parties your dad took me to. He's really handsome, tall and manly, and sooo sexy..."

"Mum! I did not just witness you lusting after Gregor," I spluttered, laughing at the dreamy look on her face.

"Yes, you did, and I think every woman in the room was going weak at the knees for him and the rest of those guys. But Gregor seemed to have that dangerous edge to him and... you know."

"What do I know, Mum?" I prompted as she fanned her face with the lid from the biscuit tin.

"Well, if I'd been younger and single, I would have definitely gone for some of that." Mum winked and carried on fanning her face.

I laughed so hard at my mum's dreamy yet embarrassed

look that I nearly wet myself, and after a few moments, she laughed along with me.

I was enjoying all the girly conversations I was having with my mum. I felt that we were becoming a lot closer than we had been previously.

I left home for university when I was eighteen, then moved to live with Gavin straight after. So I hadn't spent much time as an adult with my parents unless Gavin and I were visiting—or if they came to us. That time was always shared; we were rarely on our own.

When I came back home after the accident, I wasn't good at communicating my feelings with either Mum or Dad. I made a silent promise to myself right then: I would build a better, closer relationship with my parents, especially my mum.

We packed a few more of my things together, and I took them to my car. As I placed them on the back seat, I felt I was being watched.

I turned to my left and saw a tall man with blond hair looking my way. He was wearing a black, Barbour-style wax jacket with the collar up so it covered his nose and mouth. He made it obvious he was watching me and didn't move at all.

The man was leaning against the bushes surrounding the neighbour's garden, about twenty-five feet from my car. At first, I froze, not knowing whether to get in my car or run back into my parents' bungalow.

In the end, I did neither. I started questioning him instead.

"Hey, who are you? What do you want?"

He stood as still as a statue, but I couldn't make out anything else about him because it was getting dark. Stepping away from my car, I took my phone out of my pocket and called Alex.

The man moved away when I put the phone to my ear. And when I say move, it was super quick. Inhumanly so.

Alex answered, and at first, I couldn't speak; I was too busy looking around, trying to make sense of what I'd just witnessed. But after hearing a car engine start close by, I finally found my voice.

"Alex, there was a man watching me outside my mum and dad's bungalow. He's gone now, but he was staring and—"

"Julia, where are you now? Are you still at your parents'?" There was panic and fear in Alex's voice, but I chose to ignore it.

"Yes, I'm outside. He's just got in a car around the corner. Hang on; I think he's driving away."

"For fuck's sake, Julia, get in your parents' home. Now!" Alex yelled. I could hear him telling Josh what I'd said. Then I heard the sounds of gravel crunching underfoot and the familiar sound of his SUV starting up.

A car came from the junction at the side of my parents' home and drove away up the street. I recognised the type of vehicle; Gavin had one as a company car last year.

"Alex, he's driving a Vauxhall Insignia, registration number NE64 U... something something. Sorry, I can't see the rest. Oh, hang on," I said as I ran onto the road. "It's UBL."

"Please, Julia, just do as I tell you. Go inside right fucking now!"

The last bit came out as a growl, bringing me back down to earth with a bang. I hung up the phone but still didn't move. Mum came outside and asked if everything was all right. I nodded my head because words failed me.

She put her arms around me and said I looked like I'd seen a ghost. Not a ghost, Mum, I thought.

A vampire.

A centuries-old immortal who'd been following Alex.

That had set fire to the lorry trailer.

And was now following me.

That was when the fear hit me, and I started shaking. I seemed rooted to the spot, and it took some effort for Mum to get me back into her kitchen.

"Julia, you feel ice cold. What's the matter? Are you feeling ill? Talk to me, love. You were fine when you left."

"I'm okay now, Mum. I thought I saw someone watching me. I shouted, but they ran away, and it scared me a little, that's all."

"I'll call the police. Did you get a good look at them?"

"No, Mum, I didn't. It's probably nothing. I've called Alex, and that car door you've just heard slamming is probably him now."

It was Alex. He came storming in, followed by Josh. He picked me up from the chair I was sitting in and hugged me tightly.

"God, Julia, I was so scared. He didn't hurt you, did he?"

"No, Alex, I'm fine, I swear. I'm just a little shaken, that's all."

"What's going on here, Julia? There's much more to this than you're letting on." Mum was really worried, and I wasn't sure what to tell her.

"Sue, it's nothing to worry about, I promise," Alex assured her. Yet the tone of his voice told a different story.

"Hang on a minute, Alex. If someone is stalking my

daughter, I need to know about it. Just because she lives with you now doesn't mean I can't look after her. And I say we should call the police."

Mum looked so angry she even frightened me. I could see Alex trying to calm himself, but it was a slow process. And Mum staring him down wasn't helping in the least.

"I'm sorry if I offended you. You have every right to be concerned, and I didn't want to keep you out of the loop. The thing is, I think someone's targeting the business—me in particular. And I think because they've seen me with Julia, she could now become a target herself," Alex told her.

"What do you mean by a target? Oh my God, you mean like the trailer fire the other night? Julia, you need to come home until they find this person."

Josh stepped forward and spoke to Mum, looking directly into her eyes.

"Sue, there was no one watching Julia. It was just a misunderstanding. We came to pick Julia up because she was having some problems with her car. It wouldn't start, so you brought her back inside. I will have a look at it, and Alex can take her home."

Mind control! I wasn't sure how I felt about him using it on her, but when I saw my mother's worried expression change to a smile, I felt relieved. I didn't want this keeping her up at night.

"Would you like some tea, Josh? It's cold outside, so I'm sure a nice hot brew will keep you warm while you look at the car. Can I persuade you to have a cuppa, Alex?" Mum asked.

"No thanks, Sue. Julia and I have to go to work. We can pop round again soon, though."

"That will be lovely. Make sure you do." Mum smiled.

We said our goodbyes, and Alex threw Josh my car keys as he guided me to his car.

"See you back at the office," Josh said.

"No, we're going back to the cottage. Look up the car reg plate and see what you can find," Alex barked.

"Calm down, Alex. It won't do us any good if we can't keep our heads about this," Josh insisted.

"When we find the bastard, it will be him that won't keep his head," Alex growled.

"Don't take it out on Julia. This isn't her doing," Josh said before he got into my car. The concerned look on his face made me nervous.

Alex put the keys in the ignition but didn't turn them. He took slow, deep breaths as if to keep himself focused. He appeared both anxious and angry, his fingers drumming rapidly on the steering wheel.

Though I was still quite shaken, I didn't regret my actions because we finally had information about the mysterious vampire, so I wouldn't apologise for ignoring Alex. Instead, I sat back in my seat and waited for him to take us home.

Chapter Twenty-Nine

Julia

We'd been driving a couple of minutes before I dared speak. "Do you want me to descri—"

"Don't," yelled Alex. "I can't deal with this right now."

Again came the deep breaths and pinched expression. I could feel the tension rolling off his body in thick, icy waves. I didn't know what else to do, so I kept quiet and stared at the road ahead.

We drove through security at the compound and down the small lane to the cottages at the back. It was dark now, and although the area around the cottages was well-lit, it still felt like someone was waiting to step out of the shadows. So I took my time taking my seatbelt off while I looked all around. What I didn't expect was Alex to grab me out of my seat and more or less drag me to the front door.

"Alex, what the hell are you doing? I nearly fell."

"Just do as I say for once and get inside, Julia," he yelled. As soon as we got inside, Alex slammed the front door behind us and pushed me up against the wall. He didn't switch on the light.

"Why didn't you listen to me and go straight inside your parents' home, Julia?" he questioned, breathing heavily. "Why did you blatantly disregard your own safety and try to play detective?"

"Alex, it wasn't like that at all. I didn't think about the danger I was in. I saw him staring, so I shouted at him. When he disappeared, I looked where he went, then I heard and saw the car, that's all."

"That's all? You had time to shout at him. To find out the type of car he was driving, and you can't see how stupid that was?"

"Alex, I'm not stupid. It's just that I was shocked when I saw the man watching me."

"You didn't see a man, Julia. You saw this!"

Alex flicked the light switch at the side of us, and when my vision adjusted, I looked up to see silvery eyes with red rims. His fangs were so clearly visible that they protruded below his lower lip.

"Alex, why are you being like this? Don't you think I've had enough of a shock today?"

I wasn't sure what to make of his behaviour, but I didn't like it one bit.

"You should have fled indoors and armed yourself, Julia. You should have listened to me. I was trying to keep you safe, but you thought you could take him on."

"No, Alex, you've got it all wrong. I think the shock kicked in at first and controlled my actions. The fear didn't come until he'd gone."

Alex's grip on me tightened as he pressed me further to the wall. I felt the back of my neck grow damp with sweat.

"Fear should have been the first thing you felt. It

would've taken nothing for that vampire to rip out your throat." He bent his head to inhale around my throat and lick my damp neck, allowing his fangs to graze the skin.

"Or he could have gutted you with his claws," Alex growled. His nails turned to claws before my eyes, and then he ripped my dress straight down the middle.

I couldn't understand why he was being like this. Did he want to scare me away? If that was his intent, he was doing a good job.

Alex placed his hand against my chest and let his claws tear through my bra. My knickers and tights received the same treatment.

"I can smell your fear, Julia. Think about how you are feeling now; multiply that by a thousand, and you'll still not be anywhere near how scared I was when I took that phone call today, knowing you weren't taking yourself to safety. It's like you wanted me to suffer."

He leaned in close and ran his lips up and down the side of my face, inhaling deeply, taking in my scent. I could feel his erection straining against the fabric of his jeans, and the need for him hit me hard.

"If anything happened to you, Julia, I wouldn't survive. You are my woman, my hope, and my future. I can't be without you; don't you get that?"

I ground my sex against his leg and kissed him hard. I felt his fangs against my lips, but I didn't stop. Despite his actions tonight, I knew he wouldn't hurt me.

When his grip on me released, I shook off my coat and shredded clothing. Then I unzipped my boots and kicked them to the side, my ripped tights following.

Alex was staring at me. His eyes were still that startling silver grey with deep red rims, and his fangs were exposed, although he no longer had claws.

This was the man, the vampire, the immortal I'd agreed to spend my life with, but although there was still a tiny amount of fear running through me, it was quickly overtaken by lust. I placed my hands on his shoulders and my head against his heart. I wanted him to hold me, but he still wouldn't move.

"Alex, please, come back to me. I wasn't hurt, and you came for me. Protected me. I'll be more careful next time, I promise."

"If you were already mine, I'd have known you were in danger by sensing your fear. I could have been there sooner, so you wouldn't have had the chance to act so foolishly and put yourself at risk," he grumbled.

I was getting angry now. Sick and tired of repeating myself for my words to just be ignored. And I was standing here naked, for crying out loud! Well, if Alex didn't want me, I wasn't going to hang around.

I let go of his hand and stepped away from him. He grabbed my arm and pulled me back.

"Where do you think you are going?" Alex's tone was menacing.

"I'm going to get dressed. We're late for work."

"We won't be going to work, Julia. We'll not be leaving this cottage for some time."

"What do you mean?" I asked, glancing up at him warily.

"Tonight, you are mine, Julia. Body and soul. And I will be yours; to have and to hold; till my death do us part. Because I swear, I will protect you with everything I have so that nothing will ever hurt you." With those words, Alex carried me to the bedroom and kicked the door closed.

I watched him remove his clothing. His actions were slow and steady, his silver and red eyes never leaving mine,

the determination clear. I knew he wouldn't be swayed from whatever he wanted tonight.

Alex came towards me and ran the fingers of his right hand over my breasts, leaving out my nipples. Then he ran his hands over the rest of my body, everywhere but my sex. He turned me around and did the same on my back, arms, and legs, then back up again until he reached my bottom. Gripping my cheeks in his hands, he kneaded them firmly before parting them and stroking in between.

"I'm going to have all of you, Julia, including this. And you're going to love it. Demand it. Like you do when I'm fucking you here." His other hand moved lower, and he slipped a finger inside my sex. Thank God his claws had disappeared!

A gasp escaped me, and I wanted him to continue, but he removed his finger and came around to my front again. Alex lifted me with ease and dropped me in the middle of the bed. I bounced a little awkwardly, and his eyes fixed on the movement of my breasts. He climbed on the bed over me, and I reached out to run my hands down his chest, but he grabbed them and pinned them above my head.

I gasped when his head dipped as he took my nipple into his mouth. The sucking and tugging reverberated through my body, ending up at my clit. I tried to free my arms from his hold to pull his body against mine, but I couldn't. The more I struggled against him, the firmer his grasp became. Still, he kept sucking and tugging on each of my nipples, and I could feel the wetness from my sex coating the inside of my thighs.

He brought my hands down to my sides and pinned them there. In his eyes, I saw a myriad of emotions, yet his face was impassive. I licked my lips, and the colour of his eyes almost seemed to glow. The silver inside his red-rimmed irises was mesmerising, and I found myself wanting to lick all around his fangs.

I don't know what that said about me, or my sanity, but I wasn't in the least bit bothered anyhow. He was mine, and I would take him any way I could.

Alex placed kisses all over my belly and followed them with little brushes of his fangs. When his mouth ended up just above my mound, I thought my heart would beat out of my chest.

I heard Alex let out a throaty chuckle, then his head dipped lower, and his lips went straight to my clit. He sucked hard, then licked a figure eight motion rapidly without stopping. I came screaming with my hands pinned to my sides, unable to move anything but my head.

Alex dipped his head lower, thrusting his tongue inside me, and I wasn't the only one moaning this time. I raised my head to look down at Alex and saw he was enjoying this as much as I was. That, combined with the magic he was creating with his tongue, set me off again. This time, I felt my whole body become boneless, and I didn't have the strength to move anymore.

Alex let go of my hands and crawled up my body, guiding his throbbing length inside me as he went. His movements were firm and deep, and it was pure bliss. Yet he didn't hold me like he usually did. He created distance between our upper bodies by propping up on his hands with his arms extended. I needed more. I wanted all of him.

I wrapped my arms around Alex's neck, trying to pull him against me. But he wasn't having any of it.

"Why won't you let me hold you, Alex?" I asked, frustration seeping through my lust-filled haze.

Alex stopped moving, and his vampire gaze met mine. "I'm trying to hold back from forcing you, Julia, and it's getting harder to do each time my body moves within yours."

"How can you be forcing me, Alex? I *want* to have sex with you. God only knows how hard I have to try not to jump your bones on an hourly basis," I said, smiling as I reached up to touch his face.

"You don't understand. I want something so bad right now that I was going to force it on you. And I can't do that. But right here and now, I want you to do my bidding."

"Alex, whatever you want tonight, just tell me, and I'll do it."

For a moment, Alex said nothing, then he let out a sigh and closed his eyes.

"I want you to Bond with me, Julia. Not tomorrow, tonight. Now, in fact. I want you to take my blood as I take yours. I will hold you and give you my love for all eternity. I want you to become pregnant with my child and for us to be a family. I want everything with you, for always. Will you do this with me?"

"Yes, Alex," I said as I wrapped my legs around him and pulled him closer. "Just show me what you need me to do."

He looked at me a few moments longer, and in that time, his eyes changed from silver and red back to his beautiful grey. He leaned down to kiss me and wrapped his arms around me. My emotions were all over the place, but his kiss kept me centred.

When he moved again, it was slow and deep. My hips rose to meet each thrust, our kiss never-ending, despite the breathy sounds coming from my mouth. When I felt the familiar throbbing of a building orgasm, I looked into his eyes and silently acknowledged what needed to happen next.

Alex tilted his head to the right and cut into the side of

his neck with a nail he extended into a claw. At first, I hesitated when I saw the blood running from his neck to his chest, but he lifted my head and guided my mouth to the cut.

I fastened my mouth around it and took my first suck—the metallic taste familiar and so very addictive. From the very first drop, I knew I wanted more, so I took it, swallowing it down in frantic gulps. Alex moaned out his pleasure.

Seconds later, his fangs slid deep into the carotid artery in my neck. The sharp pain was fleeting, quickly morphing into ecstasy. As he drank me down, every erogenous zone on my body heated, throbbing incessantly, as though being stimulated all at once by unseen hands, fingers and tongues. For a moment, I could hardly breathe—like something had sucked all the air out of the atmosphere. Then my orgasm hit.

Pleasure like I had never felt before rolled through my body in turbulent, never-ending waves. I let go of Alex's neck and screamed his name over and over.

The pleasure intensified when Alex's orgasm quickly followed my own. I felt him in my head, my body, and more importantly, in my heart—a connection building second by second, like the thudding of a heartbeat.

We were both still panting when he rolled us over, and then we lay on our sides facing each other. Alex stroked the damp hair out of my face and pressed a kiss to my forehead. I had to keep touching him because not doing so didn't feel right.

His hand was still in my hair, stroking away, and I heard him say, "*I love you*," yet his mouth didn't move at all.

"I love you too, Alex," I told him. But I couldn't stop the confusion creeping over my face.

"Did you hear me say that to you?" I thought I heard him say. Although, again, his mouth never moved.

"Yes, I heard you say it, but your mouth didn't move."

"It's the Bond," he stated. "Sometimes, in the beginning, you can only sense each other and communicating telepathically comes later. Our Bond must be strong from the start if you can hear me now."

"Will you be able to hear me?" I asked hopefully.

"I don't know. Why don't we try it?"

In my head, I told him he had to buy me a new dress for ruining the one I wore today; then I waited to see if his expression changed.

It didn't change.

He didn't say anything back.

Disappointed, I asked, "You couldn't hear me, Alex. Does that mean the Bond hasn't worked for you?"

He kept a serious face for a few more seconds, then burst out laughing.

"You can have as many new dresses as you want, my love, as long as you don't mind me tearing them off you."

"Oh, you rotten sod, Alex. It really upset me when I thought it was all one-sided," I chided as I slapped him across the backside in a loud, hard wallop.

"Ouch!" he yelped. "You little minx. If anyone deserves a spanking, it's you, Julia, for not listening to your lord and master today."

He grabbed me, rolled me onto my belly, and slapped me hard across my bottom.

"Oww!"

"Take your punishment like the good girl you're not," he said as he quickly slapped me twice more on each buttock.

"Oh, fuck. Her arse cheeks are jiggling with each slap," I heard Alex say inside his head.

"I heard that," I said out loud as I turned my head to glare at him. But what I saw in his eyes and sensed through our Bond surprised me.

Alex was hugely turned on.

He licked his lips and ran his hand over my bottom in a light caress. Then he bent over and licked each cheek where his handprints were.

I could hear his voice in my head, telling me he wanted to lift me onto my hands and knees and fuck me hard and deep. So I knelt on all fours, put two pillows under my hips, and told him in my thoughts that I wanted him to do it.

I couldn't believe how quickly the need had spiralled inside me, but I also felt Alex's need, and I knew our Bond was the cause of my libido going from zero to sixty in two seconds flat. I would never survive this Bond. I was beyond help; I was sure of it.

"Oh, I know what you mean, Julia. If you can die from a hard-on, then I'm pretty sure I'm done for," Alex said. Then he slapped each arse cheek again before sinking his cock deep inside me, groaning as my wet heat enveloped him.

"I wish I had fangs so I could bite you again," I thought. Or did I say it out loud? At this point, I wasn't so sure. However I'd said it, Alex heard me. He bent over me, caging my body with his, then whispered in my ear, "You can have my blood, Julia. But I want to hear you beg for it."

I could tell from the Bond that this was something he truly desired. And though I wanted to rebel, I gave in, and in a breathy voice, I begged, "Please, Alex, let me have your blood."

Alex roared and took hold of my shoulders to slam into

me even harder. I cried out his name, on the verge of orgasm yet again. Alex stopped his movements and ran his hands down my back until he came to my bottom. He reached underneath me with one hand and ran his fingers from my clit down to where his cock met my entrance, running them around his shaft as it slowly slipped in and out of me. Then he brought his wet fingers back to my arse and rubbed them against my puckered hole.

I stilled.

I'd never had anal sex. Gavin wanted to try it, and we talked about it once or twice during sex, but we never actually did it. I wasn't sure Alex would fit in there either, not without splitting me in two. But he kept rubbing his finger against me, and I found myself enjoying it more and more.

Alex whispered, "I'm glad I'm the only one to fuck you here." Then he pushed a finger past the ring of muscle at the same time as he slid his cock back inside me. I tried not to tense up, but the movement was involuntary. I couldn't help it.

"Try to relax, my love. When I push in, you push back on me," Alex said breathlessly. I did as he asked, and two fingers invaded me this time. It felt good, better than I thought it was going to feel.

"You are so beautiful, Julia, all stretched out before me, my cock sliding in and out of you and my fingers fucking your arse. But I want you to take my cock in there."

He was still thrusting both his cock and his fingers inside me while he spoke. I pushed back onto him to take more, but he removed his fingers and his cock simultaneously.

Then he pushed the head of his cock past that tight ring. The stretching stung a little and left behind a burning pain that caused me to tense up. I cried out, so Alex paused for a few seconds. I heard him in my head, saying how fucking sexy it was seeing the head of his cock where no man had been before, and he swore he'd make this good for me.

He told me to breathe in and out slowly, and I complied, feeling his wet cock push further past the almost painful barrier. Then the feeling began to change. It morphed from pain to pleasure, although a dark pleasure, one I was sure I shouldn't like.

But I did like it. The deep grunts and groans coming from Alex thrilled me, and I found myself wanting more of this sinful act. Alex was in my head, reading my thoughts, and began moving more forcefully. I was enjoying this way too much and kept pushing back on him, taking him deeper than I ever thought possible.

I sensed the change in Alex as his climax built, and I knew what would take him over the edge, hard.

"Alex, please, let me have your blood. I need you."

He leaned over me, pressing me into the mattress while fucking me deep, then he bit into his wrist and placed it against my mouth. I sucked hard on the bite, and he almost screamed out his release before biting down on my shoulder and losing himself in the taste of my blood. This, combined with my clit rubbing against the pillows, triggered my own climax. The sensation of coming with his cock buried deep in my arse felt strange yet so good, and I knew I wouldn't be opposed to doing this again.

"Well, that's good to know, love," he said as his softened cock slid out of me.

"Stop invading my thoughts, Alex. Can't a woman have some privacy?"

"I couldn't help it. The stuff that went through your head when you thought you shouldn't enjoy it, but you obviously loved it made me come like a rocket."

"You're a bad boy, Alex Staithes. But you're my bad boy," I said, smiling. "But you can't have what we just did all the time. I don't think my poor arse could handle it."

Alex laughed and pulled me towards him. "Come on; we need a shower. And because you've made all my fantasies come true, I'm going to wash and tease every inch of your body until you're humming with pleasure."

Chapter Thirty

Alex

After taking a leisurely shower with Julia, we both dried off and settled on the bed. I held her naked body in my arms, and I should have felt at peace, but I was still so worried about the encounter she'd had with the vampire who'd followed her.

"Alex, I'm worried about my mum and dad. This vampire knows where they live. What if he goes back?"

"Do you think they could pack up and go on holiday tonight?" I asked.

"Well, yes, but it's a bit short notice. And my dad will be at work now, so he'll need to arrange time off. What would we tell them?"

"I'll text Josh to sort out two weeks paid holiday for your father. We can tell them one of our clients has given us the use of a villa, but none of us can go. I can get one of our planes ready. Or we could get them a package deal with a hotel and flight to somewhere nice. You choose."

Julia left my arms and climbed off the bed. "I'll get my purse and book them an all-inclusive late deal for tonight or first thing in the morning."

"I'll pay. My cards are in there," I said, passing her my wallet.

"I'll pay for it, Alex. I have the money from my share of my old house, so it's no big deal."

"It's a big deal for me," I told her as I walked over to where she sat. She'd put on a bathrobe and switched on her laptop.

"Alex, I was saving that money towards a deposit for a house, but I'm living with you now, so I no longer need it."

"I'll pay for this, Julia," I insisted, "and everything else we buy. I have more money than I could ever spend, so let me do this for your parents and provide for us, too."

Julia stared me down but gave in after I got a text back from Josh. It said George Browne's holidays were now in place, and his shifts had been covered.

She found a holiday in Lanzarote at a five-star all-inclusive hotel, and the flight left at 7 a.m. from Doncaster Sheffield Airport.

"I'd better ring Mum and Dad to let them know," Julia said with a smile. She seemed pretty excited, and I could sense through our connection that she'd like us to go, too. I made a note of the hotel so we could holiday there when the threat from this vampire had ceased.

I laughed to myself when I heard the disbelief in her mum's voice when Julia told them about the free holiday they were getting, courtesy of a made-up client. Her mum went from excitement for a holiday to panic that they wouldn't be able to get everything packed in time. She was anxious that she wouldn't be able to fit back into the dresses from her last holiday, and she was worried that Julia was hiding something, too.

Sue Browne was very perceptive, and Julia was finding it hard to lie to her mother. So I asked to take the phone from Julia, then spoke to Sue myself.

"Hi, Sue, it's Alex. Thanks for taking this holiday for us. I know it's short notice, but the client has offered us a room at this hotel before, and we had to turn him down, so I'm glad you and George could take the trip for Night Movers. George is a valued member of our team, and I'm sure he'll welcome the break. I've booked you a flight from Doncaster in the morning, so I won't keep you as I'm sure you have a lot of packing to do."

We said our goodbyes and I winked at Julia. She had a wary look about her, and in her mind she was thinking that lying came easily to me.

"I've had a lot of practice in the art of deceiving people, Julia. It comes with being immortal. There are few people who know what we are—for their sake and ours. But we live alongside the human population, so we have to make up various reasons why we don't age, and why Made vampires avoid the sun. You can use mind control but not on a grand scale, so a few white lies here and there stop questions being asked that could cause us problems.

"For instance, Mr Singh and others in the village think Josh, Nik, and I inherited this business from each of our fathers a few years ago. You will hear Mr Singh say how I look exactly like my father, apart from the fact that he thinks my father wore glasses and had a squint. Mind control, a few white lies and no public photographs. Small steps, but otherwise, we wouldn't have been able to keep the business going in the village."

Julia shook her head. "I just hate lying to my mum. And now we have to go through it all again with my dad."

"I don't think they're in danger from this vampire, Julia," I reassured her. "But I don't want to take any risks. We can drive by later to see if he's still hanging around if you want."

"Thanks, Alex. Now give me the phone so we can get my dad home to help Mum pack."

George was easier to convince than his wife. I told him to drop by the office to collect something and got Josh to get a thousand euros out of the safe for him, along with the E-tickets Julia had emailed him to print off. If I knew George, he wouldn't want to take the money, but Josh was to tell him it was a gift from the client. I wasn't sure what the Brownes' financial situation was, but I knew that holidaying in Europe didn't come cheap.

When Julia handed me a cup of tea, I suddenly felt deflated.

"Did you want coffee instead?" Julia asked, sensing my disappointment.

"No, love, tea is fine. I just imagined that when we Bonded, it would be an all-night thing, with candles and other romantic, sexy stuff, making it a night we'd both remember. Instead, we're drinking tea and trying to stay one step ahead of this vampire stalker."

Julia giggled. "Alex, I don't think romance entered into what we did at all, but you have a lifetime to make up for that. The sexy part was off the charts good and extremely naughty, so I guarantee I'll remember this night forever."

I was about to ask her to take off her robe when I received a text message from Josh, telling me he'd had news about the car Julia saw the vampire drive away in.

I called Josh and put him on speakerphone. He said the

car came from a hire service based at Manchester Airport. He was trying to get the name of who'd hired the car so he could try to see where he'd flown in from. I knew this would be tricky, but Josh said that once he had a name, he'd get in touch with Viktor over in Russia.

Viktor was an extremely introverted vampire and an essential part of Gregor and Sergei's team. Although he was an equal partner, in general, he preferred to avoid business meetings.

We'd joined part of our business with the Russian team in the last ten years but still operated under separate umbrellas, as it were. This stopped anyone from either country looking into our businesses in too much detail. When you're around for hundreds of years, it's best not to draw attention to yourselves if you can help it.

Viktor was an IT genius, and I don't think he'd found a computer system yet that he couldn't hack. I know he's worked for various government agencies in the past, and his knowledge and skills are in high demand.

Viktor was known by many different personas, which kept his real identity hidden from all but those closest to him. He and Josh were good friends, and it was because of Viktor that Josh was so good with computers and technology.

Julia went to the wardrobe and took out trousers and a sweater, before going to the chest of drawers and taking out her underwear.

I ended the call and asked her what she was doing.

"What does it look like I'm doing, Alex?" Julia replied as she pulled on her underwear.

I strode over to where she stood and slipped my arms around her waist, feeling her soft skin beneath my fingertips.

My cock had gone from semi-hard to hard when she bent over to put on her knickers, and I couldn't help but press the hard ridge against her bottom to let her know my intentions.

"Oh no, mister," Julia chided as she stepped out of my arms. "You can forget about sex until we get more information about this vampire. I want to make sure he's left the country so I can relax again."

She was deadly serious. I didn't need to see the determined set of her jaw to know that. The Bond told me that Julia wasn't willing to budge on this, no matter what I did. I stepped towards her and tilted her chin so that she looked into my eyes. Julia read the need in them and softened towards me.

"Alex, I know you want to make love to me and make all this disappear from our thoughts, but it will only be a temporary fix, and I need something more. I need to be proactive in eradicating this threat. That's what made me want to get that number plate, and now we have a lead on the car. Let's get over to Josh and Nik and see if we can make a bit more progress tonight. We have the rest of our lives to make love, and I'll enjoy every moment you spend seeing to all my sexual needs."

Julia winked and stepped back to put on her trousers and sweater.

I didn't say anything to her; just watching the way her body moved bewitched me. The emerald green sweater brought out the blue in her eyes and the highlights in her hair, just like the dress she'd worn last week. I decided to buy her an emerald pendant and a diamond engagement ring if she'd wear them. Julia didn't seem to wear much jewellery.

"Yes, I'd wear them, Alex. But if you're going to

propose to me, then I suggest you wait until my divorce comes through."

"Damn, I forgot you can hear my thoughts. I need to get the hang of this telepathy business, or I'll never be able to surprise you with anything. I think because it's so new, we can't put a block up yet."

"What do you mean by a block?" she questioned curiously.

"We should be able to select when we communicate telepathically. Like when you choose to speak or stay quiet. At the moment, it's pretty full-on because the Bond is so new and seems so strong right away. Some Bonded couples wait weeks for this to happen."

"I suppose that makes us special, then. But when I think about our relationship, everything about us has happened so quickly. I'm happy about it, though, and I know you are, too."

"I am. If it weren't for this mysterious fucking vampire, everything would be perfect," I grumbled.

"That's exactly my point. So get dressed, and let's go see Josh and get some answers."

Twenty minutes later, we walked into the offices. Nik and Josh sensed our Bond immediately and came to hug Julia and shake my hand.

Maggie got all teary and hugged us both for what seemed like forever before she went to the bathroom to sort out her makeup. Because of her tears, most of it had ended up on my black shirt, and I was trying to wipe it off with a tissue.

I loved Maggie dearly and wished I could keep her with

us always. She'd chosen to grow old with her husband and family over the immortality we offered, and I couldn't blame her. Although, selfishly, I wished she would reconsider.

"We checked the car hire firm, and the man who hired the car that Julia saw was called Brian Vargan. Does that name ring any bells with you?" Nik asked.

"No, not at all," I told him. "The surname sounds German, definitely European anyway."

"I rang Freya. She doesn't know the name either," Josh remarked while rubbing the stubble around his jaw. "Of course, we've all chosen different names to adapt to immortal life in whichever country we live in. I did it, and so did you, Alex. So the name may not be any help at all."

He was right, of course. I don't think my Nordic name would fit in so well in Yorkshire. Josh's mobile started ringing, and he announced that it was Viktor on the line. He put Viktor on speakerphone and asked him what he'd found.

"Hello, my friends. I have some strange news for you."

"Go ahead, Viktor, and thanks for your help, by the way," I said, leaning in towards the phone.

"No problem, Alex. I hope you are all well. I hear you have a woman now. Gregor says she is very beautiful, but Sergei tells me she kisses women."

Everyone in the office laughed while Julia groaned. "I'm never drinking with Sergei again," she said, shaking her head.

"Ah, is this Julia I hear now?" asked Viktor.

"Yes. Hello, Viktor."

"Hello, Julia. You must come to Russia soon and visit with us."

"Julia and I Bonded tonight, Viktor," I told him. I couldn't hide the pride and love in my voice even if I tried.

"That is great news, my friend. I am happy for you. I must tell Gregor and Sergei. Unfortunately, I cannot pass the news on to Ivan as he is still missing, and even I cannot trace him. Although, I am sure he will turn up soon. He always does."

"What did you find for us, Viktor?" Josh asked.

"This car we traced to the airport, yes?"

"Yes, Manchester," replied Josh.

"Well, the name on the hire paper, Brian Vargan, no one of this name has flown in through Manchester Airport in the last two months."

Josh and Nik both looked at me and then back towards the phone.

"I assume you have more news for us, Viktor?"

"Yes, my friends. I checked every other airport in the UK, starting with those closest to you, and still came up with nothing. But then I checked the ferry ports and found that a Brian Vargan sailed in from Calais to Dover the day before the car was hired from Manchester Airport three weeks ago. He came in with a car, the registration number, make, and model I have emailed to you, Joshua. I am running a trace on the car as we speak and should find more information soon."

"Thanks, Viktor, I owe you one," I said gratefully.

"You always say this, Alex, and the ones you are owing me are all adding up," Viktor replied with humour in his voice.

"Come over and work in Yorkshire. You can even have your own office," I said.

"No chance, my friend. There are too many fields and sheep."

Everyone laughed. Viktor's fear of sheep was hilarious.

"You all laugh at Viktor. I know this. But sheep are sent

from the devil. One day you will see this, and then you will not laugh at Viktor," he declared, his tone serious.

"Goodbye, Viktor," Josh chuckled. "And keep in touch."

"Goodbye, my Yorkshire friends," Viktor replied before ending the call.

"Does he really hate sheep?" asked Julia.

"It's more like a phobia," Nik replied. "When he came over with Gregor and Sergei one time, we got drunk on vampire-made vodka and absinthe that we'd sneaked into the Red Lion, and we ended up walking home. Viktor never drinks, so it hit him hard. We went over a wall into a field for a piss, and somehow we lost Viktor."

"I thought you lot couldn't get that drunk," Julia said.

"This stuff was made *by* vampires, *for* vampires, and it was lethal. Anyway, Viktor woke up the next morning hungover and surrounded by sheep. He's had a sheep phobia ever since. He insisted they spoke to him. We both said that will have been the absinthe, but Viktor disagrees. Then Josh sent him clips of that film, Babe, where the sheep talk to the pig, and he's refused to come back to Yorkshire ever since."

"Josh, that was an awful thing you did to poor Viktor," Maggie admonished. She walked into the room looking as pretty as ever, her make-up all back to normal.

Julia couldn't stop giggling, and it was a lovely sound. She was running her hands over my shoulders, and I was thoroughly enjoying her touch. I could tell she wanted me to hold her. I sensed it through our Bond. So I took one of her hands and brought her around to sit on my lap.

Josh opened the email Viktor sent and went through the details. We were still none the wiser as to who this vampire was, but at least we had something to go on that we didn't have before. That, I realised, was thanks to Julia and her sighting of the car.

I felt sorry for getting so angry with Julia, but I was still annoyed she'd put herself at risk.

Julia kissed me on the cheek and said I should stop fretting about it. For a second or two, I'd forgotten she could sense my feelings and hear my thoughts through our Bond, but I was grateful that she tried to soothe and calm me.

I noticed a change come over Julia, and I felt it, too. She lay against my chest and licked my throat, giving me the most erotic thoughts I'd ever had.

Standing swiftly, I hooked an arm around her, grabbed our coats from the rack and ushered her towards the door. The Bond was kicking in, and if I didn't get her home soon, I would fuck her right there over my desk, in front of everyone.

I heard Nik chuckle and say, "Get used to this feeling, you two. You have days of this left."

I didn't reply because Julia and I were out of the door and home much faster than I ever thought possible.

Chapter Thirty-One

Alex

At first, being Bonded with Julia was exhausting, yet exhilarating too. I drank both from her and the bagged blood we brought in from our donors, but it never seemed to be enough. The sex we had was phenomenal, and I can honestly say that committing myself to the woman I loved was the best thing that had ever happened to me.

Humans often moan about being tied down in a relationship, but when we're together in each other's arms, I feel like I'm soaring high above the clouds, and all is good with the world.

We found out that the vampire, Brian Vargan, had left the UK for France the same night that Julia had seen him. I wish we could have known who it was from her description, but tall, blond and well-built wasn't much to go on. After all, that kind of described me. But at least he was out of the country, and Viktor had placed alerts at every UK airport and ferry port, so we'd know if he came back.

Julia's parents were having a great time on their holiday, so they weren't around to interrupt us in our first few days as a Bonded couple.

Freya had done enough of that already.

On hearing from Josh that we'd Bonded, she immediately left his cottage to come and congratulate us. Unfortunately, we hadn't locked the door in our race to make love, and Freya caught us in an *extremely* compromising position.

After apologising, she hid behind the kitchen door and congratulated us on our Bonding. You didn't need to have vampire hearing to know how hard Freya laughed once she'd closed the door behind her. The very next morning, after giving us another red-faced congratulation, she left for her home in Aldbrough on the rugged East Yorkshire coast.

By Monday, the effects of the Bond had settled down enough for us to go to work, although we ended up having sex in the conference room, and at home on our midnight break.

Everything was going great, but I sensed a big mood change in Julia by mid-week.

I couldn't seem to do anything right, and it was like treading on eggshells around her. By Friday, the source of all the anger became apparent.

Julia got her period.

I don't know why I didn't recognise it before; the office used to be a terrible place at *that* time in Maggie's younger years. Then she became menopausal... When she went on HRT, we were all so relieved we sent her doctor a gift.

Now I'd have to deal with Julia's moods when she had PMT. But it was easier said than done.

I came home on Friday to Julia being in a rage because I'd eaten all the chocolate chip cookies she'd bought from the work's canteen. So I went over to the canteen and bought whatever cookies they had left, as well as four of Moira's famous cupcakes. When I got back home, I made her a large mug of tea and brought her a plate full of cookies and cupcakes. I thought she'd be pleased, but I didn't expect her to be in tears at my thoughtfulness. I dried her tears, kissed her on the cheek, and then went for a shower.

When I came out of the shower, I put on my jogging bottoms, went to sit at the side of her on the sofa, and just happened to mention that Julia must have enjoyed the cookies and cupcakes because she'd eaten all of them.

BIG. MISTAKE.

The yelling and plate-throwing that followed was bloody scary, and the Bond didn't help matters either. It got to the point where I wasn't sure if the words were coming out of her mouth or her head. When she walked off into the bedroom and slammed the door, I felt relieved…until I heard her cry again.

So off I went to the bedroom, asking her what was wrong. This time, Julia said she was upset because she felt all bloated and fat after eating all the cookies and cupcakes in one sitting. After thinking for a moment, I suggested we go to the gym together the next day.

ANOTHER. BIG. MISTAKE.

More tears came because, apparently, my suggestion that we went to the gym together meant that I was going off her because I thought she was fat, and that her thighs were too big.

Then she got angry again because, "Who did I think I was anyway, telling her she was fat?"

After five minutes of defending myself repeatedly, telling her I didn't think she was fat and that I loved her more than ever, she finally calmed down. Then Julia got up off the bed like nothing had happened and suggested we watch a movie.

So that's what we did until Julia fell asleep, and I searched my smartphone for anyone local who could perform an exorcism. Because I've seen a lot of things in my years, and what had just transpired couldn't only have been due to PMT, could it?

Freya called, and I spoke to her quietly while Julia slept. I explained the situation, and Freya—the oracle of all things immortal—told me that everything is heightened when a female is newly Bonded to an immortal male. Not only their senses and emotions that link them to their Bonded mate, but all senses and emotions linked to their hormones, too.

Apparently, she'd be this way until her body became fully accustomed to being Bonded by blood.

I suppose it's like when you first become a vampire. When you feel anger, it's uncontrollable, and your need for blood sends all rationality out of the window.

Freya told me to remind Julia that this effect was only temporary, and at least it meant she'd be fertile. I apologised to Freya for talking to her about this, but she said I was being silly to do so.

As far as we know, an immortal female was no longer fertile. Freya had plenty of information she'd collected over the years, and of course, we'd met many immortals. Yet we knew of no female vampire who had become pregnant. Therefore, it didn't seem fair that an immortal male could impregnate a human female. I often wondered if this was why Freya hadn't entered into a relationship with anyone. Freya had enough admirers over the centuries, yet she remained single.

I hoped that Julia and I would be blessed with children.

I knew Freya would be a wonderful aunt and would spoil any little ones we had.

In the past, she'd looked after orphaned children during the Spanish Flu outbreak. Freya became like a mother figure to them and has kept an eye on their families ever since. I hoped she'd become a mother again one day, in whatever capacity that may be. Freya was a complete natural when it came to motherhood. I could only hope that I'd be a good father. Between Brandr and Sebbi, I hadn't had the best role models.

I ended the call after telling Freya I'd bring Julia to see her soon.

Julia stirred in her sleep and then moaned something unintelligible. I felt terrible that the Bond was affecting her this way. It was scaring me, so God only knew what she felt like.

I got up and brought the quilt and pillows out of the bedroom to cover us because, although she still looked like my sweet Julia, I conceded that I just wasn't brave enough to wake her.

Chapter Thirty-Two

Julia

The fortnight my parents were away seemed to fly by, and so much had happened since they left.

It became apparent that the Bond with Alex was going to take a while to settle down in my system. My hormones raged, even without the bad case of PMT I'd had.

In one way, I felt sorry for Alex having to put up with me, and I truly believed him when he said he wasn't aware of how much the Bond would affect me hormonally. Alex said he hoped to have me pregnant as soon as possible, so I shouldn't let the worry of another period bother me.

In all honesty, I wanted to spend some time getting to know Alex one on one before we started a family. We were rarely on our own unless we were going to sleep or making love. The cottage being down the lane from the works compound and offices didn't help.

When I mentioned this to Alex, he told me he owned twenty other homes in the UK, so we could move to one of them—or buy another—if I wanted. He proceeded to tell me about the other houses. Some were regular three-bedroom properties, scattered about the UK in various rural areas, but there were also four large manor houses.

Alex went to the dresser in the kitchen and took out a photo album containing lots of photographs of his larger properties and their surrounding gardens and land.

I was extremely impressed and wondered why he wouldn't want to live in any of them. Alex carried on flipping through the pages quietly. Then he looked around his cosy home and said he felt lonely in those large houses. But here, in this cottage, he'd found the best of both worlds.

Alex had privacy in his cottage but had Josh and Nik as neighbours if he needed them. He was pretty much on site for work, and because you had to drive through the compound to get to the cottages, it meant that the security cameras from work could pick up any threat that came down the lane.

There was another photograph album showing pictures of Freya's house in Aldbrough. It was stunning, and like Alex's larger properties, it appeared as if it had been around for at least two hundred years.

Alex informed me that he and Freya had the property built around five hundred years ago. He said it was the only home that Freya felt happy in.

Freya had human staff who'd been with her since 1898. Her butler was called Leonard and his wife, Millie, was her cook. They didn't age due to them consuming a shot glass of Freya's blood once a week, and Frank, the gardener, along with his wife, Sally, the housekeeper, did the same.

I could tell that Alex had a great fondness for these people. He showed me photographs on his phone he'd taken of them one evening.

Alex, Freya, and Josh were on a lawn around Freya's home—playing cricket or something similar. I wondered why he'd thought he was lonely when he had so many people in his life. I must have sent him my thoughts telepathically because he said, "I was lonely because I didn't have you, Julia. And a property with twenty-eight different rooms in it, including an unused ballroom, can take some filling."

I assured Alex that I loved it here at the cottage. It felt like my home already, and my parents lived nearby, so that was a huge bonus.

My mum and dad were due back in the early hours, so we called at their home to drop some fresh bread and milk in for when they arrived.

We'd visited every other day of their two-week holiday to check the bungalow and move their post away from the door. We also made love in my old bedroom, which seemed quite a naughty thing to do. You couldn't even tell we'd been in the room, yet I was worried that my parents might somehow know when they saw me.

There were quite a few letters in the post, but only one addressed to me. It was my decree absolute, which meant that my divorce was final. I thought I'd feel upset, or relieved, or *something*. But I just felt numb.

Alex looked at me when he saw what the papers were, trying to gauge my reaction. But he mustn't have been able to read anything from my expression because he took my hand and asked, "Are you okay, love? You seem to be blocking your thoughts from me because I can't tell how you feel about this." He gestured at the papers in my other hand.

"I'm okay, Alex. I just feel numb," I told him truthfully.

He kissed me on the lips and said, "Come on, love. Let's go home for a bite to eat before work."

I nodded my head and let Alex lock up before we climbed into his SUV. Although he was wealthy, he didn't drive anything fancy. He said he wouldn't want the attention an expensive car would bring, so the Honda CR-V executive model with heated leather seats suited him fine. Alex switched on the heated seats as soon as he started the engine. The weather had turned extremely chilly over the last couple of days, and there'd been a thick frost over the Pennine hills this morning.

We drove in relative silence until we got back to the cottage. After placing my divorce papers on the kitchen table, I walked into the bedroom to change my shoes ready for work. I must have been in there a while because Alex came in and told me he had made us chicken curry with rice.

We sat and ate our meal, the radio playing with the sound down low in the background. The curry was so tasty, and I was really enjoying my meal until suddenly, I couldn't seem to swallow it down.

Alex crouched in front of me. Holding both my hands, he urged, "Just let it out, Julia. Don't keep it locked away, love."

I cried silent tears, unable to speak until Alex picked me up out of the chair and set me on his lap.

"I'm not crying because I wanted to stay married to Gavin," I assured him.

I didn't want Alex to think that I was still in love with Gavin, so I continued to explain my feelings. "I just feel like I've wasted years building a life and a home, only to receive a piece of paper telling me it was all for nothing."

"It wasn't for nothing, Julia. You had some good times, didn't you? I know you travelled a lot because your dad used to tell me all the places you'd been to. I watched you sometimes when you were at uni, and when you first got engaged. You looked so in love with him, though it tore me up inside. But you were having such a good time together. Maybe that got you through your studies so successfully."

More tears came, a little harder this time. I ran my fingers across his jaw and chin and spoke to Alex telepathically about my fear of being in the same situation all over again. I couldn't bear it if we ended.

"Oh, Julia, you should never doubt my love for you. You are my life, my love, forever. There is no paper that could break our Bond. Only death can do that. And even then, I'd love you. My ghost would find you and stay with you. My spirit wouldn't do that moving on shit they talk about. When I come back to haunt you, I'm staying put. I might do some of that cool floating-through-walls stuff to get to you, and I'd want to do some weird, scary, poltergeist stuff to Sergei to freak him out."

His words and the comical face he pulled made me giggle. He tugged me closer and stroked my hair.

"Julia, this is probably the wrong time to ask, but do you think you'd like to get married again? If not, it won't matter, because you're Bonded to me now. And legally, since a week ago, you own half of everything I do. Freya, Josh, Nik, and Gregor would take care of you if anything should happen to me and—"

"Yes, Alex. I think I'd like to get married again," I told him.

"You would? So if I got down on one knee right now and proposed, you would say yes?"

"Well, I don't want to get off your lap so you can forget about getting down on one knee. But if you were to ask me, I'd say yes."

He looked at me lovingly, and I expected him to ask me to marry him, but he didn't. Neither did he ask me when we got back in from work the next morning. Even after a wonderfully satisfying session of lovemaking, the proposal didn't come.

I thought about proposing to Alex instead, and the idea really appealed to me. Gavin had proposed to me during a night out to see one of our favourite bands, so he had all the excitement of planning the perfect evening and buying a ring.

My mind was so occupied with thoughts of a proposal that I'd almost forgotten about my divorce papers, and they no longer bothered me in the slightest.

Alex had done it again. He'd taken away my hurt and replaced it with a way to look forward.

I would marry this man, this Born Immortal vampire, and show him how much he means to me every single day of our lives.

Chapter Thirty-Three

Gina

I'd been one of the organisers of the Barrowfield bonfire night party at the Red Lion for several years. Night Movers sponsored the firework display, and the villagers supplied the wood for the bonfire. It was a great night for the community. We held a raffle with loads of prizes—also supplied by Night Movers—which raised money for the Barrowfield Youth Club.

I called at the post office to find out if Mr Singh had the raffle ticket books for us. He usually sold a lot of tickets and always attended the bonfire. There were a few people in the queue, so I looked around the chilled food area of the shop. I saw a tub of twelve profiteroles drenched in thick milk chocolate, and I knew that Nik and I could have lots of fun with those later.

I thought I heard my name mentioned, and I glanced to the side to see who it was. Sandra Jackson was a real bitch to me whenever she got the opportunity, and by the sound of it, today wouldn't be any different.

"Yes, I heard Gina had been having an affair with Nik Harding from Night Movers for years. I don't know what he sees in her, though. She's always been fat," Sandra stated.

That bit stung. I'd been on a perpetual diet for years, and no matter how much Nik told me he loved my curves, I would never feel happy with my shape.

Sandra carried on with her gossip.

"I feel sorry for her lovely husband, Steve. She deceived him for such a long time, but I think a good woman would help him get over it. Their kids must be so upset and embarrassed by her behaviour. I bet that—"

She could talk about me, Nik, and Steve all she wanted, but there was no way she was talking about my kids.

Strolling towards the gossiping cow, I said, "Hello, Sandra. Still busy sticking your nose into things that don't concern you, I see."

"Just saying what we're all thinking, Gina. If you didn't want people talking about you, you shouldn't have been having an affair," Sandra exclaimed loudly so everyone in the shop could hear.

"For your information, Sandra, I wasn't having an affair. But now I've sampled the goods on offer, I wish I'd done it sooner. I mean, you have to admit, Nik is one hell of a man. Oh, and if you want to be the good woman to help Steve get over me, then be my guest. I think you deserve each other."

I closed the gap between us and felt a sliver of satisfaction when Sandra's back hit the shelf behind her as she tried to retreat. "Now listen up, because I'll only tell you this once. If you ever talk about my children again, I'll beat you all the way to Rothley and back. So if you want to keep your teeth, you'd better keep that big mouth shut. Do you understand me, Sandra? You mean, gossiping, bitch?" I said with my finger poking her flat chest.

I took the profiteroles to the till and sorted out the raffle tickets with Mr Singh before making my purchase. I didn't look back to see Sandra's face and held my head high as I walked out of the shop.

Nik was pulling up to the kerb when I walked out of the door. He'd been to collect the raffle tickets from Barrowfield Motor Repairs, which was down the road from Mr Singh's Post Office and General Store. He stopped the car abruptly and slammed the door behind him as he came towards me.

"What's wrong, Gina? Why are you upset?"

I knew Nik could sense the anger and hurt coursing through me, and it was good to know he was here for me. If there was anyone who could keep me grounded, it was Nik. But I wasn't sure how he would respond to this incident today.

"Let's just get in the car, love," I said, already opening the door and climbing inside. Nik captured my face in his hands before looking into my eyes and telling me he loved me telepathically through our Bond.

When he got in the car, I told him what had happened and everything that had been said. Nik looked at the profiteroles and mumbled, "I think we need more of these." Then he got out of the car and headed towards the shop.

I chased after him, telling him through our Bond not to do anything rash. But Nik had a very determined glare on his face, which he focussed on Sandra.

He went straight towards his favourite foodstuff in the

world other than my blood—Nik's words, not mine—which was a large jar of chocolate and hazelnut spread. Then he turned to Sandra and said, "It wasn't long ago that I bumped into you in here when buying some of this heaven in a jar, and if I remember correctly, you insinuated you'd be more than happy to lick this chocolaty, hazelnut goodness from certain parts of my anatomy, and you were a married woman at the time."

Sandra turned to her friend and spluttered, "I don't know what he's talking about. He's making it up."

Her friend glanced from Nik to Sandra, then me, with an undecided look on her face.

Nik carried on speaking, totally ignoring Sandra's protests.

"You told me I'd get to see the butterfly tattoo on your left breast. Although to be fair, it must be a small tattoo because there's not a lot of space to put one, is there? But I turned you down that day because I like my women to look like women, not a man in a frock. And the nasty, gossiping type doesn't do it for me either.

"Now, I would never physically hurt a woman, but I take exception when someone bad-mouths the woman I love and my stepchildren. So if I hear that you or anyone else in your circle of backstabbing, gossip-mongering bitches are talking about any of them, then I'll spread some gossip of my own. Perhaps I'll start with the night you propositioned Alex and Josh at the same time. You also asked Sergei and Yuri to double-team you when you'd had a little too much cider at the Red Lion, which is a regular occurrence, by all accounts. So, I'm giving you a choice here, Sandra, which I think is quite generous of me. Keep your trap shut and stay away from Gina and her kids or suffer the consequences."

And with that, as cool as you like, Nik walked to the till

and spoke with Mr Singh about how he hoped the weather stayed dry for tonight's bonfire. Then he took my hand, kissed me on the lips, and led me outside.

On our way home, Nik sang along to the radio like nothing had happened, while I tried to process everything I'd heard.

One thing that stood out for me above all else was the fact that Nik had called my grown-up kids his stepchildren. I knew he wanted to play a part in their lives, and I was thrilled about that. He'd invited them and their partners to our cottage for dinner, and that had gone down well.

Nik had also mentioned about us buying them both a car for Christmas; he wasn't happy with the ones they drove. Although their cars were old, they were well-maintained and still got them from A to B. I wasn't sure how I felt about Nik spending so much of his money on them, but I'd been told once again that it was our money now, and we had more than enough to go around.

Nik had instructed a solicitor to make me the beneficiary of his entire estate. I'd assumed he was just a partner in the business and owned the cottage we lived in. I wasn't aware that he owned several other properties, both in the UK and Europe. And now I co-owned everything he did.

It didn't seem fair that I was now worth a small fortune just because someone fell in love with me. Nik laughed when I told him that. He said he'd had the money to himself for all those years, so sharing it with me was okay with him. He also said I should know by now that what we had together was more than being in love, so I should stop worrying and enjoy the rest of our lives.

And I was enjoying life. There were some things that

rattled me, though. Like the mystery vampire that was stalking Alex and Julia, and comments from bitchy cows like Sandra and her cronies.

I couldn't believe what Nik had said in the store. So nasty Sandra had made a play for my man, but he'd turned her down. That made me feel good. Although I despised the woman, she was quite pretty and super slim, so to know that Nik preferred me did a lot for my ego. I'd make sure Nik was rewarded for what he did today by way of profiteroles and chocolate spread…if you get my drift.

Later that afternoon, we went along to the gym at work. Nik had placed some workout mats in a room off to the side of the main workout area, so he could train me how to kickbox.

To be honest, it was his own brand of boxing, kickboxing, judo, and wrestling, all wrapped up as *self-defence.*

Nik did this because he didn't like the fact that my kickboxing trainer was a man. He was quite jealous and extremely possessive of me around other men, although Lord only knows why. So, to save argument, I agreed to stop going to that class and let Nik train me instead.

Because of Nik's blood, I had more energy and was becoming much stronger, so Nik stopped being as gentle with me in our training sessions. I think part of that was because he worried about the mystery vampire and wanted me to at least try to defend myself.

I'd never be able to fight a vampire, but if I could get away from one, or defend myself until help arrived, that would be something.

Although I knew I didn't stand a chance against an

angry vampire who wanted me dead, Nik told me how to kill one. Stabbing them in the heart, cutting off their head and burning them generally did the trick. So nothing at all like it was on the re-runs of Buffy.

"I hope you're ready for a good workout, Nik, because I'm ready to *kick some ass*," I said in a poor attempt at an American accent.

"Actually, I'm ready for a good fuck," Nik replied as he walked into the room he'd set up at the back of the gym.

I dropped my gym bag on the floor and placed my water bottle beside it. Hands on my hips, I declared, "No, Nik, you promised me a good workout, so that's what's going to happen."

Nik smirked and raised one eyebrow. "Gina, when we fuck, we both get a good workout."

"Well, not now, Nik. I want to really go for it today. I need to relieve some of the tension and stress that bitch Sandra caused me. So when you're ready, let's get to it."

"Fucking also relieves tension and stress, Gina. And with much less bruising. Unless, of course, you're in one of those moods..."

I blushed profusely, thinking about the wild, passionate night we had at the weekend. I couldn't get enough of him, and the rougher he was, the better. I didn't know I had it in me. But now Nik was laughing at me because he knew he'd made me think about it. Oh, I was *so* going to take him down today.

The thing we'd worked on most of all was upper body strength. Typically, women don't have as much upper body strength as men, so I'd been using the machines at our gym and swimming every other day. Julia came to the pool at Rothley with me, and both Julia and Keeley came to Zumba. I felt so much better for toning up, but try as I might, I couldn't get rid of my muffin top and bingo wings.

Still, it felt good to be able to take Nik down when he made a grab at me from behind. I took his arm, twisted it behind his back and swept his feet from under him to bring him to his knees. When he cried out in pain, I quickly let go and apologised. It was then that he laughed and spun around, sweeping both my legs from under me, dropping me flat on the floor with a whack. It knocked the wind out of me, and it took a few seconds to catch my breath.

"Never let your guard down, Gina, even if you think you have the advantage." The cocky smirk on his face soon died off when he knew I was genuinely hurt.

"Baby, I'm sorry. Are you okay?" he asked, concern marring his handsome face.

I nodded as my breathing became more even. I placed my hands on his shoulders as if to put my arms around him, then thrust my knee towards his balls as I threw him off me.

He made a grunting noise as my knee made contact with his nuts, but I'd held back at the last minute, so there was very little impact. Just enough to let him know that smirking at me would not be tolerated in today's workout.

After another twenty minutes of the most gruelling training session we'd ever had, I decided I'd had enough. Sure, I was learning a lot, and Nik had been much tougher on me than he had previously, but try as I might, I found it hard to hurt him.

Trouble was, I didn't want Nik to see that I was giving up. Since the slight kneeing him in the balls thing that happened earlier, he'd had the upper hand in most of what we'd done.

I'm not stupid. I knew he had the strength and speed of a comic book hero, but I still wanted a little power over him.

So, I pretended that something was irritating me in my bra. First, I scratched at the side of my boob. Then I looked down my top and into my bra as if to see what was wrong. I took a quick drink of water and scratched at my boob again.

"What's up with your tits?" Nik asked, staring at the hand that was rubbing the side of my breast.

"I don't know. It feels like something's sticking in this boob," I said, trying my best to keep a straight face.

Then I turned around and bent over at the waist to put my water bottle back on the floor. With my arse in the air, I took my time unzipping my bag and removed the towel I'd put in there earlier. Once upright again, I patted my forehead with the towel, then I glanced down into my tank top, swiping the towel inside my bra—as though wiping away whatever was irritating me. After I'd done, I bent over again to put the towel back before turning around with a pained look on my face.

"Are you okay? Have you had enough for today?" Nik asked.

"Oh, God no," I said, shaking my head. "I thought we were just getting started, but maybe I'd feel better if I take this bra off."

I turned and lifted the back of my tank top, unclipping and removing my bra, making sure my fingers brushed over my nipples as I did so.

When I turned around, the relief must have shown on my face because Nik said, "I can tell you're feeling better now. Maybe it's because you need a sports bra instead of what you've been wearing."

Damn!

My plan seemed to have failed. He didn't even look at my boobs and pointy nipples.

"What shall we do next then, Nik?"

"We could try some more floor work, but that's up to you."

"Okay," I replied, stretching my arms above my head, one after the other. Wait, did Nik just look down? I was sure he did, but...maybe not.

Suddenly, the impressive package Nik had in the front of his sweatpants began to twitch.

Bingo!

He had looked, but now I was looking at where his rapidly expanding penis was hiding. I glanced up at his face, and he licked his lips while staring at my own.

I swallowed nervously. Maybe this was a bad idea after all because the sexual tension had grown so thick you could almost see it. I tried to make up some funny comment to diffuse the situation, but the words wouldn't come. I looked towards my gym bag, ready to pick it up and run.

"Oh, no, Gina. You don't get to play me like that and run. Strip. Now."

"No, Nik. I mean, not here, at least. Let's go home... We've got chocolate spread."

I saw his eyes flick to the side. Good, he was thinking about it.

"I said strip, Gina, before I come over there and remove your clothes for you... forcefully."

I looked towards the door, and Nik shook his head. "The door is locked, Gina. No one's getting in or out of this room, and I'm becoming impatient."

I began by kicking my trainers across the floor. I wasn't wearing socks, so I peeled down my sweatpants and knickers at the same time. I was standing there in just my tank top, which thankfully covered my flabby tummy. Nik gestured with his hand for me to lift my top, but I shook my head and looked down. Nik stalked forward until he was standing in front of me.

Because I was looking down, I could clearly see the outline of the raging hard-on he was sporting. As if in response to his arousal, I could feel myself becoming wet. When I lifted my gaze to his, he silently asked me one more time through our Bond to remove my top. And this time, I did. However, what he asked me to do next caused my arousal to dissipate.

"Take me down, Gina."

"What?"

"You heard me. Take me down. Fight with me and show me your moves."

What the hell? I couldn't do that naked. With all my flabby bits exposed and wobbling as I moved? No way, José.

Nik pushed me and made me stumble backwards, struggling to steady myself. "What the fuck, Nik? I don't want to do this."

He took off his clothes slowly as he came towards me again. "Fight me, Gina, or are you too chicken to do that?"

"Piss off, Nik. Whatever you're hoping to achieve just now, it's not happening," I yelled, picking up my clothes. He pulled them out of my hands, then swept my feet out from under me. Before I could fall flat on my back, he dropped to the mat and caught me in his arms. I was still upset with him, so I pushed his face away with my palms when he tried to kiss me and used my legs to flip him over onto his back.

"That's my girl. Give me what you've got."

"No, Nik. I'm going home. You can take care of that hard-on yourself because there's no way I'm going near it."

As I turned and once again walked back to my clothes, Nik rolled over and grabbed my shins, causing me to drop to my knees.

The bastard.

Now the man would pay.

As Nik bent over me and cupped my breast, I brought my elbow back and slammed it into his ribs, then gave him a backwards head butt, delighting in his groan. As he went to put his hands up to his nose, I jumped up and grabbed his arm, twisting it around his back. Placing my knee into the small of his back, I forced him flat to the floor.

"Ow, fucking hell, Gina. Where did all that come from?"

"It came from being pissed off with a vampire who needed to be put in his place."

There was a momentary silence, and then Nik started laughing.

"I knew you could do it, babe," he said while freeing himself from my hold. Then, using his vampire speed, he flipped us over, pinning me underneath him, his chest against mine.

"Why did you do this, Nik? Why, when you knew I would hate to do this naked?" I sobbed. He ran his nose up and down the side of my face and inhaled.

"You're still uncomfortable with your body, Gina. I knew that the last thing you'd want to do was fight me naked. Even though it's one of the biggest fucking turn-ons I've ever experienced. Anyway, because you felt so uncomfortable, you got upset, which eventually turned to anger. Then you gave me the most honest fight we've ever had. Normally, you hold back as if you're afraid of hurting me. Something changed today. When you kneed me in the balls earlier, I knew I could push you into using all your training. In the end, you played right into my hands and did that funny thing with your bra." His expression stopped me from giving him a smart-arse remark.

"I need to know you're going to be as safe as you can be when I'm not around," he said sombrely.

"Why? Are you going somewhere?"

"I can't always be with you twenty-four-seven, Gina, so I need to know you're safe if I'm not there. Today is the only day that Alex has left Julia on her own, and that's only because she's in the office sorting the raffle prizes for the firework display. We all know Alex never does bonfires, so he's asked Josh and me to guard her tonight. If this mystery vampire shows up and you're even three steps away from me, I need to know you can defend yourself until I can get to you."

"You know I'm going to stick by you, Nik."

"Oh please, Gina, don't make promises you can't keep. As soon as someone asks you for help, you won't hesitate to do so."

He was right, of course, so I didn't argue.

"Gina, you just can't help it. You're one of those people who can't say no when someone asks you to do them a favour, even if it spoils your plans. You would rather do that than risk upsetting someone. So, if we are separated tonight, please, even if you have to picture yourself fighting naked, draw on the anger and rage you felt today and take the fucker down. At least it will give me enough time to recognise through our Bond that you need me."

"You really think something's going to happen tonight, don't you?"

"I can't explain it, Gina. It's like I feel it deep in my gut. I don't know whether it's going to be tonight, but I know that something bad will happen, and soon."

I wrapped my arms and legs around him and held him as close as I could. Now he'd finally revealed his feelings about this vampire, I could see how hard it must have been to keep those emotions from me. Fear for my safety, anger for the disruption in our lives, and worry that he wouldn't be near enough to protect me.

The love he felt for me was the base from where all these other emotions grew, and it was becoming stronger each day. I was so blessed to have him in my life. Loving me, protecting me, and wanting me. I just wish I'd been smart enough to accept his love sooner.

He kissed me softly and pushed himself inside me, slow but deep. We made love right there on the gym mats in that small room. It was sweet and beautiful, and when we climaxed, the feelings I got from Nik were so strong, it felt like Bonding with him all over again.

I loved him, heart and soul, and he returned that love tenfold. This was the life I wanted. No, this was the life I needed, and there was no vampire on this earth that could take it from me.

Chapter Thirty-Four

Freya

I hate bonfires. They bring back terrible memories for Alex and me. Whenever he stayed with me on bonfire night, we'd remain indoors all night.

Today, however, Alex was visiting me for a different reason.

He arrived at my home at eight this morning and was treated to a full English breakfast by Millie, my cook. Afterwards, she spoiled him with homemade croissants and honey from the hives in my garden.

The rest of my staff had a cuppa with Alex and spent most of that time enquiring about Julia. They couldn't wait to meet her so they could fuss over and spoil her.

Alex enjoyed their fussing. I knew he missed my staff when he'd not seen them for a while.

Leonard and Frank treat him like a son, and whenever Millie and Sally try to coddle him he laps up the attention.

Joshua was the same when he came here. It must be a man thing.

Anyway, today was a very special day as far as I was concerned. Alex was going to ask Julia to marry him next week, so we were travelling to Whitby to see a friend of mine who made bespoke jewellery.

Alex had decided to have a ring made for Julia. He'd taken her old wedding ring from her jewellery box so we could get the size right, and he'd chosen a few words that he wanted engraving on it.

It was the first time since Bonding with Julia that Alex had been without her for more than two hours, and I could tell it made him uncomfortable.

It had taken us an hour and forty minutes to travel up to Whitby. We went straight to Maxwell Farley's shop, which was on a back street a few minutes away from the harbour.

Alex chose a platinum wedding band for Julia and requested that the words My Love Forever—written in old script—were engraved on the outside of the ring. On the inside, Maxwell would put the infinity symbol.

Unbeknownst to Alex, I'd already spoken with Maxwell before we left my home. You see, I had a very interesting conversation with Julia last night. She wanted my help in finding Alex's ring size as she was going to propose to him. I turned the conversation around and mentioned I was paying my jeweller friend a visit, so I could source a ring from him. And oh, what if we could have it engraved with something meaningful?

Julia was thrilled. She couldn't go far without Alex because of the mystery vampire, so she agreed for me to arrange for the ring to be engraved.

So, while we were in Maxwell's back room, I had Alex

try on a few rings. When he found one that fit him, I gave Maxwell a nod, and he put it away for me.

I couldn't wait to see their faces when they realised they had matching rings.

Alex said Julia's ring needed to be a size up from her old wedding band. Julia had mentioned the old one was too tight the last time she wore it.

He paid for Julia's ring and was looking at other jewellery for her when I slipped Maxwell my card. We did it so surreptitiously, and I loved every minute of it. Alex purchased diamond earrings set in a platinum base, along with a platinum chain with a diamond pendant. Jokingly, I asked him why he didn't finish it all off with a matching bracelet and a watch.

Alex nodded enthusiastically and selected a pretty, delicate bracelet and a watch with a mother-of-pearl face. He also selected an eternity ring instead of an engagement ring, even though he planned on marrying her as soon as the rings were ready.

When Maxwell asked if Alex would like anything engraved on the back of the watch, he said he wasn't sure. Maxwell suggested an important date or name, perhaps, and Alex immediately said, "Megan." Then he gave him her date of birth and explained the details to him.

I already knew what had happened to Julia and her baby, and I couldn't help the tears that welled in my eyes. My brother was such a thoughtful man, and I was so happy that he'd finally found love with Julia. She would adore the watch, and the engraving would mean so much to her. It was a way for Julia to carry the love and memory of her baby daughter, somewhere other than in her heart.

After sorting out the rest of the jewellery and arranging for me to pick it up next week, we set off to a florist I'd been in touch with. They'd made me a set of wreaths, as per my request. Each wreath was a different size, and they were all made with carnations. All were block coloured, apart from one.

We headed up the coastline to Staithes—the little fishing village where Alex and I landed when we first arrived in England. The pretty colours of the painted houses were a welcome sight on this chilly yet bright sunny day.

Alex and I made our way to the church called *Our Lady Star of the Sea*. My husband and children's burial site was now a busy road, and the village where we'd lived was just farmland. So I preferred to lay my family's wreaths on holy ground.

My husband's wreath had red carnations, and Brisa's was always in pink. My little Tobias had lemon-coloured flowers, which looked so pretty against the stone wall of the church.

Alex held me while I cried for my family, and we spent a little time telling each of them how much they were loved and missed.

I always wondered, if my Brisa had lived, would she have been the image of my mother when an adult, like I am? She'd seemed to favour the both of us, having the same grey eyes and fair hair. And would baby Tobias have looked like his father and namesake or like his uncle Alex? Both were strong, kind, handsome men, and would have spoiled him all the time, just like they did his sister.

Alex took my hand and led me down towards the harbour. We'd timed it so the tide was in, and Alex volunteered to place the wreath on the steady waves.

My mother's wreath comprised deep fuchsia carnations with a singular cream one in the middle for my father. It might seem strange to others that I do this, but to my mind, I lost my father the day my mother drowned.

He was with us physically—until the day I killed him, of course—but he lost his soul and his goodness when he lost the woman he loved.

Before her death, Sebbi was a kind, respectful, and loving father. Although, who knows how he would have turned out if our mother had survived.

The journey back to my home in Aldbrough seemed to take forever. Apart from tuning into the local radio station, we drove in silence until we reached Hornsea, which is ten minutes from my home. Alex went over the details of what would happen when I collected the rings. He wanted to plan his proposal to Julia so that everything would be perfect.

I tried to listen, but my mind wasn't taking it in. I was still wrapped up in thoughts of my family, and I wanted to disappear to my room and sleep for a while. Also, even though Alex and I were Born Immortals, being out in daylight hours had made us tired.

I called Leonard, letting him know we were nearly home. I knew we'd have a warm meal waiting for us, as well as bagged blood.

Alex looked as weary and heartsick as I did, and I felt sorry that he'd done all the driving. I told him he could stay the night, but I knew he wouldn't take me up on the offer. He was already anxious after being without Julia for most of the day.

A newly Bonded couple needed to stay close for a few weeks, so as soon as Alex eased his weariness with food and blood, he was back in his car heading home to his intended. Whereas I was alone, dreaming of my family, mourning their loss—longing for the kind of love I may never experience again.

Chapter Thirty-Five

Alex

Traffic was minimal on my drive home from Aldbrough. Even the motorway wasn't as busy as it would normally be at 6:30 p.m. As it was bonfire night, people would be with their families, either at an organised event or something in their own back garden. It had been dark for over two hours, and already I could see fireworks going off in the distance.

I never went to any of the organised displays, even though Night Movers had sponsored the firework display at the Red Lion for years.

My life as a Viking meant I'd seen many funeral pyres, so the ritual of burning the guy to represent Guy Fawkes wasn't something I desired to see. Although, that wasn't the only reason. The night Freya and I had burned our father's body was forever etched in my mind, as was the night of the fire that killed little Brisa and Tobias.

Julia had been sorting out prizes for the raffle in preparation for this evening's event. She was attending the bonfire with her mum; her father was working this evening.

I'd asked Josh and Nik to guard her in case the mystery vampire showed up. Viktor hadn't let us know that any airline or ferry tickets had been purchased in the name of Brian Vargan, but he could have another alias he used for travel purposes. If that were the case, we'd never know where he was.

With this in mind, I waited outside the front of the Red Lion when I got back to Barrowfield.

The firework display was impressive this year. I usually watched from the outside of my cottage as it gave a good view of the fireworks lighting up the Pennine landscape. It wasn't as good when watching it from the inside of my Honda, so I got out and leaned against the door.

There was so much *oohing* and *aahing* coming from the spectators, and I wondered if one of those voices was Julia's. Could I stand next to her and watch the fireworks from there? I felt a little nauseous at the thought, but I needed to see her, touch her, and ensure she was safe. A loud bang followed by a succession of cracks spurred me on, and I left my vehicle—striding forward with determination.

The heat on my face was the first thing that struck me, and I almost panicked. Julia was by my side within seconds, sensing my discomfort through our Bond. She threw her arms around me, gave me a candy-floss-flavoured kiss, and then hugged me tightly, letting me know she wasn't going anywhere until I felt okay again.

I glanced around and saw Josh, Nik, Gina and Julia's

mum standing beside us. Josh and Nik gave me an enquiring look, silently asking if I was okay, reminding me I had their support. I realised at that moment just how lucky I was to be surrounded by such great people. After the emotional day I'd had with Freya, I really needed that.

"Alex, we can leave if you want; we don't have to stay here."

I kissed Julia on the tip of her nose and shook my head. For the first time ever, I wanted to stay and watch a bonfire night celebration. I wanted to carry on watching Julia's face light up with all the colourful fireworks and see the smile she wore when some made funny sounds.

"Alex, would you like some bonfire toffee?" Julia's mum held out a tin.

"Have some, Alex; it's homemade." Nik reached for the tin and took a piece.

"Better get some quick before Nik steals the lot," Gina told me, giggling. "You know what a sweet tooth he's got."

Nik really did have a sweet tooth, especially if he was stressed. I watched him bend to kiss Gina on the lips, then whisper something in her ear. She giggled again, her pupils dilating.

It appeared I wasn't the only one looking at the loved-up couple. As I took a piece of toffee and thanked Julia's mum, I noticed quite a few people staring at Nik and Gina.

A quick scan of the crowd standing around the bonfire told me that several women were talking behind their hands while nodding towards the couple.

Now, normally, no vampire likes to attract attention, but I had the feeling Nik was playing up to the crowd tonight. When Gina's son, Jack, came towards Nik and Gina with a couple of beers and a glass of wine, I took the opportunity to speak to Julia.

"What's up with all the dirty looks coming their way?"

"Apparently, Gina and Nik had a run-in with some super bitch at Mr Singh's earlier today. It appears that Gina's been the topic of village gossip for leaving her husband."

I knew that would have upset Gina. She sometimes acted tough, but she was a sensitive soul, and something like this would get to her. I was glad her son was here to show support. Buying his mum and Nik a drink and laughing and joking with them would go a long way in letting the village know that he accepted Gina and Nik as a couple.

"Ooh, Alex, look at the Catherine wheels," Julia squealed.

"They were always her favourite when she was a little girl. She never liked the ones with the loud bangs," Sue commented.

"And your favourites were the traffic lights," Julia remarked. She smiled broadly and held her mother's hand.

Sue leant over and kissed her daughter's cheek. Then, surprisingly, she pulled me down and kissed my cheek, too.

"Thank you, Alex, for bringing my daughter back to me."

There were tears in her eyes, though she quickly wiped them away and turned to watch the last of the fireworks. I placed myself in between Julia and her mum and put an arm around each of them. We stayed that way until Josh came over with a tray of hot chocolate drinks in plastic cups. We all took one, warming our hands on them as the fire warmed our faces.

We stayed until the bonfire burned down to about four feet high. That's when I began to feel uncomfortable. Watching the flames dance around the charred and almost skeletal look of the old bed frames, chairs, and other unwanted furniture brought back memories I never wanted to think of again.

Julia and Josh sensed it was getting too much for me, so Josh volunteered to drive Sue home and see her safely inside, while Nik and Gina came back with us.

Josh wanted to be back at the Red Lion for last orders. He had to make sure that the fire was out before the pub closed for the night.

Julia and I held hands as much as we could on the way home. It seemed my time away from her today affected both of us. We had to be touching each other, even if it was just our fingertips.

As soon as we got home, I went to the bathroom and set the shower running. Our clothes and hair smelled of bonfire and candy floss, especially Julia's. I undressed first, then removed all her clothes, kissing her as I stripped away each item. When she was naked, I carried her into the shower.

After getting clean, we made love in the shower and drank from each other. I needed the taste of her blood tonight. So much had happened today, and I needed her essence to give me strength—emotionally as well as physically. After we'd satisfied ourselves with blood and pleasure, we dried off quickly, and Julia got into bed. I brought us hot chocolate, then we snuggled under the duvet to warm our naked bodies.

Julia asked if I wanted to talk about what happened today with Freya. She knew we were going to Staithes to place the wreaths, but not about going to Whitby for the rings. I told her it was always a sad event, and I was worried about Freya.

I explained about Freya always having a single flower in our mother's wreath to represent our father. I hoped that one day we could mourn the man my mother loved and not the monster he became. Although, after all these years, I doubt that day would ever come.

Chapter Thirty-Six

Julia

I woke up earlier than usual, and after going to the bathroom, I lifted the curtain and peeked outside. Why was the day after bonfire night always so foggy and grey? It was the same every year, so I shouldn't be surprised. I quickly adjusted the curtain so I didn't wake Alex, then I put the central heating on and got back in bed until the cottage warmed up.

Alex opened one eye and looked at me sleepily.

"Come here, love," he said while pulling me into his arms, my back to his front. I could feel the heat from his morning erection against my cold bottom. He ground it against me and fondled my hardened nipples. Alex had woken up in a good mood this morning.

He nipped the skin between my neck and shoulder, not piercing it, but enough to leave teeth marks. Then he ran his nose up my neck to the back of my ear and said, "Mmm, you smell different."

I turned over onto my back to kiss him and pulled him down so that he lay on top of me. The kiss was filled with passion and want, the type of kiss that makes you wet in seconds. But suddenly, it stopped. Alex pushed himself upright and stared down at me.

"Julia, you taste different, too."

"Alex, stop with the Little Red Riding Hood nonsense and get back to what we were doing. I'm so ready for you right now."

Alex didn't make a move; he just stared at me. Then he lifted my hand, let his fangs descend and bit into my wrist.

"Oww!" I yelped. It certainly wasn't as pleasant as when he bit me during sex.

"Alex, what on earth is wrong with you?"

He looked down at me, his eyes glazing over with tears.

"What's wrong with me? Am I going to be ill?"

He shook his head and smiled. "Maybe sick in the mornings, but no, you're not ill."

"I'm pregnant," I gasped.

"Only just, I think. But your scent has definitely changed. I thought something was different last night when I drank your blood. It had a much sweeter taste, but I thought all that candy floss and bonfire toffee you ate might have had something to do with it."

"Are you sure, Alex? I don't want to get my hopes up in case you're mistaken."

"Well, I've never tasted a pregnant woman's blood before, but I've heard from other Blood-Bonded Immortals that it has a much sweeter taste than normal. And you certainly smell like a pregnant woman does. We can get a test later if you want to confirm it, but I'm pretty sure you're pregnant, Julia."

Could it be true? Dare I even hope? I needed

evidence. I needed to pee on a stick and see for myself that what Alex said was true. I wanted to be 100% sure that my body was giving me a second chance at motherhood.

Alex sat up against the headboard, frowning.

"Aren't you happy about it, Julia?"

I hated hearing the sadness in his voice, but I needed him to know that I couldn't allow myself to get excited yet. I moved to the edge of the bed and faced him.

"I'm sorry, Alex, but I need to see a positive pregnancy test before I allow myself to believe that I'm carrying another child. I don't doubt that you've picked up something different from my scent or taste, but I don't think a doctor would confirm I was pregnant just from those anomalies, either."

"Then I'll go to the pharmacy and get you some tests. Do you want anything else while I'm there?"

"If I *am* pregnant, I'll need some folic acid," I told him.

"What the hell is folic acid? That doesn't sound healthy for a pregnant woman. And where on earth do you put it?" he asked while hastily getting dressed.

I could tell through our Bond all the different places Alex imagined I would put folic acid. He thought it was like an exfoliator to slough off dead skin.

"It's one of the extra vitamins and minerals a pregnant woman needs."

He still didn't look convinced, and I couldn't help laughing.

"Alex, can you go to Rothley for it? If you go to the pharmacy in Barrowfield, it will be all around the village before I even do the test. I want us to tell everyone together, especially my mum and dad."

"I understand, love, and I'll be back as soon as possible."

He grabbed his keys, kissed me on the lips, told me he loved me through our Bond, and then he hurried out of the door.

We'd been together for almost two months. In that time, we'd gone from being friends to committing to each other forever. And now we might have a baby on the way. Alex said he wanted me pregnant as soon as possible, but I didn't think it would happen so quickly. It took years for me to get pregnant with Megan, and I thought it would take just as long to get pregnant again. I should have known Alex would have super sperm.

I felt butterflies in my tummy as the excitement kicked in. But I couldn't allow myself to get too hopeful. Not until I had the pregnancy test in my hand. I needed to take my mind off it all until Alex came back.

As if I could. This was too big to switch off and wait.

I set the shower running and got in. I'd washed my hair last night, but still, I washed and conditioned it again to kill time. After shaving my legs and underarms, I ran out of things to do, so I rinsed off and grabbed a towel.

I glanced at the alarm clock beside the bed. Only fifteen minutes had passed since Alex had left, so I needed to kill more time.

After blow-drying my hair, I used my straighteners to give it some soft curls. Then I applied moisturisers and body creams before putting on a little make-up.

I tried to remember the date of the next ladies' night. If I were pregnant, I wouldn't be able to have any alcohol, but I could still dance and have fun with everyone, although I'd give the karaoke a miss.

Forty minutes had passed, and the butterflies in my tummy had grown exponentially. We hadn't had breakfast yet, so I put some bacon and mushrooms under the grill and eggs in the poaching pan.

Music! That's what I needed. Alex usually had the radio or CDs on, so I took my cue from him. After another ten minutes of anxious dancing and cooking, Alex finally walked through the door.

I pretended not to be bothered about what he had in the carrier bag for all of ten seconds, then I grabbed it and tipped the contents onto the kitchen table. There were three different pregnancy tests, a tub of folic acid, a book about pregnancy, and some prenatal vitamins. I asked if Alex wanted to eat his breakfast first. He looked at me and shook his head.

"Let's get it over and done with, Julia. The emotions swirling around your head right now are too much for either of us to handle."

I'd forgotten that Alex could feel everything I felt through our Bond. I often forgot that he was a vampire. Sometimes things are just so normal that it's easy to forget.

I picked up the tests and went to the en-suite bathroom. After opening one of the boxes, I stared at it without moving.

"Stop stalling, love, and do the test."

"I didn't realise you were behind me, Alex. You don't need to stay for this bit."

"I'm staying, Julia. So hurry up and pee on one."

I took one out of the box, skimmed through the instructions, and then got down to pee. Once done, I placed the test on the side of the sink and washed my hands. Alex was timing the five minutes of waiting time on his phone, watching the test the whole time, but I couldn't look, and neither of us spoke. When the phone beeped, I looked up and saw the biggest grin on Alex's face. He picked up the test and placed it on the instruction paper.

"Two blue lines, Julia. That means you're pregnant, love."

He picked me up and twirled me around the small space before placing my feet back on the floor and dropping a big, wet kiss on my lips. I couldn't help the tears that fell as I gazed at Alex and smiled.

"I'm so happy, Alex. Our baby will be loved and cherished by everyone around them."

"That it will, love, just like I love and cherish its mummy."

I went to take the test and put it back in the box to throw away, but Alex snatched it from me.

"You can't throw it away, woman. I'm keeping it."

"Why on earth would you want to keep something I've peed on?" I asked.

"Because it told me I'm going to be a daddy," he replied, grinning from ear to ear.

He didn't need to know I'd be using the other two tests to make sure.

After we ate breakfast, Alex wanted to tell everyone our good news, but I asked him if we could keep it to ourselves until tomorrow. I knew that Josh and Nik would be able to scent the pregnancy on me as Alex had, so I told him I wasn't going into the office as planned. I wanted to get used to the idea myself before we told anyone else, but I felt bad for Alex because he was bursting at the seams to let everyone know. I told him that some couples wait three months before telling anyone else, just in case anything was to happen. Alex shook his head and told me not to worry about that. He said he would take good care of me and give me his blood more often, keeping me strong and healthy. Alex also suggested an appointment with a doctor and midwife to ensure everything was okay.

"They don't need to see you until you're ten or twelve weeks pregnant," I pointed out.

"Then we can go private, love. I'm making sure everything is okay from start to finish for you and our baby. Our baby... I love saying that." Alex beamed. "We didn't take our time, did we, Julia?"

"It's because you have super sperm," I told him.

"Would you like some of my super sperm right now? I think it would be better for you than that folic acid stuff," he said as he grabbed his cock through his jeans.

"Oh, yeah?" I laughed. "And how do you suggest I take this super sperm? Would it be orally or vaginally?"

"I think a dose in each, morning and night and anally once a week," he suggested with a wink.

I pretended to look shocked and embarrassed, but I wasn't fooling him. He'd given me ideas, and my libido had sprung to life.

"I can tell my woman is feeling a bit randy this morning. Tell me, Julia. Is it because you found out that we're having a baby, the bacon and egg butty we've just consumed, or talking about taking my super sperm?"

I got up from the table and walked towards the bedroom, taking my top off as I went.

"I think my man ought to come and find out for himself," I said, then turned and threw my bra at him.

Chapter Thirty-Seven

Josh

The evening went as most other Saturdays did at work. We got the stock brought forward for tomorrow's deliveries, and the invoices were printed and ready to be checked.

Gregor and Sergei were flying into Doncaster Sheffield Airport next week, so I liaised with our guy there to let him know how long the aircraft would need to be in storage.

Gregor's house was nearing completion. He'd arranged to meet with an interior designer from Chester, who'd apparently worked for the Royal Family and a few famous footballers. Typical of Gregor. He always insists on having the very best for everything he does, and he seldom compromises. In fact, the only person who can get him to change his mind about anything is Freya.

She persuaded him to give Keeley a job as his personal assistant in the UK. Keeley doesn't know she has the job yet; she just thinks she's going for an interview.

I know Gregor will definitely employ her, and not only

because of Freya's influence. He'll employ Keeley because she's smart and will make a great PA.

I've always had a soft spot for the beautiful Keeley and her daughter, but recently I've had feelings for Keeley that maybe I shouldn't be having.

I've seen her work hard to provide for her little girl so that she doesn't want for anything. I also remember Keeley as a twelve-year-old who'd just lost her mother to cancer. Both she and her twin brother, Daniel, moved in with their aunt Maggie for a while when their father had a breakdown after their mother passed away.

Her mum and dad had moved to Lincolnshire before she and Daniel were born. They lived there until their mother first became ill. With all the upheaval in their lives, you would think that the twins would become little brats. But they didn't. I remember them both coming in to help Maggie with her work and being so well-behaved. Not like some of the other little sods in the village.

Their father has an ongoing problem with alcohol addiction, although he seems to behave around little Daisy.

Daisy is an absolute star, and I love her dearly. I look forward to her visits and always spoil her whenever I can. I hope that even with Keeley's new job, she still has time to visit us. I'll miss both of them otherwise.

So, on top of our busy Saturday night schedule, I drew up an advertisement for Keeley's old job.

My mobile rang with the ringtone I set for Viktor. I was hoping we had some news about this mystery vampire so our lives could get back to some semblance of normality.

"Hello, Viktor."

"Joshua, I have news regarding Brian Vargan. He purchased a ticket at Bordeaux Airport in France, flying to Frankfurt in Germany. I can tap into the live security feed to show passengers arriving on that flight. I will record it and send it over. Alex can take a look to see if he recognises this man Vargan."

"That's great, Viktor. I'll call Alex now and let him know. Thanks for doing this for us. This guy has everyone on edge here, especially after the fire and him following Julia."

"I hope this is the lead that finally helps identify the man because I do not think this is his real name. Although I may be wrong, Joshua. But we will see."

"How long until the plane lands?" I asked.

"Thirty minutes. But it will take a while for me to record all the passengers, and there may be other flights arriving at the same time."

"Yeah, I understand. I'll let Alex know and get back to you."

"Goodbye, Joshua."

"Goodbye, Viktor, and thanks again."

Thank God for that! Let's just hope we can identify this guy from the footage. He proved on the night of the fire he was dangerous. And him watching Julia didn't sit well with me at all.

I called Alex's mobile and got no answer. So I called his landline, and still no answer. I rang Julia's phone and was just about to hang up when she answered with a breathless, *"Hello."*

Julia put me on speakerphone, and I informed them about the phone call I'd just had with Viktor. Alex told me they would be over in about forty-five minutes. Just before I ended the call, I heard him tell Julia they would finish off in the shower... So that's why it took so long for them to answer the phone!

With Alex and Nik Bonding with their women within a

week or so of each other, I now felt like Billy No-Mates. I was happy for them both, but truthfully... I was lonely.

That's why I was looking forward to Sergei and Gregor coming over. At least I'd have some company for a while. Although, as usual, Gregor would split his time between Freya and us. Hopefully, it wouldn't be too long before they completed the renovations.

We'd all been monitoring the building work so that the renovations were on schedule. I was sure Gregor would want Freya to stay with him when the old manor house was ready. She normally stays with either myself or Alex. Usually, we stop at home and watch a movie or get together with Nik and play cards. Freya always wins.

Of course, all that has changed now that Gina and Julia are permanently on the scene. Everyone loves Gina, and I am no exception. She's someone I've always been able to share my thoughts and feelings with, and I doubt that will ever change.

Julia is a lovely person. She's smart and hard-working here in the office, and so brave to get details of the vehicle that the mystery vampire was driving. I was mad as hell at her for putting herself in danger, but she knew how frustrated we were with having no information to go on, and she wanted to help.

It was due to Julia's quick thinking that we had the visual evidence coming through from Viktor.

I made a cup of coffee and checked that Maggie hadn't swapped the chocolate chip cookies I bought for the low-fat crap she buys. Thankfully, she hadn't. I knew we'd need a few sweet treats to keep us going tonight.

Alex came in with his arm around Julia, and they were laughing loudly. It was almost as if this Brian Vargan thing wasn't worrying them at all. I'd never seen him look so happy. Being Bonded with the woman he loved had really changed the usually so serious Alex. He appeared relaxed and at peace with the world…instead of having the weight of it on his shoulders.

Within thirty seconds, Julia's scent hit me.

I wasn't sure if I was imagining it at first, so I went over to her, leaned into her neck and sniffed. I realised that was a little inappropriate, but I was so shocked I couldn't even find the words to apologise.

I stepped back and looked at Alex.

"Julia's pregnant."

Alex beamed at me. "Joshua, you're going to be an uncle next summer. And you are officially the first person to find out, other than Julia and me."

I felt my eyes fill with tears that I couldn't prevent falling. As I congratulated Julia and the man I'd known as a brother for over 270 years, I was an emotional wreck.

We were going to have a baby in our family. A niece or nephew for me to spoil. Freya would dote on him or her, too. I hugged Julia tightly and kissed her on the cheek.

"Julia, is there anything I can get you? You should sit down. Have you eaten?"

Alex burst out laughing and winked at Julia as she blushed.

"Josh, I'm fine. You don't have to fuss over me. I'm only just pregnant, anyway."

My email alert pinged, so I wiped my eyes and went over to my desk to bring up the video. Julia wheeled a chair around the back of my desk, as did Alex, and we waited patiently for the passengers to pass through security. Surprisingly, the video feed was in colour, so I held high hopes that we could identify him.

My high hopes were soon dashed. After fifteen minutes,

we'd seen at least twenty-five tall, blond men that Julia said *could* be Brian Vargan. She'd only seen his face from his eyes upwards that evening, so I could understand why she found this so difficult. But at the nineteen-minute mark, Julia asked us to pause the footage when another tall, blond man came into view.

"That could be him, Alex. His hair was that colour blond, and he has the same strong, broad look about his shoulders. And how he's walking… I'm sure that's him."

"Alex, do you think you recognise this guy?" I asked hopefully.

"I'm not sure, to be honest. Just rewind it back and let me look again."

I rewound it and played it from the man first entering through some doors into passport control.

"This man looks a little like the man who I believed was my father. But Brandr had a lot of facial hair, like most men in our village. It can't be him, though. He died over nine hundred years ago. We were told by Sebbi he died in battle, but I believe it was Sebbi who killed him. It was the look on his face when he told us about his death that gave him away."

"Do you think he could have been lying about him being dead, Alex? I mean, did they say he had a proper Viking funeral?" I asked, knowing a little about the way they would send a Viking to Valhalla.

"I can't remember everything that was said about his passing, other than what Sebbi told us. I don't even remember the others who readied the settlement ever speaking about it."

Alex turned away from the computer for a moment, then spun back around and asked me to play it back again.

After starting and stopping the image too many times to

mention, we carried on looking at the rest of the footage to see if we could spot anyone else who resembled the man Julia saw. But there was no one who sparked any recognition for either Alex or Julia.

"If it was Brandr, then why would he wait until now to make contact?" Julia pondered.

That was a good question. But Alex just shrugged his shoulders.

"Honestly, Julia, I'm not sure it is him. Sebbi claimed Brandr had died in battle, and no one contradicted him."

He said this to reassure the woman he loved, but I had known him as a brother for centuries and could easily pick up the doubt and confusion in his voice.

"Alex, I can email this footage to Freya to see if she recognises him," I said as I began typing the email.

"No, Josh, we can leave it for tonight. I want to be with her when she sees the footage, in case it triggers any bad memories. I'll speak to her tomorrow and tell her that Julia and I are expecting a baby. But for tonight, we want to keep the news to ourselves."

"Can I buy the pram?" I asked. "Then I can say I bought them their first set of wheels. I'm a good babysitter, Julia; just ask Keeley. I even change nappies," I told them.

"That's good to know, Josh," Julia said, smiling. "I hope Alex will change nappies, too."

"Of course. I'm going to be the best dad ever!"

I'd no doubt he'd be a great dad—this man who stood smiling before me. The same man who saved me from death all those years ago at Liverpool docks. This good, kind soul who'd brought me into his family and treated me like a brother. I swore a long time ago that I'd lay down my life for him and Freya because they'd given me my own. They both told me they loved me, and their love didn't come with any conditions, so I must stop feeling obligated to them.

But I would do it anyway.

However, looking at Julia and knowing what precious cargo she carried, I vowed to be both her and the child's protector always, no matter if Alex was there or not. This woman held the future of our family, and I'd make sure she was safe, whatever life threw at her.

Chapter Thirty-Eight

Alex

We visited Julia's parents the next afternoon. She wanted to tell them before we told anyone else, and I respected that, even though I was desperate to tell Freya.

Sue and George Browne were quite shocked by our news, which was to be expected. But once they got over the shock, they were thrilled. Then we hit them with the rest of our news: that Julia and I had Bonded.

I explained it meant that Julia and I shared blood to seal our love and commitment to each other. I told them that because of our Bond, as long as Julia had my blood regularly, she wouldn't age or get ill. Also, Julia would become stronger than a normal human and would heal from any injuries much quicker.

George looked at his daughter for the longest time before saying, "I'm happy that you're happy, Julia. I think you could have waited a while before you started a family, but I can see that you love my daughter, Alex, so I'll say no more about that. Can I just ask about our grandchild? Will it be human or vampire?"

A valid question that deserved a full answer. So I explained that their grandchild would be a Born Immortal who'd have a choice in whether they wanted true immortality. I also told them about my background and how old I was.

I thought Sue was going to faint and that George's jaw would hit the floor. Perhaps I should have held back with that one.

After our visit with the Brownes, we went back home to video call Freya.

On hearing about the baby, Freya squealed so loud she had Leonard running in to check on her. When he heard the news, he went and brought everyone else in the house to join in on the call. I was glad that Freya had people around to share her happiness. When everyone had finally calmed down, I told her that Viktor had been in touch about Brian Vargan.

Freya opened the video we sent her and minimised our screen. She skipped through the recording until nineteen minutes to see the guy I thought looked like Brandr.

Freya said she thought he might have looked like him but couldn't really remember. She was nine years old when he sailed to England, and he'd been away in battle for months at a time before that. Even when Brandr was home, he'd avoid being in the same room as her.

We concluded that it probably wasn't him, but she said she would watch the full video, anyway. Freya was coming down to visit us again next week with Gregor. I thought Gregor might try to convince her to stay in Barrowfield so she could oversee the renovations at the manor, but I knew she'd go back to Aldbrough.

I also knew that Freya would bring the ring and the rest of the jewellery I'd purchased for Julia. Maxwell had been true to his word and was making the engraving a priority.

Julia and I were going to visit Nik and Gina before we started work tonight, so I rang Nik and told him to expect us.

Although impressive, the modern decorating and contemporary furniture in Nik's cottage hadn't appealed to me. I preferred a traditional cottage look, with wood and stone finishes and sumptuous fabrics. Nik opted for neutral-coloured fabrics, a large corner sofa and angular wood and metal furniture. So you can imagine my surprise to find a decidedly more feminine home when I entered.

"Excuse the smell of paint," Gina said as she hurried around the room, rearranging throw cushions. "They're delivering the new furniture tomorrow, so we wanted to get all the painting done before it arrived."

They'd painted the walls in a pale mint green, and Nik was hanging up cream-coloured curtains with mint-green flowers across the bottom. He was shirtless, and it seemed funny to see Nik's large, muscle-bound chest splattered with such a pretty pastel colour.

Gina handed us a pamphlet showing a three-door cabinet, TV unit, coffee table, and side table, all made from oak. Julia loved the furniture and the light airy look, and I felt guilty at that moment.

I hadn't even considered that she might want to change the look of our cottage to something she preferred.

Gina offered us tea or coffee, but Julia declined. Apparently, caffeine wasn't good for the baby, so Julia was only having decaf. But I could never say no to a cuppa. We sat and waited for Nik to finish hanging the curtains before we announced our news.

He came straight over to sit by me but turned towards Julia and leaned in to take in her scent. "You're pregnant. Only just, but the scent is definitely there."

"Wow, that was quick work, you two. Congratulations," Gina said, handing me my tea. "I bet you're both a bit shell-shocked."

"I am, but Alex did say he was getting me pregnant as soon as he could. I just didn't think it would be this quick," Julia admitted.

"Well, congratulations to you both. When do you think you'll be due?" Nik asked.

"Early August, I think." I glanced at Julia and pictured her as she would be in the coming summer. Beautiful as ever, but with a radiant glow and her belly round with our child.

"I am so lucky."

I didn't realise I'd said that out loud until Nik slapped me on the back and said, "Yes, you are, Alex. You have your woman and now a child on the way. What more could a man want?"

"When I saw her at that party all those years ago, Josh asked me what I wanted from her, and I remember saying everything. Now I have everything I ever wanted, and it's all because of Julia."

Julia blushed, but through our Bond, she told me I was getting some good loving for that remark.

"You'll have to let us know what we can buy for the baby when the time comes, Julia. And as you can see, Nik is a dab hand at painting," Gina said as she gestured around the room. "So when you decide what colours you want for the baby's room, Nik can decorate for you. Although, if you're anything like me, I had my babies in the bedroom with me until they were a year old."

"Thanks for offering my decorating services, Gina, you slave driver," Nik joked as he poked Gina in the side. "And why ever would you want to keep babies in your room for that long?"

"I just wanted to know they were okay, and I needed to hear them breathing. That probably sounds like I lay awake all night listening to them, but it's not like that. You become so in tune with your baby that when they start to wake, you are instantly alert, even from sleep, and can deal with it accordingly.

"I breast-fed both my babies, so I didn't have to get up and warm bottles. When they'd murmur and become restless, I'd pick them up and put them on my breast. It's better than letting them get to the screaming stage because they take a lot longer to calm down then. When they were snuffly with a cold, it was better for them to be in the room with me."

"Didn't your husband mind?" Julia asked.

With a shrug of her shoulders, Gina replied, "He slept in another room."

"Selfish bastard," Nik muttered under his breath.

"Well, we better get to work and see what Night Movers has for us tonight," I said.

After handing Gina my empty cup, I pulled Julia up off the sofa and slipped my arm around her. She looked tired, and it was no wonder. We'd been up late last night, both restless due to all we'd learned that day. We'd been busy today, too, telling everyone our joyful news.

"Nik spoke to Josh last night. He told him about the guy on the security footage you thought you might recognise. Are you any nearer to finding out who this vampire is?"

"Sadly, no. It looked like the guy on the video could have been my stepfather, but he died many years ago, so it can't be him. Well, it's hard for me to imagine that it *could* be him from what I know."

"Alex, me and Julia are living and working with vampires. We're happy to exchange blood, and we'll be Bound to them forever. If you'd asked either of us fifteen years ago if we could imagine that, then I'm sure we'd have had you committed."

She was right, of course. But after seeing that look on Sebbi's face, I knew he'd killed Brandr. That still didn't help us find out who this Brian Vargan was, though. Now that we had a baby on the way, it was even more important that we find him to eliminate any threat he posed.

Chapter Thirty-Nine

Nik

Gina had become quite subdued after Alex and Julia left. She was pottering around the room, putting things from my old cupboards into boxes until our new furniture came.

When I asked her if she was okay, Gina said she was stressing about getting the cupboards emptied, so they'd be ready when the local animal rescue charity picked them up to sell in their shop. I knew she was lying, but I let it go.

Yesterday we went to the garden centre and noticed a display of paintings by a local artist. There were paintings of the duck pond and of various countryside views around Barrowfield and Rothley. He also had some of East Yorkshire's seaside resorts, particularly Bridlington. I purchased a painting of the harbour and hung it in the hallway just outside our bedroom. Gina said that was a good place to put it because she'd see it before she went to bed, and it would give her sweet dreams of a place she loved. Gina had such a fond, faraway look in her eyes when she'd said that. I decided to buy us a home there so we could go on our nights off.

It was time I sold some of the other properties I no longer visited. The upkeep was a burden I didn't need.

Vampires used to move around a lot a few years ago to avoid our immortality being discovered. When you don't age and are around for centuries, that can be a problem, especially when there are people hunting your kind. But that hasn't happened for over a hundred years now, so I think we're safe in modern-day Britain.

We also used some of our smaller properties for when we were transporting Made vampires to and from Europe, so they weren't travelling in daylight. But now we have planes, we rarely need the houses.

Gina finished clearing out the cupboards and had six boxes of stuff for me to go through. Crouching down to look inside the hoard, I was surprised at the amount of utter crap I'd amassed over the last few years. I glanced up at Gina and said, "Apart from my photographs and legal documents, you can bin the fucking lot."

"What about these CDs and DVDs?" she asked, producing yet another box.

"I've got all the songs I like on my iPod, and I've seen those DVDs, so they can all go. Apart from all three Godfather movies," I quickly added. I couldn't let my all-time favourite films go.

"And what about all those books that are in the back bedroom? Have you decided what you're going to do with them?"

"I don't know yet. Some of the modern stuff can go, but there are a few old ones in there that my grandfather gave me. I'll save those."

I picked her up and set us both down on the sofa. Then I took her hand and asked her what was really wrong.

"Nothing's wrong, Nik. As I've said, I'm just stressing about the furniture."

"That's bullshit, Gina. Now stop blocking me from your thoughts and tell me the truth!"

Gina looked a little sheepish but didn't deny she'd been blocking our Bond. After a minute or so of her not speaking, I'd had enough. I pushed her off my lap, walked over to my toolbox and took out some black electrical insulation tape. When I turned around, I could see she had a wary look in her eyes.

Good. She had a right to be wary.

I went over to lock the door and heard her get up from the sofa.

"We can do this here, Gina, or in the bedroom. Your choice," I stated. Then I removed the belt from my paint-splattered jeans and emptied my pockets.

Keeping the belt and tape in my left hand, I stalked towards her. Just before I reached her, Gina ran towards the bedroom.

"I know that look, Nik, and I'm not in the mood for any kinky stuff right now," she yelled before slamming the bedroom door behind her.

There was no lock on the door, not that one would have stopped me, so I went into the bedroom after her.

Gina stood next to her side of the bed with her hands on her hips and a defiant look on her face. I couldn't wait to wipe that off. It was about time she learned that she had to share what was worrying or upsetting her. I walked to her slowly and pressed her up against the wall.

"Are you going to tell me what's worrying you, Gina? This is your last chance before—"

"I can't give you children, Nik."

Wow. I didn't expect that to come out of her mouth.

"What made you think I wanted you to?"

"Alex looked so happy, and Julia is the reason for that. She not only loves him; she can also give him a family. I can't do that for you," she sobbed.

I picked her up and set her on my lap. After wiping the tears from her eyes, I placed my hand on the back of her neck and pulled her face towards mine. I kissed her with all the love and tenderness I could manage without wanting to rip her clothes off. Unfortunately, I couldn't hide the growing erection I was sporting, but I tried to ignore it, and Gina didn't mention it either. It wasn't my fault that I couldn't kiss her without getting hard. She was just too beautiful and sexy for me not to get aroused whenever we touched. It killed me to see the sadness in her eyes, and I needed to put her mind at rest over this.

"Gina, I love you. I don't need you to birth babies for me. I need you for you alone. To be with me and to love me right back. Besides, you've given me a stepson and stepdaughter. So you have given me kids in a way."

"It's not the same, Nik. I can't give you babies of your own."

"And thank fuck for that! They're noisy, smelly things that are a lot of hard work. They're not something I've ever wanted."

"But don't you want what Alex has? He can build his family and have someone call him Dad. Haven't you ever wanted that?"

"Do *you* want more kids, Gina? Do you want us to have a family? Because I know for a fact that I've never mentioned it. I knew you'd had a hysterectomy, so obviously, you couldn't have children. But it didn't stop me Bonding with you. I've never aspired to be a father, Gina.

"I was brought up in an orphanage in Romania with Sergei and lived there until my grandfather came for me. So if *you* wanted more kids, I'd be willing to adopt an orphaned child or two with you. But I'm sorry, love, I don't want babies. They'd have to be about six or seven years old before I would consider adopting them."

That surprised Gina. I could tell she hadn't thought about having more kids. But with Alex and Julia's news, Gina felt bad that she couldn't give me a child of my own.

"Personally, Gina, I'm happy with what we have. There's so much that I want to do with you. I want us to travel, have great holidays and nights out as a couple. Spend time together doing normal, everyday couple things.

"In a few years' time, we'll become grandparents when your son and daughter have children, and then I'll have no choice but to spend time with babies. But for God's sake, woman, when that happens, I don't ever want to change a nappy.

"I remember Josh making me hold Keeley's little girl when she was a baby. She pulled a face and shit straight through her nappy and sleep suit. It was bright fucking yellow and was all over my T-shirt. It went right up her back into her hair. Everybody laughed, and they left her in my arms until Keeley got all the baby stuff out of her bag so she could change her. She offered to wash my T-shirt, but I binned it. There was no way I wanted that back."

Gina was laughing now, thank God. I never wanted her to think she wasn't enough for me. She was it for me, for always. When she unblocked our Bond, I made sure she knew how I felt.

"I've told you, Gina, time and time again. Like I told you for all those wasted years before we Bonded. I could have been a father to your children. I would have loved you like you wanted and needed to be loved. But you doubted my love and commitment then. What will it take for you to believe that—in my eyes—we as a couple are perfection, just as we are?"

I moved Gina off my lap and went to get my iPod. After scrolling through the songs, I selected what I wanted. Then I put my iPod in the docking station and took Gina into my arms, just as the song started.

I began singing along with Billy Joel as we slowly danced cheek to cheek to the song, "Just The Way You Are."

I twirled her around at the end of the song, then brought her back into my arms and kissed her softly. Gina deepened the kiss, then reached between us to open the buttons on my jeans. I stilled her hand and pulled away from her a fraction so I could gaze into her beautiful blue eyes. The look I saw there told me exactly what she needed, and I was only too happy to oblige.

"Nik, what were you planning on doing with that tape and your belt when you came into the bedroom?" Gina asked as she lowered her gaze.

This shy side of Gina seemed to war with her bold and brazen side. I was lucky that my woman loved sex, and she especially loved a bit of kink with her sex. We'd tried a little bondage, which we both enjoyed, and last week we did some online shopping, buying nipple clamps and a vibrating cock ring. The nipple clamps really did it for Gina, and I loved seeing them on her bouncing tits when I fucked her.

"Gina, strip for me and get on the bed. On your back with your hands above your head."

My good little woman obeyed my command. As she moved up the bed, I dropped my jeans and boxers, picked up the tape, and crawled up the bed towards her. When she raised her arms above her head, I traced the shape of her breasts with my tongue, and her moans went straight to my cock.

I loved the sounds of pleasure that came from Gina when we were intimate. They stroked my ego and made me want to please her even more. She said she was making up for lost time and was enjoying everything we did together. I'd always been dominant in bed and was glad Gina liked that side of me.

I took the insulation tape and bound Gina's wrists together. The black tape stood out against her soft pale skin and turned me on even more. I looped my belt through the bars of the headboard and back through her bound wrists, then I asked through our Bond if the tape was too tight. She shook her head and licked her lips. The action prompted me to straddle her chest and drag my cock up her neck towards her mouth. She licked the head, then opened her mouth to take me inside.

I kept my thrusting shallow and steady, so I didn't cause her to gag. Gina loved to suck my cock. She hummed her enjoyment, which vibrated down to my balls. When I took my cock out of her mouth, she whimpered.

"Sshh, baby, I have something else for you." I leaned further forward with my balls above her lush lips. She lapped the underside, then drew my balls into her mouth one at a time.

Fucking hell! That felt so good. She had a wicked tongue and used it well. When she heard me groan, she moved to bite the inside of my thigh, just like I did to her. The only difference being, she didn't pierce my skin and drink my blood.

"Enough," I groaned. I moved down her body so I

could return the oral worship, kissing from her breasts to her slit. I gave her long, firm licks all over her sex. She was dripping wet, and I lapped it all, loving her taste as I always did. Her pretty pink pearl stood out from its hood, and I swirled my tongue around it gently. Gina's moans grew louder, and she tried to pull away from me. I held her still, licking and gently sucking until she came. I loved Gina's taste, but after she came, it was the sweetest, tastiest cream I'd ever had, and I couldn't get enough.

I turned my head to the side and bit into her femoral artery, thrusting two fingers inside her hot, wet heaven. She came again, and I was torn between drinking her blood and tasting her cream.

"Nik, please fuck me," Gina begged, panting and bucking her hips.

I lapped at the bite on her thigh, ran my tongue through her folds and then pushed myself up the bed to kiss her roughly.

I thrust my tongue in her mouth at the same time as I thrust my throbbing cock inside her. I yelled her name as I began to move. I wanted to fuck her hard, but I was almost ready to come after less than a minute, so I slowed my pace and gave myself time to recover.

"Untie me, Nik," Gina panted.

I reached up and extended my nails into claws, cutting through the tape carefully. Gina flexed her arms and wrists, then put them around my back.

I moved in that steady rocking rhythm guaranteed to make her come. The trouble was, I was so far gone by now that I couldn't hold off much longer. I was inside her to the hilt, dominating her body, and yet, when gazing down at her, I felt almost powerless. Gina owned me. Without her love, I would wither and die.

"I love you, Gina." The words didn't seem enough, but I said them anyway.

"I love you too, Nik, more than ever. You've made my life worth living."

Now, why didn't I say that? Women seem to be a lot better with words than men, but I hoped Gina could tell that she would always be my world.

We came together, and for a few blissful minutes, I swear I'd entered the promised land.

Gina's stomach rumbled, reminding me how long it had been since we'd eaten.

"Come on, woman, let's get in the shower. I have to get this paint off my chest hair, and we both need to eat." I rolled Gina over and slapped her arse.

"Only if you promise to make it worth my while," she said, getting up and stretching. So I slapped her arse once again, harder this time, which caused her to yelp. My cock came back to life when I saw my handprint on each cheek.

Gina looked down at my rapidly rising shaft and smiled. I guessed this was going to be a long, enjoyable shower, and I hoped there was plenty of hot water.

Chapter Forty

Julia

Freya called on Monday to let me know she'd bring the ring I'd had engraved for Alex today. It was Friday now, and I'd been both anxious and excited about proposing to Alex since she rang.

My mood seemed to have rubbed off on Alex, too, as he was behaving in the same giddy, loved-up way as me. We were both so thrilled about my pregnancy that life couldn't get any better.

On Tuesday afternoon, I went round to Gina and Nik's to see their new furniture, and I told her I was planning on proposing to Alex when Freya brought the ring. We discussed different ways I could do it, and Gina gave me a great idea.

She told me that when we'd visited her and Nik to tell them about my pregnancy, she became worried that Nik would also want a child. Because Gina had a hysterectomy a few years ago, she obviously wouldn't be able to get pregnant, so Gina had felt like she was letting Nik down.

Nik reassured her that he didn't want children. Then he'd sung the Billy Joel song "Just The Way You Are" to her. Apparently, Nik was a talented singer and had sung it while dancing with her. Gina told me it melted her heart, and I could understand why. She'd stopped questioning if she was enough for him ever since.

The fact that Nik Harding was a big romantic came as a surprise. That tall, good-looking hunk of man-flesh was just about everything a woman could want by the sounds of it. All women apart from me, of course. I had my sexy blond Viking to drool over.

Hearing what Nik had done gave me an idea regarding my proposal. I wouldn't sing to Alex because, to be honest, my voice isn't that great. Oh, who am I kidding? It's actually terrible. And apart from my drunken karaoke episode on ladies' night, I avoided singing in public. But I thought that playing love songs in the background while I proposed would be a good idea. Gina gave me Nik's iPod to borrow so I could browse through all the different ones he had. Nik's song collection was enormous, and I was sure I'd find quite a few I liked that had words I wanted to say.

I thought I'd cook a main course followed by dessert, proposing before we ate. Gina and I bounced ideas off each other about the menu, finally deciding on beef cobbler and some profiteroles from Mr Singh's shop that Gina recommended.

Freya had dropped the ring off earlier, and I absolutely loved it. But handing over the ring while getting down on one knee wasn't something that appealed to me. I looked on the internet for ideas, but they nearly all seemed to involve flowers or putting the ring in a glass. Then I happened upon an advert for helium balloons. I thought about weighing a helium balloon down with the ring box and a champagne weight.

Getting a clear picture in my mind of what I needed, I rang the florist across from the Red Lion in the village and told them what I had planned. We decided on a dozen red roses in a vase, a red heart helium balloon with a gold ribbon, and the champagne weight I'd envisaged. I also called Mel at the Red Lion for a bottle of champagne. I wouldn't be able to drink it, but Alex would celebrate for the both of us.

Alex had meetings all day, so I could prepare everything without him knowing. Nik and Sergei were with Freya and Gregor, looking at building plans, and Josh would probably be at home sleeping. Gina was going out for lunch with her son, so I couldn't ask her to go with me, and my mum and dad were visiting their elderly neighbour in Barnsley hospital. I was the only one available to drive down to the village to collect what I needed.

I knew I'd probably get shouted at for going out without telling anyone, but I needed to go as soon as possible to collect it all, then I could get back and prepare our food.

If I'd opted for the florist to deliver everything, people would see her drive down the lane and could ask Alex about it. That was the trouble with living alongside work and between Nik and Josh. We had very little privacy unless we were behind closed doors. If I hurried, I could be back before anyone noticed I'd left.

I threw my car keys, purse, and mobile phone into my new Kipling cross-body bag, then I got in my car and drove the short distance to the florist's.

As soon as I pulled up outside the shop, I was immediately enchanted by the brightly lit Christmas display in the window. It wouldn't be long before the big day was upon us. Less than five weeks to go, and I hadn't even thought of any gifts. My life and the important people in it had changed dramatically over the last nine months, and I became distracted by the memories.

The crisp November air nipped at my fingers, so I left my melancholy moment outside the shop and went inside to plan for my future.

Chloe, the florist, was an absolute star who listened to everything I had to say and put together a balloon masterpiece. The main balloon was a deep-red shiny heart with a plaited bronze and pewter-coloured ribbon attached to it. Instead of the champagne bottle weight I'd initially asked for, Chloe suggested a small charcoal-grey wicker basket where I could put the ring box. She also did two miniatures of the larger balloon and placed them on sticks, slotting them in with the dozen red roses and white gypsophila, which she called babies breath. I touched my lower tummy when Chloe said that. I was determined to feel this baby's breath on my skin as I held them. No one would take that away from me this time around.

As I turned to pay for my items, I caught a beautiful scent coming from candles to the left of the till. They were by a famous brand my mum liked to use, but the name of this one made me smile. It was called *First Christmas*. I bought two of them—one for Alex and me and one for Nik and Gina, as it was their first Christmas together, too.

I wondered if Alex put up Christmas decorations. I hoped so because I loved this time of year. There was nothing prettier than twinkling Christmas lights to welcome you home on a cold winter's night.

Chloe said she was bringing in more decorations over the next couple of days, so I promised I would call back and have a look. She joked that the *'Santa Stop Here'* signs would probably be her biggest sellers when children saw them. I thought of Alex, Josh, and Nik and their playful office banter with Maggie. So, for the office, I picked a tiny Christmas tree covered with snow spray before adding one of the Santa signs to my growing list of purchases.

The sign was about a foot in length and was all metal with a sharp, spiked end. It had a vintage look with muted colours that stopped the sign from looking too babyish.

After I'd paid for everything, I popped the sign in my bag along with the candles, and Chloe helped carry the flowers and balloon to my car. Once everything was secure, I popped over to the Red Lion to get the champagne from Mel. The draymen had just pulled away, so I went around the back of the pub to where the cellar door opened.

Looking down the cellar steps, I shouted a quick hello to a busy Mel, who waved a bottle of pink gin and told me to come down.

I was just two steps from the cellar floor when I heard a noise behind me. Before I could turn to check it out, a large hand covered my mouth while a strong arm grabbed me around my waist.

I didn't need to see them to know who it was, and for a moment, I stilled as panic swept through me. But as quickly as that happened, it disappeared and was replaced by anger.

I kicked out and jabbed my elbows into the vampire's sides, but he laughed and said, "I knew you would fight me, little female, but as a mere human, you will not cause me harm, so your resistance is futile."

His English was heavily accented in either German or Scandinavian, making me think of how the actors who played Germans in old war movies spoke. I couldn't help laughing at the thought, and the vampire released me from his grip.

I turned around and got my first proper look at the vampire we knew as Brian Vargan. He was well over six feet tall and extremely handsome, with classical features and deep-blue eyes. He was powerfully built with broad, muscular shoulders; if he were human, I would have said he lived at the gym to get a frame like that. He wore a black leather jacket and blue jeans, which seemed too casual for him.

"Like what you see?" he questioned with a smug look.

"Not really," I answered truthfully. "I don't think this look works for you, Brandr."

He gasped and took a step back from me, and I knew Alex was right when he tried to identify this vampire.

Not two seconds later, Mel came forward and tried to wallop him around the head with what I suspected to be the bottle of champagne I was going to buy. But Brandr was too quick and grabbed the bottle with vampire speed. Then he punched Mel hard enough that she fell back onto the concrete floor and didn't move.

I scrambled to the floor after her, turning her face towards me, and I noticed blood coming from grazing at her temple and hairline. I tried to feel for a pulse, but my heart was beating so fast I couldn't tell if hers was faint or strong.

Brandr yanked me back from Mel, and I swear I saw her eyes open slightly as I was dragged away. With a fierce grip on my ponytail and coat collar, I was pulled towards steps leading up to a trapdoor behind the main bar. I lost my footing as my feet stumbled over bottles that had yet to be put away from the recent delivery. Brandr held on tighter to my hair and coat, not caring about what I bumped into.

He didn't stop until we were in front of the main bar, pushing me down on a bench next to the jukebox. I still wore the cross-body bag, so the candles knocked together against my side, and I thought I heard one smash.

"Tell me how you know my name," he demanded angrily.

I *could* tell the truth, I thought, as I studied his scowling yet interested face. Or I could turn it around and try to reason with him. But I wasn't sure how I could do that or even if I should. I tried to access the Bond I held with Alex, but he'd closed himself off for his meeting. I'd welcomed that fact earlier when planning and buying for my proposal. Now I wished the Bond was open so he could sense my fear at this possibly life-threatening situation.

"You are refusing to speak to me," he stated, studying me closely. "I have all the time in the world for you to tell me, Julia."

Brandr smiled sadistically.

So he knew my name. It came as no surprise. He'd followed me to my parents' home, and in a small village like Barrowfield, everyone knew who you were and who you were seeing.

"Don't move. I will be back momentarily, and you will be punished if you disobey," he said.

Brandr went behind the bar and closed the trapdoor to the cellar before pouring himself a drink.

Chapter Forty-One

Josh

My phone rang while I was getting dressed. I thought it would be Alex letting me know how his meeting with the local vicar had gone. We were on good terms with the last one because Night Movers had contributed enough money to get the roof fixed on the church. But, as Alex wanted to get married within a couple of weeks, I had a feeling the church would receive another large donation so Alex could get his way. A quick glance at my phone before I answered told me it was Mel, my bar manager from the Red Lion.

"Hi, Mel. What can I do for you?" I asked while putting my trainers on.

"Josh, I need you to come down here. Now! There's a man—who I think is a vampire—and he has Alex's girlfriend in the bar. I tried to stop him, but he's really strong and quick. He almost knocked me out when he punched me. I can hear him talking and moving around behind the bar. I'm down in the cellar, and I've left the outside doors open for you. Hurry, please, Josh. I don't think I can take him on my own."

What the... Oh, fuck! Vargan was here, and he had Julia. I wouldn't let him harm her and the baby.

I quickly grabbed my car keys and a few long sharp knives out of my kitchen while I tried to calm Mel.

"Now listen to me, Mel. Under no circumstances should you try to get near him. Just stay where you are, keep your phone on silent, and expect my call shortly. I'm just setting off to you now, but I'll park in the car park so he doesn't hear me pull up. Okay, Mel?"

"Yeah, okay."

"I'll be there in five minutes."

I sped away from the compound and called Alex. The call went straight to voicemail, so I rang him repeatedly until he answered.

"Josh, what's up? I'm busy with Father Stevens at the moment. Can I call you back?"

"Vargan has Julia at the Red Lion. I'm on my way now. Mel's still there, but she's hurt."

I heard a chair fall over as Alex got up and ran, then listened to the vicar yelling in the distance, asking if everything was okay.

"Is Julia hurt, Josh? Did Mel say he'd hurt her?"

"No, Alex, she said she could just hear talking. Listen, I'm parking my car across the road from the pub, and I suggest you do the same. We don't want to alert him to our presence. I'll keep my phone on so you can hear what's being said. Go through the drayman's entrance around the back. I'm just heading there now, so I'll let you know what I find out, okay?"

"Just keep her safe for me, Josh. Julia and the baby mean everything to me. I can't live this life if they aren't in it."

Alex's voice broke on those last words, but as much as I wanted to speak kind words back to him, now was not the time.

The scent of blood hit me as I descended the cellar steps; when Mel came out of the shadows to greet me, I could see why.

"Thank God you're here, Josh," Mel whispered as she threw her arms around me and hugged me tightly.

I had never seen Mel looking scared before, and she wasn't normally the touchy-feely type.

"Let me take a look at you." I tilted her head to see grazing at the side of her temple.

"Do you trust me?" I whispered. "I can give you a little blood to help you heal from your injuries, but only if you want it. It won't do anything other than heal the grazing and any swelling, but I'd sooner have you at full strength so you can help if I need you."

She hesitated for a few seconds, then whispered, "Okay, Josh, I trust you. And I want to see this bastard take a fall."

She seemed to stand taller in that instant, and I could see that the Mel I knew was coming back to me. I bit into my wrist and offered it to her. Mel placed her mouth on top of the cut, looked directly at me, and then sucked.

Fuck me! If that wasn't the single most sexiest thing a woman had ever done. I was instantly hard and throbbing, but I had to get my mind back in the game.

I pulled my wrist away and wiped some stray blood from Mel's mouth. Her cut would heal within minutes, so I took off my T-shirt, grabbed a bottle of vodka, and told her to clean the blood away from her head.

She did as I asked, and I climbed the concrete steps up to the bar as quietly as I could. The trapdoor had been closed, but I could hear words being spoken by a deep-voiced male. He had a European accent and kept asking Julia how she knew who he was. Vargan said he thought it was funny that he'd been able to watch Alex for years without his knowledge. He told her he'd used herbs from a witch in the Black Forest that masked his scent from other vampires.

According to Vargan, he'd been watching and waiting for the right moment to strike out at Alex, and Julia would be his weapon. I didn't like the sound of that at all. He also said we'd only sensed him recently because he'd become resistant to the herbs.

He mentioned they'd dulled his other senses, but he could still scent the fear in Julia. She laughed loudly and said she had no fear of him. Not while Alex and her vampire family were around. But Vargan laughed too and remarked, "Look around, dear Julia. There is no one here except you and me."

Mel tapped my leg. I looked down and found she had a huge machete-type knife in her hand.

"Mel, what the fuck are you doing with a knife like that?" I whispered as I climbed down the steps.

"I thought you could use it to kill the vampire. I've got others if you don't think this is suitable," she whispered.

Mel crooked her finger, asking me to follow her. She opened up what used to be a cleaning cupboard and switched on a light. To say I was shocked was an understatement. Mel had been in the army before she came to be my manager at the Red Lion, but I don't think the army would have trained her to use the weapons on display. There were knives ranging from about four inches to two-foot-long swords. I touched the handle on the largest one and turned to a grinning Mel.

"This is wrong on so many fucking levels, Mel. I mean, look at them. This one is huge," I said, taking the sword/knife from its shelf.

"If you think that's big, you want to see the one under my bed," she whispered with a smirk.

A gun cabinet was attached to the wall on the right. Mel produced a key from her jeans pocket and opened the tall cabinet. Inside was a shotgun, two handguns, and a semi-automatic rifle.

Mel retrieved some ammunition from the bottom of the cabinet and took out the shotgun, a handgun, and the rifle. She loaded each one quickly and with great ease, handing them to me as she went. When she was finished, Mel turned to face me and whispered, "I need you to tell me how to kill him, Josh. Then we're good to go."

The weapons were impressive, but I wouldn't put Mel in harm's way.

"Mel, a vampire needs to be staked through the heart, then you have to remove the head and burn the body. Just shooting him won't kill him like it would a human."

"I'm keeping the rifle and handgun, Josh. You can take the machete and whichever sword you want."

"Mel, I can't risk you getting hurt. The speed a vampire can move is like a bullet being shot from a gun. Before you know it, you're lying on the floor with a broken neck. I can't let anything happen to you."

"Not your choice, big guy. I swore I would never let another man hurt me again, and this fucker knocked me out. I'll let you do your thing, but if I get the chance to shoot him, I will."

I nodded my acceptance and walked back towards the

steps. She'd said she wouldn't let another man hurt her. I'd never asked Mel about her past, but after this was over, I think we were due a long conversation.

The vampire kept asking Julia how she knew his name was Brandr.

So, Alex was right. It was the guy he thought was his father. That made him an extremely powerful vampire, and I didn't think he'd come for a nice catch-up. Julia had a steely determination in her voice; I couldn't help but admire her resolve in the face of what could be her death. She told Brandr that Alex often spoke of him and thought he'd died in battle.

I became aware of Alex's presence behind me and felt relief at knowing he was there. I started to whisper what I'd heard, but he put his fingers to his lips.

"Our Bond is open; Julia has told me everything he's said. Right now, he's next to the dartboard, so that places him around ten feet away from her. I'm going to open the trapdoor and speak to him. You can follow me up but stay behind the bar."

Alex noticed Mel approach the steps with the rifle in her hands and shook his head. He took my phone from my back pocket and gestured to Mel.

"Flick through the contacts and call Nik. Tell him what's going on." She nodded and took the phone but didn't let go of the rifle.

"On the count of three," Alex whispered.

After counting down silently, Alex opened the trapdoor into the bar.

The squeaking noise wasn't that loud, but it was noticeable even to human ears. We heard a scuffle as Brandr grabbed Julia. Alex stood as I silently climbed the steps and hid behind the bar.

"Brandr, I assume you've come for me and not my woman?" Alex said calmly.

I was anything but calm at that moment. Through a slight gap in the woodwork, I could see that Brandr was holding Julia, his chest to her back and his hand in her hair, pulling her head over to the side. His fangs had descended, and his eyes had turned red.

I crouched in readiness and placed the large machete on my knee. Mel came up the steps behind me as Alex spoke.

"Why did you hide yourself from us? You should have let me know you were alive—that you were a vampire like me. I mourned you, Father. And all this time, you hid from me."

"I am not your father, Aðalbrandr, you know this. Sebbi fathered you and Freya with my beautiful Brisafreya. He took my woman from me and made me into this."

"Why did he make you immortal? And when did he do this?" Alex asked.

"It was on the night we were due to sail back to Norway. Our settlement was established, and we were leaving good warriors behind to protect it. I took a walk in the woods every night we were there, and on that particular night, I set off later than usual. After I had been walking for a while, I heard a noise behind me. Sebbi came up to me as I drew my sword. He moved so fast and held me in a tight grip, forcing me to drop my weapon. I could not believe his strength; it was far greater than anyone I'd ever encountered. When he wrestled me to the ground and bit into my neck, I knew why.

"I'd heard the legend of vampires from the village elders, but I didn't believe them to be true. I thought they were stories to frighten little children.

"I don't know how long he drank from me, but I could

feel myself growing weaker. When black spots appeared before my eyes, he stopped drinking. That's when I saw the monster in him for the first time. His eyes were red, and my blood dripped from his sharp, pointed fangs. I thought he would end my life, but instead, he told me a story.

"Sebbi said he'd met my wife the day we were married, when Gamall introduced them at our wedding feast. It was the night before I was due to sail to Bretland for the first time. He said he was able to control my mind and convince me that I didn't want to sleep with my wife. Instead, I took one of the willing wenches that had been flirting with me all night. That was the first night Sebbi took your mother and might have been the night she conceived you."

I kind of felt sorry for this guy. Sebbi was a real bastard and deserved everything that Freya did to him.

After a heavy sigh, Brandr carried on speaking.

"Sebbi told me that when I'd come back from Bretland, he used mind control on me every night thereafter to prevent me from sleeping with your mother, although I was convinced I had lain with her. He was there to see you born but let everyone believe you were mine. I was proud of my son. You were growing strong and handsome with your mother's grey eyes and fair hair.

"When Freya came along, I knew she wasn't mine. She had her mother's hair and eyes and was a beautiful child, but something inside me told me she came from another man's seed."

Alex sighed and looked towards Brandr with sympathy. "You hurt her with your indifference, and Freya tried so hard for you to love her. She was a lovely little girl."

"But I could not love her, Aðalbrandr. I loved you, though. But that love was misplaced because *you* did not belong to me, either."

"What else happened the night that Sebbi drank from you?" asked Julia.

"He explained what it would take to make me a vampire. He said he would drink from me once more, then give me his blood. Then he would tie me to the trees and leave me so that I would burn from the inside out when the sun came up."

That was harsh. Even if Brandr hadn't been father of the year, there was no need to punish him. And especially making him face that kind of death.

Brandr carried on talking but released Julia from his grip and set her on his lap, his arm around her waist.

"After Sebbi told me what he was going to do to me, he said he would bring you and Freya over to Bretland to the settlement we had built. He said because you were from his seed, you were a Born Immortal. Sebbi told me that when Born Immortals drank human blood, they had the strength of a vampire yet could walk in the sun. That is how I knew you were not my child, Aðalbrandr.

"When he finally took my mortal life and gave me his blood to make me a vampire, I felt both fear and despair. Sebbi laughed when he left me tied up. I was weak and in the change from human to vampire. The sound of that laugh has stayed with me for over nine hundred years.

"Unbeknown to Sebbi, my friend Kafe—a warrior who had fought at my side in many battles—had witnessed what Sebbi had done. He untied me and carried me to a cave at the far side of the woods. He made a small cut on his wrist and dripped blood into my mouth. Kafe stayed with me until the sun rose high in the sky, and I fell into my first immortal sleep. He left for the settlement but came back every night and gave me his blood until I was no longer weak.

"I left that place and moved to other areas of Bretland at night, taking human blood and keeping myself strong. I swore I would go back and finish Sebbi when he returned with you and your mother from Norway. But I wasn't as strong as him and was unable to walk in the sun, so I knew I could not beat him. I returned instead to take your mother from him, but I found out from Kafe that your mother had drowned during the journey over. I watched you and Freya go about your life for years, oblivious to the fact that I was watching you. You both seemed happy about my supposed demise.

"I came back to find you some twenty years later and discovered that Sebbi and Gamall had both passed away. I was told that Freya's family had perished, and she was living with that grief. You had not yet taken a wife and were caring for your sister—still living in the settlement that I helped build.

"I decided to wait until you took a wife, then I'd take that woman from you so you would know my pain."

Bastard. Just when I felt sorry for the guy, he had to come out with something like that. I couldn't see Julia's face from where I was, but Alex shook with anger.

"Brandr, why would you want to do this? I did you no harm, and I wasn't happy about your demise. You could have forgotten about us and lived your own life. Why haven't you met and married someone else?" Alex asked, trying to control the anger in his voice.

"I was like you, Aðalbrandr. I used women for my pleasure when I felt the need. I did not want one enough to take a wife. I knew I would prefer yours," he said with a smirk. Julia tried to wriggle away from him.

"I travelled all over Europe, coming back to Yorkshire to find you at different intervals. About twenty-four years ago, I found a woman in this village. She, too, was recently married, and I used mind control to make her Bond with me. Her husband was working away from the village, and I had her every night for weeks. I discovered she was having my child three weeks into our Bond. She cried because she knew the child wasn't from her husband's seed. I kept using mind control to make her forget and keep me satisfied in bed. She was a beautiful woman, with long blonde hair and pale blue eyes. She reminded me of your mother. I thought about taking her back to where I had made my home in France and forgetting all about you."

"You raped her," Julia spat. "You used mind control to force her to sleep with you. I'd felt sorry for you earlier, but you're a true monster who needs to be stopped."

Brandr laughed at her. I saw Mel tense up beside me and lift her rifle. I also felt the presence of two more vampires, so I knew Nik and Sergei had arrived.

"Why didn't you stay with her and raise your child? I thought you would have welcomed a son or daughter with this woman," Alex asked.

"I had to leave the village. You and that Russian vampire you associate with had almost discovered me. So I went back to Germany to see the witches for a stronger brew of their herbs. When I came back, the woman had moved. Because she didn't want the Bond, she was able to shut me out, and I could not locate her. I felt her death years later through the Bond she so despised. I still do not know whether I have a son or daughter on this earth."

I wondered who the woman was, glad that she'd escaped him and that her child would never know this evil man.

"Do not try to get away from me, Julia. I promise you

will find me to be a good lover," said the evil bastard as Julia tried to pull away from him.

I saw her hand reach into the large, patterned bag she carried. Alex shook his fist where I crouched, then gave a command with his hand: three, two, one.

I couldn't see what Julia pulled out of her bag, but whatever it was, she hit Brandr in the face with it. I heard glass smash, followed by a roar of pain from him.

Alex jumped over the bar, and I followed, but it was too late. Brandr had his hands around Julia's neck.

"I will kill her if you come any nearer, Aðalbrandr. You know this to be true. So if you want to keep her alive, you will let me leave with her."

A shot rang out from behind me.

Brandr's head snapped back, and blood splattered on the wall behind him. His hands dropped from around Julia's neck as soon as the bullet Mel fired hit him. Julia reached into her bag and pulled out a long metal object, which she thrust into his chest on the left side. When I saw Brandr drop to the floor, I knew she'd hit her mark.

Alex pulled Julia into his arms to comfort her, but she pushed him away.

"Alex, we have to finish him; we can't let him come back. You need to chop off his head and burn him. Where can we burn the body?"

Alex picked her up and moved her away from Brandr.

"I'll take care of this, Julia. You can go with Mel and calm down. I can't let you see this next bit, love. I can't let you have the nightmares that have plagued me for years."

As soon as she turned away, Alex went over to Brandr's body. He took hold of his head and placed his foot on the vampire's chest.

Oh, fuck no! He was going to pull Brandr's head off.

Quick as a flash, I leapt over to Alex and knocked him onto his back. I put my hand on Alex's arm and showed him the machete I carried.

"Let me take care of this, brother. This isn't something you have to see either."

"Josh, he came here to hurt me because of what my father did to him. He was going to take Julia. It's my mess, and I will see it done."

I offered Alex my hand. Pulling him up onto his feet, I looked him in the eyes.

"Let me do it, Alex. Consider it payment for saving my life. Then we'll be equal... up here, anyway." I tapped a finger against my temple and saw him flinch.

Alex sighed heavily and brushed a tear from his cheek before he spoke.

"Josh, we have always been equal here," he tapped his temple, "and here," he said, as he touched his chest where his heart lay. Then he hugged me close and whispered, "Never think otherwise, my brother. Now let this day be an end to it."

"Go," I told him, my voice choked with emotion. "Julia needs you. Make sure she and the baby are okay."

Alex released me and nodded. Then he walked towards Julia and escorted her to the back of the bar. They both went to hug Mel and thank her for her help in taking down Brandr.

Nik and Sergei came up behind me and took in the scene.

"Come, Joshua, let us get this done," said Sergei as he went to take the machete from my hands. Nik held a couple of sacks and was moving towards Brandr's body.

"No, Sergei, it's fine. I can do it," I declared as I went to stand by Brandr's bloodied head.

The gunshot wound had already begun to mend, and if we pulled the sharp object out of his chest, Brandr would heal and carry on hurting the people I loved. But to remove someone's head is not an easy task, and I was dreading what was to come.

"You need to strike here," said Sergei, pointing at a spot two inches below his chin. He looked around at the carpeted area where we were standing. "It is too late to cover this up, and there's blood on the walls already. Nik and I will stand back while you strike, but depending on the sharpness of the blade, it might take two strikes to remove his head—even with our strength. Nik, can you lift some of this carpet so we can carry the body outside to burn him? He is too big for the sacks, but the head can go in one until we start the fire."

Sergei seemed to know what he was doing. I was glad about that because my mind felt scrambled.

Nik took one of the kitchen knives I'd brought and began lifting the edges of the carpet.

"Joshua, it is time," Sergei prompted. "You have no love for this man. He tried to hurt Alex and his Julia and does not deserve to live. He could hurt them again or someone else. Now do it, Joshua. Take his head."

I raised my arm, and with as much force as I could muster, I brought the machete down to the place where Sergei said to strike, removing Brandr's head on the first go.

It was a relief to hear the machete cut through the carpet and scrape against the concrete floor. Sergei nodded, confirming Brandr's decapitation, so I pulled the bloodied weapon away, then staggered towards the bar.

Mel returned and handed me a whisky. She came around to me and took the machete from my hands.

"Sit down, Josh, before you fall down," she said, looking at me with concern.

I gestured at my jeans, which were splattered with blood, so she pulled up a wooden stool and set me down on it.

"I've put a sign on the door saying we're closed due to a water leak, and I've cordoned off the car park with the cones we used to keep people away from the firework display. We can burn the body on the bonfire site to save people seeing you take it in any of your vehicles. I have a can of petrol we use for the lawnmower, so the body will burn quicker."

"Yes, that is good thinking, Mel," Sergei said as he placed Brandr's head in a sack. Then he and Nik rolled the body up in a piece of carpet and asked Mel to open up the door to the back of the pub.

I helped Nik carry the body while Sergei carried the sack containing Brandr's head. Nik doused the body in petrol, and Sergei sent Mel down to the garage to get two more cans.

Sergei and Nik seemed so efficient, but I was a wreck. It wasn't the first time I'd witnessed a gruesome death, though the way in which you destroy a vampire is beyond horrific. When Freya had done it, she was dealing with a twisted, vengeful anger and unimaginable grief. Yet I know it still affected her considerably.

It took four hours and three cans of petrol for the body to burn to ash. Alex came back after leaving Julia at home with Gina. When I asked how she was, he said she was fine. She was glad that Brandr was dead and had no qualms that she'd staked him. Julia was just annoyed that she'd lost the Santa Stop Here sign in the process. I couldn't believe that's what she used to stake him, but I was glad Julia had that and the candle in her bag.

I thought Julia showed real bravery for a mortal woman. Alex said it was more to do with the fact that she was pregnant. Julia was determined that no one would harm her child. Or separate her and Alex.

Women truly surprise me. When I'd been falling apart today, Mel had taken over and helped sort everything out. I couldn't believe how strong she'd been in the face of such a nightmare, military training or not. And what was with the weapons she had hidden in the cellar?

While we were cleaning blood off the walls and tables, I asked her about them. She'd said that was a conversation for another day, and if I respected her at all, I wouldn't push her on it. I respected Mel, now more than ever, so I let it go —for today. But I was concerned about her need for them and why she had so many.

Once everything was taken care of, Mel gathered together some clothes and toiletries so she could stay with me for the night. I didn't blame her for wanting to be away from the place. I wouldn't have stayed there either.

After switching off all the lights, we locked up the pub and headed back to my cottage.

I offered Mel the shower first, but she shook her head and said I needed it more. As the warm water beat down on my weary body, I felt the door to the shower cubicle open, with Mel's scent saturating the wet heat. She placed her arms around me, her bare breasts pressing into my back, then she lay her head against my shoulder and sighed.

I threaded my fingers through hers, and we stayed that way for a few minutes before I turned around to face her.

Even through the splashes of water from the shower, I could tell that Mel had been crying. I held her close while she let out more tears, and I cursed my erection. It had been so long since I'd been naked with a woman, I couldn't help getting hard when I felt her body against mine.

When she stopped crying, I kissed her on the forehead and washed her hair. Mel had soft brown, shoulder-length hair that she nearly always wore in a ponytail. After I rinsed out the shampoo, she asked me if I had any conditioner. I shook my head, so she shrugged her shoulders and grabbed the body wash. Mel soaped up her hands and washed my chest and arms, then she turned me around and did my back. Her hands moved lower, and I held my breath. She ran them over my tense buttocks, then dropped to her knees to wash my legs.

When Mel asked me to turn around, I hesitated but did as she asked, holding my cock away from her face.

She washed my thighs and then looked up at me. I let my hard cock fall free of my hands and closed my eyes as Mel touched me. She washed my now-aching manhood thoroughly, then I moved my body directly under the shower spray so I could rinse off.

Taking the body wash, I soaped up her arms and back as we leaned together, chest to chest. Then I stepped back and poured more body wash into my hands and began to wash her breasts, taking my time around her rosy-brown nipples.

Mel's cheeks were flushed, and her breaths came faster when I moved lower until my right hand reached her smooth-shaven core.

I slipped my fingers between her folds and ran them along her slit. Mel was wet and hot, and I desperately wanted to taste her, but for now, I let my fingers work to bring her to orgasm. I dipped my middle finger inside her, and she let out a gasp. I added another finger and let my thumb press on the area above her clit, dragging it around in circles until she ground herself against my hand, panting and moaning. When Mel came, she let out a loud gasp and opened her eyes to look at me. The moment she came down from her orgasm, I pulled my hand away.

We hadn't spoken many words to each other since she entered the shower, and I wasn't sure whether she wanted to take this any further.

I looked into her eyes, needing to know whether she wanted more. Mel put her arms around my neck and pulled me down for a kiss. It was soft and sensual, and we both groaned at the pleasure it gave. Grabbing the back of her thighs, I lifted her up against the tiled wall. She wrapped her legs around me and sighed when my cock found her sex.

I pushed inside her tight, wet heat and moaned out loud with pure pleasure. I was a big guy and was careful not to hurt her as I pushed in further, but she angled her hips to take me deeper. I pressed her harder against the wall, my thrusts slow but deep. I was desperate to come but tried my best to keep my climax at bay. When I felt Mel's orgasm hit and heard the noises she made, I lost it totally. I fucked her hard and fast until I came, grunting and groaning against her shoulder. It was a strong, cathartic release that I felt deep within my soul, and I could only hope that it gave her the same type of healing.

I lowered Mel until she was standing once again, then kissed her. Neither of us spoke as we finished washing, or I turned the shower off and grabbed each of us a towel. After drying off, she went over to my bed and climbed in naked.

"Will you hold me tonight, Josh?" she asked, looking up at me.

I nodded and climbed into bed beside her, holding her

back against my chest. Within minutes, Mel was asleep, but it took me a while longer to follow.

I was trying to process in my mind everything that had happened today. From Mel's frantic call to cutting off Brandr's head, then sleeping naked with Mel after having sex in my shower. I understood that sex was a way to forget the horrors of today, even for a short time, and I expected nothing more from it.

I got up to get some blood because I suddenly felt so drained. I was glad that Mel was sleeping. I didn't think seeing me drink from a blood bag would help her feel safe tonight.

I was careful not to wake Mel when I slipped back in bed and put my arms around her. My dark skin was like a silhouette against her paleness.

Today had been a lot to take in, and I thought I'd never get to sleep. But somehow, the sound of Mel breathing softly against my skin lulled me into one of the best night's sleep I ever had.

Chapter Forty-Two

Alex

Sergei brought Julia's car back. He was staying with Nik and Gina, so he'd followed us home. Mel had opted to stay the night at Josh's cottage, which I was thankful for. I didn't want to leave her at the Red Lion after everything that had occurred there today.

Julia had fallen asleep by the time I got back. Gina had kept her company, and they'd been trying to watch a movie, but they turned it off halfway through when neither of them could concentrate on it. Gina whispered goodnight and kissed me on the cheek as she left.

I looked at Julia curled up on the sofa and didn't have the heart to wake her. I could understand her wanting to see Brandr dead. She'd rebuilt her life, and he would've taken that from her. After the tragedy of her past, I knew Julia wouldn't let that happen without a fight. But I also knew the fact that she'd helped kill a man today would eat away at her bravado, and she'd feel the effects of our actions at some point.

I covered Julia with a fleece blanket and then took a shower. I welcomed the spray of hot water, washing away the sweat, dirt, and blood from today. I wished it could wash away my emotions just as easily, but from experience, I knew that would take many years, if ever.

When Brandr relayed what Sebbi had done to him, I initially saw him as a victim. One who'd endured unforgivable hurts. But when he spoke about the woman he'd forced into Bonding with him and his intent to take Julia, he became a monster, just like Sebbi. It made me sick to my stomach to think that both men I called father ended up twisted and evil.

My impending fatherhood made me wonder what my child might think of me. I couldn't do a worse job than my father, that's for sure. I'd want my child to know I loved them and that their opinion mattered to me. That I was proud of even the smallest achievement they made and would always be there for them, no matter what.

I suddenly felt the need for blood come over me, although I wasn't surprised. When we find ourselves under a great deal of stress, whether physical or emotional, a vampire needs blood more.

Made vampires find it harder to cope without blood in stressful situations, more so than Born Immortals. So I hoped that Josh would take enough to sustain him. I didn't think he would feel comfortable drinking blood in front of Mel, even though she knew he was a vampire. Josh would never willingly frighten a woman. He had a soft heart where women were concerned, and I knew he'd look after Mel tonight.

He'd have to re-carpet the Red Lion after today and will probably want to redecorate. I would pay for it all. It was the least I could do in the circumstances.

After drying myself, I put on some pyjama bottoms and went to the fridge to get some blood. I drank enough to lift my energy levels and warmed some milk to make Julia one of the creamy hot chocolate drinks she loves. I placed the cup on a plate with some cookies and carried it into the room where Julia slept.

To my surprise, a red, heart-shaped helium balloon and a vase of red roses and gypsophila were on the coffee table.

"Surprise!" Julia said in a tired, croaky voice.

"Where did these come from?" I asked, confused, though smiling nonetheless.

"I bought them for you today, just before Brandr got me. I was calling at the Red Lion to get a bottle of champagne to go with them, but Mel tried to clobber Brandr over the head with it when she tried to save me."

"What are we celebrating, love?" I asked, wondering if it was the pregnancy.

Julia got down from the chair and knelt in front of me. Pulling the balloon over to us, she spoke the words I will remember for the rest of my days.

"Alex, will you marry me? Will you be my love forever?"

She pulled up a basket at the end of the balloon ribbon, then took out a little ring box that looked very familiar. Inside was a larger replica of the wedding ring I'd purchased for her, with the same engraving: *My Love Forever*.

"How did you know?" I almost whispered. I took out the ring and slipped it on the third finger of my left hand.

"Does the fact that you're wearing the ring mean you accept my proposal?" Julia asked as she smiled up at me.

"Yes, of course, but…just wait there." I dashed off to

retrieve the jewellery I'd purchased for her—which I'd hidden at the bottom of my wardrobe—and came back to find Julia sitting on the sofa, looking somewhat puzzled. As I dropped to one knee in front of her, she grew even more confused—until she saw the same style box that had held my ring.

I took her left hand in mine, looked into her eyes and smiled as I said, "Julia, I'll get my proposal in even though you beat me to it. So hear me out, my love." I made a dramatic show of clearing my voice before asking, "Julia, will you do me the honour of becoming my wife, my partner in life, and my love forever?"

"Yes, of course I will."

I showed her the ring, then slipped it on her finger. She glanced briefly at the engraving, then smiled.

"It's a perfect fit, Alex. Thank you."

"I'm glad it fits you, but it can go back in the box now."

"What, no, why?" Julia whined.

"Because it's your wedding band. I've something else for you to wear now."

I took out the other small box that contained the eternity ring I'd bought her. Julia gasped when she opened it.

"Oh, Alex, this is beautiful," she said as she replaced the wedding ring with the sparkling eternity ring.

"I bought you some other jewellery to go with it," I added, relieved that Julia liked the ring.

I opened the box that contained the diamond earrings, necklace, and pendant. They were set in the same platinum finish as our rings. I put the chain around her neck, and she carefully took out her earrings before replacing them with the new ones.

Julia went to look at the jewellery in the mirror, but I

stopped her and handed her the next box. Julia's mouth dropped open in surprise.

"More jewellery?" she questioned through our Bond.

I opened the box and took out the bracelet. There were so many diamonds sparkling away on this piece of jewellery that it appeared to bring the rest alive, creating facets of light that enhanced those on the pendant and earrings.

I took out the watch and turned it over so Julia could read the inscription. The engraving said *Megan* and had her date of birth underneath her name with a heart underneath that. It was simply done but held a lot of meaning. Julia's eyes instantly filled with tears.

"Thank you, Alex, for this, for us. For what you did for me when I had Megan," she sobbed. "I love you so much."

Julia threw her arms around my neck, sobbing uncontrollably.

I could do nothing but hold her until she finally stopped. I knew her tears were a combination of many things, including what had happened today. Julia pulled away and grabbed some tissues from the box on the coffee table before blowing her nose. Her cup of hot chocolate was no longer hot, so she picked it up to take it to the sink.

"We got carried away with all the proposing and the jewellery, and I forgot about the lovely hot chocolate you made."

"How about I make you a fresh one while you get in the bath?" I suggested, guiding her towards our bedroom. Then I went into the bathroom and set the bath running.

I lit a few candles around the side of the bath and came out to find Julia admiring all her new jewellery.

"Let's not forget to take this off," I said, removing the watch and placing it on top of the drawers. I helped Julia take off her clothes, then left to make another hot chocolate.

When I returned to the bathroom, I found Julia lying in the bath with a washcloth over her face.

I removed it and kissed her soft lips before handing her the drink.

"So, Freya duped us then," Julia said with a smirk.

"Yes, I suppose she did. I thought it was strange when she got me trying on rings after I'd chosen yours. Freya must have told him to put the same engraving on both rings."

"She made me think it was my idea to choose those words. I hope we get to return the favour."

"I hope you're right, Julia."

I wished that now more than ever, but Freya didn't seem interested in finding love again.

"I wanted to cook and surprise you with a candlelit dinner for my proposal," Julia said sadly.

"I was with Father Stevens today, trying to get him to marry us two weeks from now—or earlier if you'd agree to it. That's why I blocked our Bond. I didn't want you to find out," I admitted.

Julia sighed. "Let's hope things go just as planned from here on out."

"I like the balloon," I told her with a smile. "No one has ever got me a balloon before. Or roses. Freya has given me daisies and wildflowers from her garden, but you bought me *'I love you'* flowers. Thank you, Julia."

Julia frowned. "I wasn't going to propose today, given what happened. But knowing I could have been taken from you, or you taken from me, made me not want to waste another day. Do you understand?"

I nodded solemnly. "I would never have let him take you. He was a strong vampire, but I'm stronger than he could ever be. Although you've yet to see my strength, I can assure you that I would have torn him limb from limb if he'd tried to leave with you. But the speed at which we immortals can move is often the deciding factor. He could have snapped your neck quicker than you could blink. But working with you through our Bond, hearing you tell me what you were going to do and reacting accordingly, that's what saved you today."

"I thought it was Mel shooting him, then me staking him with a Santa Stop Here sign that saved me," Julia said, smirking at me.

I laughed hard at that statement, but it was true. Even though there were vampires in the room, two human women saved the day.

"Didn't I once tell you that the inner strength and power in females will prevail above all else?"

"Yes, you did. But I don't think I'd have been strong enough to deal with what happened today if I didn't have something to fight for."

"Then you'll always be a fighter, Julia, because you'll always have me and our growing family," I said as I placed my hand on her lower belly.

She yawned, so I told her through our Bond it was time for her to go to bed. While Julia dried herself, I brought her the cute counting sheep pyjamas she seemed to favour.

"Don't let Viktor see these," I joked. Well, half-joked. He would freak out if he saw them.

When we lay in bed, she said, "I suddenly feel so weak and drained. Maybe I should have eaten more today."

I knew what she needed. I should have thought about it sooner.

"Julia, take some of my blood. It will make you feel

better and ensure your body has everything it needs for the baby."

She nodded, so I bit into my wrist and tried to hold back my erection as Julia drank from me. Not that we could have done anything about it; Julia was asleep mere seconds after letting go of my wrist. I put my arm around her and held her close, placing a hand over where my child was growing in her belly. And for the first time in a long time, I felt at peace.

Epilogue

Alex

The happiest day of my life so far had gone according to plan, despite the wintry weather we were having. The heavy snowfall had prevented my cousins Finn and Patrick from leaving Ireland this morning to be with us for the ceremony.

When Julia walked down the aisle towards me, I had to work hard at keeping tears out of my eyes. Then Gregor—who was my best man—had whispered, "She looks so beautiful, Alex. You are a lucky man," and I felt a lone tear slide down my cheek.

In fact, it wasn't the only tear shed in the church today. Freya cried, Gina cried, Julia and her mum cried, and if I wasn't mistaken, so did Josh.

As Josh was my brother, he should have been my best man. But he and I had both agreed that he would escort Freya today. She'd been extremely emotional during all the wedding planning, so we decided it would be better to have a family member standing beside her in church, not Gregor. He couldn't bear tears of any kind coming from my sister.

Gregor, Sergei, and Viktor had flown in from Russia two days ago and were flying back tomorrow, which was Christmas Eve. I'd wanted the wedding to happen two weeks ago, but Freya and Gina wouldn't be rushed in their *perfect wedding* preparations.

Freya was still heavily involved in textiles and design, her business frequently dealing with some of the best fashion houses in the world. So it came as no surprise that she would supply the fabric for Julia's dress, and also get one of her dressmaker friends to make the prettiest wedding dress I've ever seen. And believe me, with all the wedding magazines that have appeared in my cottage over the last few weeks, I have seen many.

Her floor-length dress comprised deep cream satin, topped with a paler cream floral lace. The lace covered Julia's arms right down to her hands, where it tapered to a V, the material looping around her middle finger to keep it in place. The colour suited Julia and highlighted her skin tone, making her appear much healthier than the constant morning sickness made her feel.

Julia had been struggling with it for the last two weeks and giving her my blood only seemed to fix it for a few hours. Whoever named it morning sickness got it totally wrong in Julia's case. She could throw up at any time of the day.

I asked Maggie to stay on at work full-time for a little longer so we could find someone to job share with Julia. That way, she could rest more on really bad sickness days.

The balloons from church had been brought back to the reception, and Daisy, our little bridesmaid, was trying to gather as many as she could. Although I don't think Keeley was too impressed about having to take them all home.

I was so surprised when I arrived at the church to see gold and cream heart-shaped helium balloons at the end of every pew. Chloe, the new florist here in Barrowfield, had done a great job with all the flowers and balloons in the church.

She was the one who'd supplied the balloons and roses the day that Brandr tried to take Julia. I think Julia organised for her to do the balloons for our wedding because she knew how much I loved them. Mine had lasted nearly two weeks, and I'd comment on them daily.

Chloe was also the one who'd sold Julia the Santa Stop Here sign, with which she'd staked Brandr. So I was very grateful to her, and her shop, in a roundabout way.

Father Stevens had proven to be a greedy bastard as far as members of the clergy were concerned, and the little church in Barrowfield would be fully central heated come February at my expense.

Sergei said we weren't allowed to use mind control on him, but I'd considered it at one point. The good father had given his objections to our marriage because Julia was recently divorced, plus December was an extremely busy time in the church calendar—the month of *Our Saviour's birthday*.

The central heating finally swung it, and today Father Stevens performed the wedding ceremony of a vampire and a human. I wondered how he would feel about that if he knew.

I could afford to hold the most lavish reception money could buy, but I wanted something simple today. Something that all the people I held dear could enjoy.

So here we all were, fifteen years later, standing in the

very same room in our compound where we celebrate the work's Christmas party.

I watched my wife as she held onto her father's arm, laughing at something he'd said. From beside me, Josh asked, "Well, Alex, have you finally figured out what you want from Julia after all these years?"

I laughed, thinking of a similar conversation I had with him when I'd first fallen for this woman.

"Everything, Josh. I want everything. And now I have it."

I walked over to Julia and gave her a chaste kiss while the DJ announced it was time for the bride and groom to take their first dance as husband and wife. So I took her hand and led her onto the dance floor.

When the first few bars of the song came through the speakers, Julia looked into my eyes and said through our Bond, *"You remembered."*

"Every single moment," I told her, smiling as Elvis Presley sang "Can't Help Falling in Love."

Next in The Night Movers Vampire Series

vinci-books.com/bloodandsecrets

She thought her life was finally on track, but secrets and shadows threaten everything she holds dear.

Single mom Keeley Saunders thinks her life is finally turning around with a new job working for a charming, billionaire vampire. But secrets lurk in the shadows, threatening to shatter her newfound happiness. When a brutal attack leaves Keeley fighting for her life, she's forced to confront the dark mysteries surrounding those she loves.

Turn the page for a free preview…

Blood & Secrets: Chapter One

Keeley

I love my job! I've been Gregor Antonov's PA for the past five months, and I've enjoyed every minute of it. He's been a fabulous boss, letting me work flexible hours to suit my childcare needs.

My daughter, Daisy, is four and a half now—you have to say the half, or she gets annoyed—and soon she'll be in full-time school. This job allows me to drop Daisy off at her nursery in the mornings and pick her up midday to take her home for lunch. When my boss is over from Russia and work is busier, a friend from my old job at Night Movers collects Daisy for me.

Today Daisy is with Joshua York, one of my old bosses at Night Movers. He's been a rock for me whenever I've needed someone to lean on. He spoils my daughter constantly, and she absolutely adores him. Last week he bought her a swing and slide set for his back garden, so he doesn't have to take her to the swings at the local park. Not that Josh doesn't want to, of course, but he's limited by how much time he can spend in the sun.

You see, Josh is a vampire. So is Gregor, my boss, as well as Nik and Alex—the other two co-owners of Night Movers. And Sergei, Yuri, Finn, and Patrick—all friends of mine, and all vampires. Does this bother me? Surprisingly, no. They are some of the nicest individuals I have ever met. I've been around most of them since I was a young girl, just a few years older than Daisy is now.

My aunt Maggie has worked for Josh, Nik, and Alex in the offices at Night Movers for thirty years, and often took us into the office with her when we used to come and visit. My parents were originally from this village, but they moved to Lincolnshire for my dad's job when Mum was pregnant with me and my twin brother, Daniel.

Sadly, Mum died from breast cancer when we were twelve, and my dad couldn't cope with her loss. He ended up having a breakdown, so Daniel and I had to stay with Aunt Mags and Uncle Dave until he was well enough to look after us again.

Freya Staithes—another vampire, who is also Josh and Alex's sister—used to take me out shopping and to her home for holidays. She became like an aunt to me, and now that I'm a grown woman, she's one of my best friends.

Freya told me about the PA job with Gregor Antonov and passed him my details. I'd met him before, on occasion, but always felt too intimidated to speak to him, which wasn't like me at all, as anyone who knew me would tell you. But Gregor Antonov, the Russian billionaire vampire, has a commanding presence that intimidates even the most powerful men and women.

Now that I know Gregor better, I feel differently about him. He's one of the most charming, respectful men I've ever met. It's like he treasures your company, and he makes you feel as though you're the most important person in the world.

The last time he came over to see the progress on his house, he brought me the diamond earrings I wore today for a job well done.

DIAMOND EARRINGS!

I'd never owned a diamond anything before, and they're not small diamonds either. Gregor said all women should own diamonds, and after seeing how these sparkled in my ears, I completely agreed. If I'm honest, I may have had a bit of a crush on Gregor. Tall, with broad, muscular shoulders, dark-brown hair and piercing blue eyes. What's not to crush on? I melt like butter whenever he says my name in that delicious Russian accent.

Keeleey… He always says it with a slow drawl, and the first time I heard it, I almost swooned.

The house Gregor is having renovated is the old Rothley Manor, which is just outside our little village of Barrowfield in South Yorkshire. He hired a brilliant interior designer who's worked for members of the Royal Family, as well as famous footballers and models in the UK and Europe. His name is Ryan Adamson. He's only twenty-six, just a couple of years older than me, and he's totally gorgeous. Unfortunately for me, he's also gay, and he's recently come out of a long-term relationship.

To help Ryan get over his breakup, me and some of the ladies from my old job took him on a night out around Rothley and Barrowfield.

What a night that was!

Daisy was staying with my ex's parents, so I could let my hair down without worrying about looking after her when I got home. My ex's parents live in Gainsborough, which is only a thirty-minute drive away. My ex, Rick the prick, wants nothing to do with Daisy, so his parents take her once a month when they know he's not going to visit. It's an odd situation, but I wouldn't stop Rick's parents from seeing her just because their son doesn't want to be in her life. Although sometimes, when she's asking me questions, I think it would make life easier for me if she didn't know them.

Our night out was one of the best I've ever had.

We danced most of the night away in Rothley, which I love to do, then came back to the Red Lion and stayed for one of their famous lock-ins. Sergei brought a bottle of absinthe that a friend of his makes. Oh my God! I have never been as drunk as that before. If it hadn't been for Josh, I don't think Ryan and I would have coped. He came with Alex—our designated driver since Julia became pregnant—and ended up taking Ryan and me back to his cottage to sleep it off.

Josh looked after us all night when we were throwing up and brought us breakfast and much-needed painkillers the next morning to kill the hangover. He also gave me a small amount of his blood, which really helped.

Josh wouldn't tell me what happened during the ride home in the minibus, but I ended up losing a shoe and somehow my bra, although I still wore the rest of my clothes. He now calls me his Cinderella, though I doubt I'll get Prince Charming riding up to me with my high heel on a cushion. Not here in Barrowfield. The only Prince Charming I have in my life right now is Josh. But he still sees me as the little girl that Aunt Mags used to bring to the office, even though I've tried to make him see me as the woman I am today.

Of course, there's always Gregor and Sergei. Though Sergei never seems to take anything seriously, whereas Gregor… Gregor is the king of the castle.

Blood & Secrets: Chapter Two

Keeley

I left Ryan at the manor to lock up while I went to get my car from near the old stables. The builders were working late, as were the decorators, so Ryan was staying to make sure they did everything to his specifications. He's only five-foot-seven but has a way of making those big, burly builders and decorators obey his every command. A true professional if ever I saw one. Even Gregor doesn't faze him.

Gregor had brought two of his bodyguards with him last time—Yuri and Maxim. Yuri is lovely, but Maxim is mean. He doesn't speak, he just grunts and looks at me like I'm shit on his shoe. I don't know what I've done to upset him, but he's always so disparaging and nasty towards me. Ryan threatened Maxim that if he heard he'd upset me once more, he was going to tell Gregor. That seemed to do the trick until they all left, and I hoped Maxim stayed away this time. I mean, it's not like Gregor needs a bodyguard in this sleepy Yorkshire village.

I threw my bag in my crappy little car that had long seen better days and sat still for a minute after closing the door, enjoying a moment of peace. Gregor would be arriving in two days' time, so the builders, decorators, and Ryan had really gone for it today. They were aiming for the interior of the manor house to be completed for Gregor's visit. There were still the cottages and stable block residences to finish, but they could be done later.

The noise from the manor today had been horrendous, so I savoured the quiet of my car for a minute before turning the key.

Nothing. That's what I got when I finally turned the key. So I tried again, pumping the accelerator a little to see if that helped—still nothing. After trying for another five minutes, I gave up and phoned Josh.

"Hi, Keeley, are you on your way home? Daisy's been a big girl and ate all her fish fingers and spaghetti."

"That's good. I hope she's behaved for you. Listen, Josh, my car broke down, and I'm going to have to call the AA, so I'm not sure what time I can pick Daisy up. Do you mind dropping her off at the manor with me? I don't want her going back to mine without me. My dad's on one of his benders again."

"I'll come and get you, Keeley. Stay put, me and my little princess will be there in ten minutes. You can call the AA out tomorrow."

"Thanks, Josh, but—"

Too late; he'd already hung up the phone.

I knew he would come for me. I think he would do anything I asked of him, except kiss me, of course. Josh would be the ideal man for me. Yeah, so he's a vampire, which means a beach holiday in Ibiza is out of the question, but in every other way, he's perfect.

Josh is about six-foot-three of pure muscle. His brown eyes often seem to have flecks of fiery amber in them, lighting up bits of me that shouldn't burn for him. Of African descent, his skin is the colour of milk chocolate, and I have more than once dreamed of tasting it. He keeps his tight curls cropped close to his head, and I'd love to run my fingers through them and feel the texture.

He's a beautiful man with facial features a model would be proud of, and where Gregor makes me swoon with a silly schoolgirl-like crush, Josh makes my heart beat faster in my chest whenever I see him. Even sometimes when I can't see him, I can tell you the very moment he walks into the room just from how my body reacts. I know it's because I'm in love with him, but since that love isn't reciprocated, I try to forget about anything more meaningful. But I see Josh most days, and it's getting harder to hide how much he means to me. And how much I want him.

Josh's Honda CRV pulled up beside my car, tugging me away from thoughts of being with my perfect man/vampire. He got out of his vehicle and walked towards me, concern marring his handsome face.

"Hey, Keeley, are you okay?" He opened the door, took my hand, and helped me out of the car.

"Yeah, I'm fine, Josh. It's this bloody thing failing to start again."

"Mummy, you said a naughty word," shouted Daisy from the window of Josh's SUV.

"Sorry, Daisy."

She was like the swear police lately. Not that I choose to swear in front of her, but occasionally something slips out and when it does… Bam! She's in there straight away. Never misses.

Josh popped the bonnet up and we went through the

motions of trying to start my car. But the engine wouldn't turn over even when using the jump leads.

"It's definitely a job for the AA, Josh, but thanks for trying. Would you mind dropping us off at home now? I want to get this little one bathed and in bed," I said, smooching a kiss off the sweetest little girl in the world.

"Of course, but if your dad's being a problem again, maybe you should stay with me?" he said.

"Thanks, Josh, but I want to keep an eye on him so he doesn't end up back in the hospital again."

"Can't Daniel watch him? I can arrange for him to have time off work so he can sort him out."

"No, Josh, it's okay; I'll handle it. Dan's moved out, anyway. He says he's done with him now. They had another big bust-up, and it got all heated. Dad punched Dan, so Dan moved out and lived at his friend's house until he got a flat. He moved in a few weeks ago."

Josh stepped closer and asked in a soft voice, "Keeley, why didn't you tell me it had got this bad at home? Maybe I could have helped."

"There's only my dad that can help himself now, Josh. But I can't leave him on his own. He nearly set the house on fire the last time he was like this. He was so drunk he forgot to switch the grill off."

"Then it's not safe for you and Daisy to be there either," he declared. "Come home with me, Keeley. As soon as one of my properties becomes empty again, you can have it."

Although I was grateful, I shook my head. "No, Josh. Thanks, but no. I need to know that he's going to be okay. He does this and then he gets better. He just needs time to sort himself out again," I insisted.

"Will he go to rehab or an AA meeting?" Josh asked.

"No. Been there and done that. You get him set up to

go, and then he just refuses, so it's pointless. But he seems to come out of it himself, eventually."

Less than ten minutes later, Josh was dropping us off at home. Daisy was in a great mood due to the in-car DVD player Josh had installed for her. She'd been watching a cartoon in the back of the car while Josh and I had been talking. I knew she couldn't understand much of what I'd been saying, but kids tend to pick up more than you think. So in this instance, I was glad that Josh had spoiled my little girl yet again with his thoughtful actions. I got out of the car, grabbed both mine and Daisy's bags, and then went to take Daisy out of Josh's arms.

"Daisy's not tired, Josh. She can walk in," I insisted.

"I'll carry her in, Keeley. You have steps down to the house," he pointed out.

Before I could stop him, he'd gone through the gate and down the path to the door. I stepped past him and opened it, hoping to God my dad was asleep. No such luck!

"Where have you been, Keeley? You're an hour late," Dad yelled, drunk as usual. He came into the kitchen and saw Josh with Daisy.

"What the fuck is he doing holding our Daisy?" he raged.

"Grandad, that's a very naughty word," shouted Daisy. Josh held her tighter against his chest.

"Dad, stop it. Josh looked after Daisy while I worked today, and then my car broke down, so he gave us a lift here."

"Well, he can get his filthy, black hands off my granddaughter," Dad bellowed.

I was mortified. My dad had never been racist. None of us were.

"Dad, just shut up, please. Josh is my friend; you can't speak about him like that."

"So, you're off whoring yourself out to him while you're supposed to be working, are you?" Dad questioned as he stumbled sideways into the wall.

Daisy started crying, and I followed suit.

"That's it. Get your stuff, Keeley. You're coming home with me, and I won't hear any arguments," Josh said as he turned towards me. He put Daisy down to stand on the floor and spoke to her gently.

"Daisy, why don't you help your mummy pack some of your clothes? You can come and stay at my cottage tonight. We can watch Ellie the Fairy Queen again, and you can show your mummy the colouring in you did for her today."

Daisy nodded and took my hand as we walked towards the stairs. I paused for a moment to tell Josh to ignore whatever my dad had to say. He looked at me and smiled, even though I knew he was angry and upset.

Grab your copy...
vinci-books.com/bloodandsecrets

About the Author

Helen Bright was born and raised in Yorkshire, UK, and often bases her novels in and around the county.

Whether she's writing paranormal or contemporary romance, her novels often have darker elements hidden inside a deep and meaningful love story.

www.ingramcontent.com/pod-product-compliance
Ingram Content Group UK Ltd.
Pitfield, Milton Keynes, MK11 3LW, UK
UKHW041513100326
468839UK00004B/1264